Shane

Remington Ranch Book Two

Shane and Cassidy

SJ McCoy

A Sweet N Steamy Romance

Published by Xenion, Inc

Published by Xenion, Inc.
First Paperback edition 2016
www.sjmccoy.com

Cover Design by Dana Lamothe of Designs by Dana
Editor: Mitzi Pummer Carroll
Proofreaders: Aileen Blomberg and Kristi Cramer

ISBN 978-1-946220-03-5

Dedication

For Sam. Sometimes, life really is too short. Few x

Chapter One

Cassidy stood up and stretched. "I'm starving," she said to Gina with a grin. "Do you want to hold down the fort here while I run to the coffee shop to get us some lunch?"

"Sure. It'd do you good to get out in the fresh air, even if it is only for a walk down the block."

Cassidy made a face. "Don't start again, Miss Outdoor Adventurer. It's easy for you to go off wandering in the mountains with your camera and call it work. I have to sit here at my easel. And when I'm not painting I'm working our connections to get the word out about this new line, or to keep the gallery going."

"I'm just saying it'd do you good to get out more."

Cassidy shrugged. "I'll give you that. I will, when I get time. For now I'm going to go grab us a sandwich."

She smiled at the feel of the sun on her back as she walked down the street. Gina was right. She did need to get out into the fresh air more. She'd been so busy working on their new line and setting up marketing channels for it, she was spending all her time inside. She never made time to get out and appreciate the mountains and all the natural beauty that surrounded her. Even walking through the middle of town like this she could see the snowy peaks of the Crazies towering above the buildings to the north. Maybe this weekend, she thought as she pushed her way into the coffee shop. She should take a drive down to the park at least. Yellowstone was beautiful at this time of year, and hopefully, it was still early enough that the place wouldn't be completely swamped with tourists yet.

She stood in front of the display case at the back of the coffee shop. Today felt like a good day for a dessert. She eyed the cakes, a smile spreading across her face when she spotted a chocolate mousse. That would do nicely. As she reached for it, a big hand came down on her shoulder.

"Got a craving for something sweet, do we?"

Shane Remington! She'd know that sexy voice anywhere, not that she needed to hear it. She'd known it was him from the feel of his hand on her shoulder. The damned man had the same effect on her every time he came close. He sent tingly shivers racing through her, leaving excited goose bumps in their wake. She couldn't let him know that though. "I don't know if we do, but I certainly do," she replied, without bothering to turn around.

His chuckle sent fresh shivers down her spine. "Well, darlin', you know I certainly do. Have done since the first moment I laid eyes on you."

She spun around to face him—mistake, biiig mistake, she realized as soon as she did. He had her cornered against the display case, his huge frame blocking her view of the rest of the coffee shop. It didn't matter what or who was behind him though. His presence and the raw energy he emanated enveloped her. They may as well be the only two people in the whole state of Montana. He filled up all her senses, making her oblivious to everything but him. Big, gorgeous, sexy—infuriatingly cocky—him.

She presented him with the mousse. "Here. This should take care of it."

He grinned down at her. Damn, he was so irritatingly good-looking! His hazel eyes glimmered with amusement as he took hold of the dessert, making sure he closed his fingers over hers as he did. She wasn't going to give him the satisfaction of pulling her hand away. Instead she coolly met his gaze.

He winked at her. "It isn't exactly what I had in mind, but thanks. I'll take it."

She couldn't drag her gaze away from his. "I hope you enjoy it. Now, if I could just have my hand back, I need to get going."

He laughed and brought her hand up to his lips. She was so surprised she still couldn't pull away. All the muscles in her belly and lower clenched as he kissed her knuckles then slowly trailed his tongue over her wrist, holding her gaze the whole time. "Mmm, sweet," he murmured. "This is what I have in mind, sweet Cassidy. What do you say?"

Oh God! What did she say? What she wanted to say—actually, more likely scream—was Yes! Yes, yes, yes! The things the feel of his tongue on her skin did to her! But no. She withdrew her hand from his grasp while she still had the willpower to do so. She shook her head. "What do I say? I say not only no, but hell no! Now, if you'll excuse me." She pushed past him and made her way straight for the door. If she didn't escape him now, she'd be dragging him out of there to give him exactly what he wanted, and more besides.

"I'll be seeing you," he called just as she pushed open the front door.

She turned back and shook her head at him with a grin. "Not if I see you first." She didn't miss his wink in the second before the door closed behind her.

~ ~ ~

"What the hell did you say to her?"

Shane's grin faded a little as he turned to his brother. "I just said hello. That's all."

Mason gave him a stern look. "I don't believe just 'hello' would send her scarpering like a scalded cat."

Shane shrugged. He'd blown it yet again, and he knew it. His grin returned as he looked down at the chocolate mousse he was still holding. "She wants me, Mase."

Mason laughed. "Dream on. She couldn't get away from you fast enough."

Shane shook his head. "I might need to up my game—change tack a little—but she wants me. I know it."

"Whatever you say. Now are we going to get some food, or what?"

Shane nodded and joined the line at the counter to order sandwiches. He groaned when the coffee shop door opened and Katie Bell came in. She smiled when she saw him and came straight to him, standing on tiptoe to kiss his cheek.

"Shane! Where have you been hiding?"

"I'm a busy man, Katie. The dude ranch is in full swing for the season now. I have guests to take care of."

She pouted at him, her shiny pink lips reminding him of the several nights he'd spent with her. "Ranch guests, huh? When are you going to take care of me again?"

His eyes fixed on her plump breasts as she folded her arms underneath them. Man, he needed to pull himself together. He forced himself to drag his eyes away and look up at her face.

Her smile said it all. “So what do you say? Take me out to dinner tomorrow?”

He considered it. He could, it’d be a great night…once they got dinner out of the way. He pursed his lips. She was cute and great in the sack, but she wasn’t having the same effect on him that Cassidy had just had. In fact, remembering Cassidy’s long, honey-colored hair and the twinkle in her honey-colored eyes while she’d brushed him off yet again, Katie looked kind of ordinary. He shook his head slowly. “Sorry. No can do.”

She shrugged. “Your loss. You know where to find me when you change your mind.” With a toss of her hair she flounced away toward a table of local girls in the corner.

“I don’t get it,” said Mason.

“Don’t get what?”

“You. I mean, she wants you. No mistake about it. But you’re not interested. Cassidy won’t give you the time of day, yet you keep going back for another shot. What happened to a bird in the hand and all that?”

Shane chuckled. “How many women were trying to hook you and you had no interest? Gina wouldn’t even set foot in the same town as you while she had a choice, yet you kept going back for more. What’s the difference?”

“I love Gina. Always have, always will. I knew if I got any say in the matter, Gina was going to be my future, my wife.” He raised an eyebrow. “Are you really telling me there’s no difference?”

Shane turned away, relieved to have reached the head of the line. “I’ll take a patty melt with everything but pickles,” he said to the girl serving.

Mason dug him in the ribs. “What are you saying, Shane?”

He laughed. "Of course I'm not saying it's like you and Gina. That'd be crazy. I like the thrill of the chase that's all. Katie's a fall back option, like she said herself, I know where to find her if I want her. Cassidy…Cassidy is…" He paused to think about it, then shrugged. "I don't know, she's a new challenge that's all."

Mason nodded, looking thoroughly unconvinced. "Whatever you say, Shane. Just do me a favor and bear in mind that she's working with Gina. I don't want you to piss her off and mess things up."

Shane laughed. "Nothing I could do would mess things up between the two of them. They're thick as thieves."

"That's true. Between Gina's photographs and Cassidy's paintings it looks as though they're going to be raking it in soon."

That reminded Shane. He'd offered to put the two women in touch with some of his dude ranch guests in the hopes of helping sell their artwork. "And I'm going to see if I can help them along with that."

Mason gave him a puzzled look, but had to order his own sandwich before he could ask any questions.

Shane grinned. "I told them I'd hook them up with some of the guests. They're the girls' ideal buyers. People who love Montana and have very deep pockets."

"That's true. Just…" Mason looked uncomfortable.

"Just what?"

"Just don't fuck it up all right?"

Shane shook his head. "I told you. I wouldn't do anything that would mess things up for Gina. I…"

Mason shook his head. "I mean don't fuck it up for yourself, Shane."

Shane stared at his brother who turned away to pay for both their sandwiches. Was he for real? Did he have the same weird feeling about Cassidy as Shane himself did?
"What do you mean by that, Mase?" he asked once they were back out on the street.
Mason shrugged. "You tell me, Shane. You tell me."

~ ~ ~

Cassidy let herself in through the back of the gallery. She closed the door, and then leaned back against it. She'd practically galloped down Main Street away from the coffee shop. She'd even ducked into the alleyway to come around the back. Why? She shook her head. Why hadn't she been able to keep her cool? Shane was just a cocky…horny…ugh! She put her hands on her hips and tapped her foot as she scowled to herself. He was walking temptation—that was what he was. She'd promised herself no more messes made with men. Shane was a man-mess waiting to happen. She needed to control herself, forget about him. Nothing good could ever happen between the two of them, she was sure of that. Well, the sex would be amazing, she was pretty damned sure of that, too! But it wasn't worth it. Shane was a manwhore of the first order. She bit the inside of her lip—so, now she thought about it, wouldn't that make him perfect? He wouldn't want anything more from her than sex. He wouldn't present any of the problems that came with men who wanted a relationship. She drew in a deep breath. Did that make sense? Or was she just trying to find ways to justify sleeping with him because he made her so damned horny?
She looked up, startled when Gina popped her head around the door that led from the gallery into the back. She cocked her head to one side. "Err, am I allowed to ask?"

"Ask what?" Cassidy tried to sound nonchalant, even as she struggled not to laugh.

"What the hell you are doing back here, pressed up against the back door like a fugitive, when not ten minutes ago you headed out to the coffee shop with the promise of bringing me back some lunch."

Cassidy pushed herself away from the door and straightened up. She made a fuss of straightening her shirt and patting her hair down. "I ran into a little obstacle. That's all. I'll go back for our lunch once I'm sure the coast is clear."

Gina shook her head. "Let me guess. That little obstacle was really a big obstacle? About six feet four inches big?"

Cassidy rolled her eyes. "How do you know? Did you send him in there after me?"

Gina laughed. "I did not. I just know the look you get whenever you run into Shane."

"Oh, and what look is that then?"

"It's the only time I ever see you flustered. Go on, admit it. For all your put downs, you like him, don't you?"

Cassidy nodded slowly. "I've told you before, I find him far too attractive."

"So what's the problem?"

"There are two problems, Gina. I am the first problem, in that I made a promise to myself not to create any more man-messes in my life. And your friend Shane there is the second problem. He is a complete and utter manwhore."

"Oh, he's not. He's a…."

Cassidy laughed. "Don't, Gina. I know he's been one of your best friends your whole life and everything, but even you can't look me in the eye and deny that he's a manwhore, can you?"

Gina sighed. "Okay, no, I can't. But he's an absolute sweetheart. He is the way he is because he hasn't found the right woman yet, that's all."

"Well, let me assure you I am not the right woman!"

"But how do you know? You might be."

Cassidy shook her head. Gina meant well. Hell, it'd be cute for anyone to pair off two of their friends. But Gina didn't know the whole story. "I am not the right woman. Not for Shane. Not for anyone. I already figured that out. Trust me, okay? No more man-messes in my life and certainly not with someone who is so close to my business partner. Okay, partner?"

Gina nodded, but she looked sad. "Why though?"

"Ugh! I've told you before. It would take a whole evening and a really good bottle of wine or three to explain it all."

"So name your evening. I want to know what your problem is with men, in general, and Shane, in particular. I'm not going to give up. I can be stubborn, you know. If you don't believe me, just ask Mason."

Cassidy was saved by the sound of the doorbell buzzing as someone entered the gallery out front. "Saved by the bell," she said with a grin. "How about I go take care of that and you do the lunch run? You might actually make it back here with some food."

"Okay, but don't think you're getting off the hook that easily. I want an explanation, and I want wine—good wine. Name your day, but it is happening."

Cassidy waved a hand over her shoulder as she went out into the gallery. Did she really want to talk to Gina about what a failure she was with men? She was too strong, too independent. Hard. She resented that word, but more than one guy had called her that. Men just had such brittle egos—that was the real problem. Once she figured that out, she'd determined that she wasn't going to allow herself to be set up as the wicked bitch of the west ever again. No matter how strong a guy might seem in the beginning, it was guaranteed that she'd bruise his ego at some point—just by being strong, being herself. She had no intention of giving up who she was; it was easier to give up on men.

Chapter Two

Shane checked himself in the mirror and grinned. He was looking good—as usual. He went back out into the living room of the cabin and plonked himself down on the couch. It wasn't the same around here anymore. Mason had moved into the little cottage across the creek with Gina. He couldn't be happier for them, but on a selfish note he was a little sad that his bachelor days with his big brother were over. He, Mason, and Chance had shared the cabin for years, and they'd had some great times. Now Mason had moved on to the next chapter in his life. Chance should be back any day now. He'd gone down to California to see his sister. He'd taken April Preston with him, helping her escape from her asshole of a husband, Guy. Shane hoped she would settle in down there and be able to build a new life for herself and her kid. He was looking forward to Chance coming back, but it still wouldn't be the same. He loved Chance, thought of him as a brother, but he was different. He was deeper and darker than the rest of them, even though on the surface he was as much fun, if not more.

He picked up the remote and turned on the TV; maybe he'd find a movie. After a few minutes channel surfing, he turned it off again. Who was he kidding? He got up and went to sit out on one of the rockers on the front porch. It was a beautiful evening, and he didn't want to spend it sitting around here by himself. He didn't know what he *did* want to do though. Mason would be home with Gina, and he didn't want to intrude on their time together. Chance was gone. He wondered about his other two brothers. Beau was out of town at some realtors meeting in Billings he'd said. Maybe he should call Carter. Carter hardly ever went out. Shane grinned to himself. He should get his brother down here and show him a good time. The current batch of dude ranch guests included a whole gaggle of chicks from Phoenix. They'd been flocking around him since they arrived, so maybe it was time to have a bit of fun with them. Women always loved Carter, so why would these women be any different? Maybe he'd indulge himself, too. Shane had to do something to salve his ego after yet another put down from Cassidy. He reached for his phone.

"Hey, Shane. Is everything okay?"

Shane laughed. "Why do you always answer the phone that way? Anyone would think I only call you when I have a problem."

"I dunno. I just worry, that's all…sorry."

"Hell, I wasn't complaining. It's sweet!" Shane felt bad. Carter was the one who cared, the one who took care of family.

Carter laughed. "Thanks, little brother. I always aspired to be sweet!"

"Well, that's your problem, isn't it? You're too sweet, too caring. You need to let loose a little and have yourself a good time. That's what I was calling for."

"You want to show me a good time?"

"I do. Get your ass on down here. There's a whole group of hot little fillies amongst this week's guests. You should come pick yourself one."

"Yeah, thanks, but no thanks."

"Aww come on. I didn't want to admit it, but I need you. The one I have my eye on hangs with her best friend all the time. I need you to distract the friend so I can move in for the kill." He waited. It wasn't true, but he knew if anything would motivate Carter to come out it would be a plea for help.

"Okay. Just for you. But you owe me, okay?"

"Okay! Thanks. Come straight out to the lodge. I'll be getting them warmed up. See you soon."

"Sure. I'll head out now."

Shane hung up and pulled his boots on. He had a crazy urge to call Carter back and tell him not to bother. He didn't really want to go flirting with ranch guests at all. What he wanted to do was head up the valley to Mill Lane. He wanted to go calling on Cassidy. He shook his head. That really was crazy. She'd probably have him arrested for trespassing. He'd do better to put her out of his head and go find himself a woman who would appreciate him for the night.

~ ~ ~

Cassidy stood in front of the big window by the fireplace to watch the sky turn from blue to pink to gold as the sun sank behind the mountain. It was so beautiful here. She loved this place. She especially loved this house. It was big—way too big—but it was perfect for her. It was a huge log built home—far too grand to call a cabin—with walls of windows looking out over the valley. The Yellowstone River wound its way through the property. Eagles and deer were daily visitors. She'd been warned that she'd have fishermen and rafters floating through daily in the height of the summer season, too, but that would be a small price to pay.

This was a long way from her native South Carolina. It couldn't be more different, but she loved it just as much. The beaches and the salt marsh had a quiet beauty that slowly crept in and became a part of you; once they had a hold on your heart they never let go. The mountains were different. Theirs was an in-your-face stark, harsh beauty. She could see how it was love or hate at first sight for most people. She felt lucky that for her it had been love.

She started at the sound of a buzzer. She still could not get used to that thing. Whenever a car entered the driveway it sounded. It was a good idea really, but it still freaked her out a little. If she wanted she could go to the control panel and watch her visitors approach on camera. She rarely did though. She usually knew who was coming. It wasn't as though she got that many visitors. She frowned. It wasn't as though she knew that many people here, and she couldn't for the life of her think who might be visiting this evening. She went out into the hallway and checked the screen.

She smiled when she saw a green pickup truck sending up a dust trail on its way down the long driveway. Carter Remington! Now that guy really was a sweetheart. She pulled on a sweatshirt and headed out front to greet him.

She had to smile at the way he tipped his hat when he climbed down from the truck. Bashful. That was the word for him. He was a good-looking guy. She'd heard—and could see—that he spent most of his time either working or at the gym. Work was his landscaping business. Ah, that must be why he was here.

He confirmed it as he came around to shake her hand. "Evening, Miss Cassidy. Pardon me stopping by unannounced,

I just wanted to drop these with you." He held out a couple of large files.
"Hi, Carter. It's wonderful to see you. Thank you. Is this the work you'd already done for this place before I bought it?"
"Sure is."
"Great. Do you want to come in? Have you got time for a drink? I haven't eaten yet, if you'd like to join me?"
He shook his head and smiled. "It's kind of you, but I'm afraid I can't be stopping. I'm on my way down the valley to see Shane. Just wanted to give you these while I was passing."
"Oh, okay." Why did he have to mention his brother? Just when she thought she'd got him out of her head for the day.
"Are you all right? I can stay a while if you need anything."
Cassidy smiled. If Shane had said that, it would have been a loaded question, full of innuendo. Coming from Carter it was full of genuine concern. Strange how two brothers could be so different. "I'm fine thanks, Carter, you get on. Thanks for these. I can pick your brain about them another time."
He smiled. "You sure can. Just give me a call whenever you're ready to go over them." He tipped his hat again and climbed back into his truck.
Cassidy watched the trail of dust follow him back up the driveway. She waved when he honked his horn before disappearing around the corner and out of sight.

~ ~ ~

Shane rested his arm around the girl's shoulders and smiled down at her. She'd done everything but straight out beg for it since she'd arrived on Saturday. He tried to steer clear of ranch guests; there were enough women passing through the resort up at Chico to keep him busy. He tried—but it wasn't exactly a rule or anything. Maybe he could make another exception for this one. She had short brown hair and bright blue eyes. A great figure, with a perky little set and the kind of rounded ass he loved. She smiled up at him.

"Is tonight the night you're going to show me what happens out in the barn?" She kept her voice low so her friends wouldn't hear.

Maybe it was. Shane looked up to watch Carter's truck approach. He smiled, maybe it was Carter's night to get lucky, too. Most of the guests in this group tended to head in early. He was pretty sure he could convince this one and her friend to hang out by the fire a while longer. "You'll have to wait and see sweetheart, won't you. For now, you get to meet my brother." He didn't miss the way her eyes lit up when she saw Carter get out of the truck. He had to hand it to him. Carter was quite a specimen. Shorter than Shane himself, though only by a couple of inches, and he was like a solid wall of muscle. He spent so much time in the gym that he had the physique of a bodybuilder. Shane just didn't understand why he didn't put it to better use with the ladies. "Over here, bro."

Carter came to join them with that shy smile of his. Watching his companion's reaction, Shane wondered whether he couldn't learn a thing or two from his quietest brother.

"Hi, I'm Lena." The girl ducked out from under Shane's arm, hand extended to greet Carter.

"Pleasure to meet you." Shane chuckled to himself. Carter looked about ready to run.

"Lena, why don't you go get Kylie to join us?" he asked.

Carter met his eye as she walked away. "Sorry it took me a while to get down here."

Shane shrugged. "You're here now. I was starting to think you weren't coming. What took you so long?'

"I stopped…"

"Kylie, this is Carter. Carter, Kylie." Lena announced as she pushed her friend toward him.

Shane resisted the urge to laugh at the way Carter backed up three steps before holding his hand out to shake with the pretty brunette. She was half his height, but Shane would put money on her wrestling Carter to the ground, if the look on her face was anything to go by. Why the hell were women like that these days? When they wanted a man, they went after him and made no bones about it. He shook his head. And why did *he* suddenly have a problem with it? It saved him from having to do any hard work, after all.

Kylie confirmed his initial impression as she took Carter's hand and pulled him in to turn the shake into a hug—the kind of hug where she pressed her breasts into his chest, or at least as far up his abs as they would reach.

He did laugh when he saw the panic in Carter's eyes. "Tell you what ladies, let us go get you a drink. We'll be right back."

Carter extricated himself from Kylie's clutches and trotted behind Shane like a grateful puppy. "Yeah, I think I'm going to beat it."

"Aw, don't go."

"You can handle those two by yourself. They scare me shitless, Shane. I don't want any of that."

"Okay, maybe those two are a bit over the top, but you need to start having some fun, Big C."

"I'm fine the way I am, thanks. Between work and the gym, I have all the fun I can handle."

Shane shook his head. "How can trees and shrubs and flower gardens be any fun? I just don't get it."

"You never did get it, and that's okay. I love what I do, I love planting things, seeing things grow. I love designing a beautiful space that people can enjoy."
"Yeah, yeah, I know." Shane grasped his brother's shoulder. "You love it, and that's great. But you need to interact with other humans occasionally, you know. Especially the female of the species."
Carter grinned. "It was human interaction with a female that made me late getting here if you must know. A female I'm going to be doing some work for, and one who not only understands, but truly appreciates my love for my work. If it weren't for you I'd still be interacting with her now."
Shane cocked his head to one side. "Who's that then? One of the little old ladies up in town?"
Carter shook his head vehemently. "None other than the beautiful Cassidy Lane."
Shane's heart dropped into his stomach. Carter and Cassidy? No! That couldn't be right. It wouldn't happen. It *couldn't* happen. For once he had no words. He just stared at his brother. If Carter liked her though…Damn, Carter hadn't shown any interest in a woman in over ten years! Why the hell did he have to start with Cassidy? With the one woman that Shane himself…what? That he what? He shook his head to clear it.
Carter gave him an odd smile. "I'm only saying that Cassidy is a woman worth spending time with." He jerked his head back to the two girls. "That may be your idea of fun, but it sure as hell isn't mine. I appreciate the looks, but someone like Cassidy has a mind, a heart and a spirit to back the looks up."
Jesus! Hearing Carter talk like that shook Shane to the core. He was spelling out what Shane already knew, but hadn't yet

faced. Worse than that though, it sounded as though Carter had not only figured it out sooner, but was deciding to act on it. What the fuck?

"Are you all right?"

Shane nodded. "Yeah. I'm sorry. I was only messing around with you. I thought it was time for you to have some fun. It sounds as though you've got more serious stuff on your mind." He shrugged. "You know I can't help you there. I don't do serious. Maybe you should talk to Mason."

Carter laughed. "I don't need to talk to anyone. Maybe *you* should talk to Mason."

"I don't think he can help me." Shane didn't want to talk to anyone right now. What he wanted was to go saddle up Cookie and ride out into the moonlight. Spend some time in the foothills and try to get his head straight. All he'd ever done with Cassidy was flirt—and fail spectacularly! There was nothing between them, and she'd made it very clear that, as far as she was concerned, there never would be. Yet he felt as though he'd been kicked in the gut. His brother was moving in on his girl. Except she wasn't his girl, never had been.

"Are you all right?" Carter asked again.

Shane met his gaze. Maybe he should tell him? Hell no! He squished that thought as soon as it popped up. He could have any woman he wanted—as many women as he wanted. He would just have to live with the discovery that Cassidy was the woman he wanted more than any other. If anyone deserved to be happy it was Carter, and if he thought Cassidy might make him happy, then so be it. Shane wasn't going to mess with his chances.

Chapter Three

The next morning Shane closed up his office and crammed his hat down on his head. The guests were all out on their daily activities. Most were on a picnic ride down to Dailey Lake, a few had taken the minibus down to the park, and the rest were hanging around the ranch relaxing. He was heading up into town again. He was only going because he needed to get to the post office. That was all. He was going to stop into the Moonstone Gallery while he was up there. But that was just so he could keep his word to Gina and Cassidy. He'd promised them a while back that he would put them in touch with some of his former guests. He really did want to do whatever he could to help them sell their new line of art. He was hoping he could provide them with a steady stream of clients. If he happened to discover anything about how Cassidy felt about Carter while he was there, well that would just be coincidental, wouldn't it?

He second-guessed himself all the way up the valley. He shouldn't go anywhere near her if Carter was interested. But he needed to know if it was mutual. That would help him do the right thing—back the hell off. He should stay away, but he had promised to help with marketing leads. He should stay away, but he wanted to see her. He needed to see if the effect she always had on him would still be as strong. Would his attraction for her wither and die once the thrill of the chase was removed from the equation? How could he still be thrilled by chasing a woman his brother was interested in? He took his hat off and threw it onto the passenger seat. What the hell was he doing? He should just turn around and head back to the ranch, put Cassidy out of his head and go console himself with Lena. He put the accelerator to the floor as he turned north—toward town.

~ ~ ~

Cassidy stepped back to observe the canvas. She was pleased. She loved working on this new line with Gina. They hadn't been working together for very long, but they understood each other so well. Gina's photographs captured the landscape and the wildlife so vividly, while Cassidy's paintings reflected the feel, the colors, and the contrasts in a much more impressionistic way. She knew between the two of them they would appeal to a very broad range of buyers. She looked up as Gina came in.

"That, my friend, is beautiful!"

"Why, thank you. I was just thinking the same thing," she said with a laugh.

"Modest, aren't we?"

Cassidy shrugged. "Honest is what I prefer to call it. I'm good. I know it. I have the millions to prove it."

"And I envy you," said Gina. "Not the millions, though of course I wouldn't mind joining you. I mean your confidence. No, that's not right. Your…what is it?"

"Self-acceptance?" asked Cassidy. "I know I come off as fairly egotistical to most people, but that's their problem not mine.

For some reason we're all encouraged to hide our light, how does that go? Under a bushel? Whatever a bushel might be. I don't see the point in that. I don't see why we shouldn't all stand up and own our accomplishments. I know I piss people off, but I really don't care. I love what I do, I happen to be talented at it, and that gives me great pleasure. People are either jealous, or too bogged down in social conventions in the belief that we shouldn't toot our own horns for the fear of offending someone else. I'm not going to curb my own enjoyment of my life and my talents. I'm not going to smallen myself just to live down to someone else's expectations. Sorry, not sorry."

Gina laughed. "Smallen? Is that even a word?"

Cassidy smirked. "If it isn't, it should be! So many people, especially women, smallen themselves in order to keep other people happy. In order not to threaten the little egos of the men around them."

Gina raised an eyebrow. "This sounds as though we're heading into interesting territory. Want to tell me more?"

Cassidy shook her head. "Not until we have a whole evening and that good wine we were talking about."

"Okay. I've told you before and I'll tell you again. You name the day, and I'll bring the wine."

"How about tonight?"

"Nope. I can't do tonight, I'm going over to see my dad. And tomorrow's no good either. We're meeting Carter at the Mint. He said he'd come out for dinner, and that's a minor miracle in itself. You could join us? It'll be more likely beer and a burger than good wine, but we'll have a laugh, and we usually have a game of pool when we go there, too. Do you play?"

Cassidy grinned. "That sounds like fun. I need to talk to Carter about his landscaping ideas for my place anyway. And as for pool—do I play?" She chuckled. "Hell yes, I play. I used to be quite the hustler in my day. Just don't tell the guys, we can play doubles and kick their asses. How does that sound?"

"Like a lot of fun," said Gina.

"Okay then. I'm in."

She looked up at the sound of the buzzer when the gallery door opened. All the little hairs on the back of her neck stood up when she saw him, sending goose bumps chasing each other down her spine. She pressed her lips into a thin line to ensure that they didn't respond in kind to the infuriatingly gorgeous smile on his face.

"Good day, ladies."

"It was, until about a minute ago. What do you want now?" she asked.

Gina shot her a *why-do-you-have-to-be-so-mean?* look. "Hi Shane. How are you doing?"

"You already know what I want, sweet Cassidy. I thought I made that clear yesterday."

She took a deep breath, remembering the feel of his tongue on the sensitive skin of her wrist—oh, he'd made it very plain indeed!

He gave her a knowing smile before turning to Gina. "I'm doing great, thanks, G. I wanted to talk to you both about hooking you up with the ranch guests to sell your pictures."

Cassidy rolled her eyes. She'd heard about Shane hooking up with the ranch guests himself. "I understand you get quite close to your guests." She could have kicked herself for saying it out loud.

He turned that smirk back on her, making her want to kick him instead. "I just like to give them what they want. Show them a good time, you know?"

"Pft! I know what your idea of a good time is, Shane Remington!"

He had the audacity to laugh. "You have no idea, but I can show you if you like?" He raised an eyebrow, as if he was honestly waiting for an answer that he might like.

"No, thank you. I prefer real men to little boys."

His eyebrows lowered, for a moment he looked angry, then he laughed and shrugged it off. "Yeah, I'm just the littlest brother. You prefer an older one, huh?"

What the hell was he talking about? She hadn't been talking about age, she'd just meant to imply that he was immature, but he seemed to be making it personal. He thought she preferred his older brother? Mason was with Gina, she barely knew Beau…then it dawned on her. Carter had been on his way to see Shane last night when he came to her place. Had Shane put two and two together and come up with five? She recovered quickly, nodding as she smiled. "I do."

Damn, she'd expected a snappy comeback, but he looked like a puppy who'd just been kicked! "Good to know," was all he said.

Gina scowled at her as she put a hand on Shane's arm. "When you two have finished bickering, do you want to tell us what you have in mind with the ranch guests?"

He nodded and held Cassidy's gaze for a long moment before his usual cocky smile returned. "Sure do. I figured if you'd like I can hang some of your pictures at the ranch, so they can buy them right off their bedroom walls if they want. If you can come up with a rack card or something, I can include it in the welcome packs, and if you can give me something to include in the monthly newsletter to previous guests, I can get that out next week."

Cassidy felt bad. He was going out of his way to try to help them. "They're all great ideas. Thanks, Shane."

He nodded and turned back to Gina. "I need to get going, but if you want to give me a shout when you pull something together, I'll come over to the cottage and we can go over it."

Oh. Cassidy's heart sank. He was deliberately excluding her and she didn't like it at all. She'd been looking forward to going over marketing ideas with him. She admired what he was doing with the guest ranch and figured he must have some good ideas for marketing and promotion. The ranch was always busy and seemed very successful. She bit the inside of her lip—not that she ever would have said anything of the sort to him. Now she'd offended him somehow and he was giving her the cold shoulder. She pulled herself together. She should be glad. Now she wouldn't have to deal with his constant flirting and innuendo.

"I'll give you a call tonight, how about that?" asked Gina.

"Sounds like a plan. Talk to you later." He tipped his hat at Cassidy as he left, but didn't say a word.

She breathed a big sigh of relief when the door closed behind him. Her moment of relief was short lived though. Gina turned on her.

"What did you do that for?"

"Do what?"

"You know damned well what! You even gave me the impression that you were interested in Carter when you said you prefer an older brother. I'd believe it, if I didn't know full well that your only interest is in his landscaping skills!"

Cassidy shrugged and pushed her hair back over her shoulders. "It got him off my back, didn't it?"

"Oh, it did that all right. You won't have to worry about Shane bothering you ever again!"

"What? What do you mean?" She was surprised at the rush of disappointment at the thought of not having to spar with Shane anymore. Especially at the thought of *never.*

"I mean, you don't know the Remington boys. They look out for each other like nothing you've ever seen. If Shane thinks there might be something between you and Carter, he'll do everything in his power to make it happen. Carter has been single for a long time; we'd all love to see him find himself a woman and be happy again."

"Oh." She didn't know what else to say. She felt bad that Shane had a decent side she hadn't been aware of, and she had inadvertently used it against him. She felt even worse at the thought that he wouldn't be bothering her anymore. Though surely that was just a prick to her ego, wasn't it? It should be a relief to know she'd got him off her back.

Gina was studying her closely. "You're not interested in Carter, are you?"

She shook her head. "Not like that, no. He's a wonderful guy, but not for me. I'm very interested in what he can do out at Mill Lane, but that's about it."

Gina shook her head. "Well I hope all your bravado about not being interested in Shane was true, too, because you won't have to worry about him now."

Cassidy nodded. She couldn't believe how disappointed she felt. "The most that would have ever happened between Shane and me would have been a one-night stand that we both would have regretted. I probably did us both a favor by averting that disaster." Even as she said it, she realized she'd rather have had that than nothing.

~ ~ ~

Shane parked up at the barn. He didn't feel like sitting around the cabin, and he sure as hell didn't feel like going to hang out at the evening campfire with the guests. He made his way down the row of stalls until he came to Cookie. The gelding nickered and came to chew his lapel. Shane grinned and rubbed his velvety nose. "How you doing, old fella?"

Cookie pawed at the ground and nodded.

Shane laughed. "You're a wise old soul, aren't you? Damn I wish you could talk. Tell me what the fuck I'm supposed to do now."

The horse head butted his shoulder, making him chuckle. "You think I'm an idiot, right?"

He turned sharply at the sound of laughter behind him. Mason.

"I've always said horses make better therapists than therapists do."

Shane laughed. "And where's the cowboy wisdom in that one?"

"Think about it. People go see therapists to help them work their problems out. The therapist lets them talk and doesn't interfere with the process so they can reach their own conclusions. When we have problems we come see the horses. We talk and, since the horses can't talk back, we have to work through it and reach our own conclusions. The end result is the same, except it costs a lot less."

Shane smiled. It was true.

"So what's your problem that you need wise old Cookie's help? You usually resolve, or at least escape from, your problems in bed."

Shane heaved a big sigh. "No problem really. In fact, I should be happy."

"Bullshit. You're a long way from happy, and that's not like you. What's going on?"

"I think Carter might finally be ready for a woman in his life."
Mason cocked an eyebrow. "And why would that be a problem for you?"
Shane sighed again. "Cassidy."
Mason leaned back against the wall and tipped his hat back. "That doesn't sound right. Doesn't sound right at all."
"Tell *him* that. In fact tell *her* that while you're at it!"
"He likes her? She likes him?"
"Yup."
"And they both told you this?"
"Not in so many words, no. But…"
"But nothing then, little brother. Don't go deciding all by yourself what people think or want. Wait for them to spell it out for you, or you're in danger of getting it all wrong. Believe me."
Shane shook his head sadly. "It doesn't matter. It's much more important to Carter than it is to me."
Mason gave him a stern look. "Is it really?"
"I don't know, Mase. I don't know what the hell that woman does to me, but it's something no one else has ever done. At the same time, if Carter has a chance with her, then I am out of the picture. He's the good guy. He's the one who hasn't even dated in years. He's the one who deserves a good woman." He shrugged.
"Well, I'll tell you what. He's coming out for dinner with me and Gina tomorrow night at the Mint. Why don't you come as well? I'm pretty sure that over the course of dinner and a couple of games of pool, it'll all come out—if there's anything there."
Shane nodded. "Yeah. It'd be good to all have dinner together anyway. Is Beau back yet?"

"No, not till next weekend. And hopefully Chance will be back by then, too. Gina was talking about having everyone out to the cottage one night."

"That'd be great, but yeah. I'll be there tomorrow. What time are you thinking?"

"We figured we'd just head up when everyone gets finished with work. Maybe six thirty or seven."

"Great. I'll be there. I think for now, I'm going to saddle this guy up and head out for a while. Do you want to come? Bring Storm?"

"I'd love to, but I've got too much to do around here."

"Okay. I'll catch you later then."

Chapter Four

"Are you ready to go?" asked Gina.

Cassidy nodded. "Yeah, let's wrap it up for the day. I'm about done."

Gina collected her purse. "I'll give Mason a quick call and see what time he can get up here. I told him about six thirty or seven, so it may take him a while."

"No problem, we can have a drink while we wait. I may even tell you a thing or two about my man-messes before your sexy cowboy and his brother arrive."

Gina shook her head. "You're still rattled about Shane, aren't you?"

Was she? She shook her head, denying it to herself as much as to Gina. "Not at all. His reaction surprised me, but…"

"But what?"

"But nothing." She wasn't going to admit how many times he'd popped into her head today. How many times she'd regretted letting him think she was interested in Carter. It was stupid. She wasn't interested in Shane anyway. So why should the prospect of him no longer flirting with her bother her?

Gina gave her a knowing look. "You might be fooling yourself, but you're not fooling me."

The sound of her cell phone ringing gave Cassidy the excuse not to reply. She reached for it with a shrug. "I'll take this; you call Mason."

Gina fished her own phone out of her purse. "Okay. I'll be outside when you're done."

Cassidy hit answer. "Cassidy Lane."

"Hi, Cassidy. It's Autumn. Long time no speak."

"Oh my God! Autumn! How the hell are you?"

"I'm doing fine. Unfortunately, I can't say the same for Summer."

"Oh no, why? What's wrong?"

"She has some health issues. I don't want to get into it right now. I haven't got time. But Alan and I were just trying to come up with somewhere she could go to hide out for a while. She needs to spend a couple of months, maybe more, somewhere quiet where she can recuperate out of the limelight.

"She can come stay with me. No problem."

"You are the best. I knew you'd say that, but I think she needs her own place. Her own space. It's not like she needs to be taken care of, she just needs peace and quiet."

"Let me ask around then, find out if there is anywhere up for rent. Is she really okay? Can I give her a call?"

"Thanks, Cass. I wanted to ask if you knew any realtors or property managers you can put me in touch with. And as for calling her, you'd be better off emailing. Her voice is the problem. She's not *sick* sick; she's got problems with her vocal chords."

"Oh no! Well, listen. I'll get straight onto finding her a place to rent. I'll call you as soon as I have anything. Give her a hug for me and tell her I can't wait to see her."

"Thanks. Will do. You rock, girl. Talk soon."

Wow! Once she'd ended the call Cassidy opened her email. She hadn't talked to Autumn, or Summer, for—what? Months? It didn't matter though. Their friendship was like that. It could be years, but it made no difference to the bond they shared.

Summer!

I've missed you, chick! I'm on the case to find you a place. Lol, and apparently I'm a poet, too! We'll get you up here ASAP. You'll love it. Wish it were under different circumstances though. Can't wait to see you.

Love n hugs

Cassidy

Oxoxoxo

Gina popped her head back around the front door.

"Sorry," called Cassidy. "That was a bit of a surprise. I'm coming now."

Once they were settled in a corner booth at the Mint and had ordered their drinks, Cassidy turned to Gina. "Does Beau handle rental properties?"

"Yeah, he does. Why?"

"That was a friend of mine on the phone. She needs a place to stay for a while, maybe a few months or more."

"I'm sure Beau will be able to find her something, but it could get really expensive. Rent isn't exactly cheap around here over the summer."

"The cost won't be a problem. Not for Summer."

"That's what everyone else thinks, too. They'll pay through the nose to be here in the summer, but you can rent a house out for peanuts in the winter."

Cassidy laughed. "I didn't mean for *the* summer. My friend's name is Summer, and she won't mind however much she has to pay."

"Lucky her! She can afford whatever she wants, huh?"

"You'll be able to afford whatever you want soon as we start selling. Don't you doubt it."

Gina made a face. "I hope so. I still won't be called Summer though. Isn't that a lovely name?"

"It is, and she's a lovely person, too. Just as sweet as she seems when you see her on TV. With some of those singers and movie stars, I wonder if it's all a front and if they're bitches in real life. With Summer, what you see is what you get."

Gina raised an eyebrow. "Summer who? Why would I have seen her on TV?"

"Oh. Sorry. Summer Breese."

"Really? The country singer?"

"Yep."

"And that's her real name? I always thought it must be made up!"

Cassidy laughed. "She always jokes that she'd never get away with making it up. It's her real name. And her sister's name is Autumn."

"Oh, the poor things! That must have sucked when they were kids. I mean, they're lovely names, but kids can be cruel."

"We were at school together. There were kids with much stranger names, and much bigger problems to deal with."

"Huh. Let me guess. Some fancy private school?"

Cassidy nodded. "Yes. And I'm not going to apologize for it." She stuck her tongue out. "You were the poor little country girl; I was the poor little rich girl. It's not where we come from, but what we make of ourselves that matters."

"It is. So why is Summer coming here?"
"Apparently there's something wrong with her vocal chords and she needs somewhere to hide and rest. That wasn't her on the phone, it was Autumn. The two of them are close. Autumn is her business manager."
"Well, let me give you Beau's number. I'm sure he'll be happy to find her something that will work. And don't worry, he's the soul of discretion."
"Yeah, he seems to be quite the mystery himself."
"He's more private than the others. More, I don't know what the word is, serious? Aloof? Not really either of those but he's more that way than the other Remingtons are."
"That's the impression I got of him. He seemed like a nice guy though."
"He is, and he's damned good at what he does."
"Well, that's all I need to know. I'll give him a call in the morning. Thanks." She smiled when she saw Carter making his way through the bar. "He's such a sweetheart, isn't he?"
Gina laughed. "Yes, he is. But you are not interested in the slightest, are you?"
"No. I wish I was though. He's going to be a great catch for some lucky lady."
Gina sighed. "I hope so. He gave up on women years ago."
Cassidy smiled. "We'll have to see what we can do about that. Find someone who can rekindle his interest."
"It'd take a very special lady."
Carter smiled as he reached the booth. "Evening, ladies. Mason said we were meeting earlier than we thought. He told me to get my a…butt over here in a hurry. Looks like I beat him to it?"

"You did," said Gina. "He was still at the barn when I called, so it'll take him a while yet. Sit down and have a beer."

~ ~ ~

Shane had to park a couple of blocks down from the Mint. He checked his watch; it was just after seven. He wasn't exactly late, they hadn't set a specific time. He was looking forward to this evening. It would be good to just relax with his brothers and Gina. Catch up, have some laughs, play some pool—and, hopefully, put Cassidy out of his head. He was expecting to hear something from Carter about what was going on between the two of them. Even if only because he knew Mason would bring it up to get it out in the open. Hopefully whatever Carter had to say would be enough to help Shane feel happy for his brother—and forget any intentions he might have had toward Cassidy himself. They were hardly going to be honorable intentions after all.

He pushed his way inside the bar and scanned the tables. He spotted Mason and Gina sitting in a booth in the corner. Carter mustn't have arrived yet. Then he spotted him—standing at the bar with Cassidy! Well, fuck! He didn't need his nose rubbing in it! Gina caught his eye as he started to turn away. He hadn't come for this. Gina waved, but he pretended not to see her. He wasn't going to be the fifth wheel. He almost made it back to the door before she caught up with him.

"Shane! Don't go."

He glared down at her. "Why not? Four's company. I don't feel like an evening of playing odd man out."

"It's not like that. There's nothing going on between Carter and Cassidy. Nothing at all."

Relief rushed through him. "There isn't?"

She shook her head, a big grin on her face. "No, but I'm pretty sure there could be something going on between *you* and Cassidy. If you're prepared to work for it."

Work for it? He'd never worked to get a woman in his life.

Gina laughed at the look on his face. "What's up? You don't like the sounds of that?"

He grinned. "It's just a novel concept. Not one I've come across before."

"Well, it's one you're going to have to try out if you want to stand a chance with her. You can bet your ass she'll make you work for it. You just have to ask yourself if you think she's worth it. If not, then don't even bother."

He looked over at the bar to where Cassidy was chatting with Carter. She pushed her long blonde hair back over her shoulders as she laughed. She waved her wineglass around as she spoke. She threw her head back when she laughed. She drove him crazy! He looked back at Gina. "I think I'm nuts, but I think she might be worth it."

Gina grinned and took his arm. "I was hoping you'd say that. Come sit down."

Shane followed her over to the booth and slid in opposite Mason who smiled at him.

"You could have told me Cassidy was going to be here."

Mason shrugged. "I didn't know she was when I asked you."

"And you wouldn't have come if you had known," said Gina. "And that would have been pretty dumb, considering you had your wires crossed about her and Carter. So how about a thank you instead of whining?"

Shane grinned. "Yeah, you've got a point. Thank you." He turned to look at Cassidy at the same moment she and Carter started back toward the booth. She didn't look too pleased to see him. "I take it *she* didn't know *I* was coming either?"

"Erm, I may have forgotten to mention it," said Gina.

Shane shook his head. He knew Gina's warning was true—he was going to have to work for this one. "Evening," he said as they approached the table.

"Hey, Shane," said Carter.

Cassidy held his gaze for a moment then nodded at him coolly, before shooting an evil look at Gina.

The server arrived with menus and Carter slid in next to Gina, leaving Cassidy with no option but to sit beside Shane. He grinned up at her and patted the bench beside him. "Come on, I don't bite."

She shook her head as she sat down. "I might though."

He raised his eyebrows with a grin, but said nothing.

She tried to hide it, but he didn't miss the smile lurking behind her scowl as she rolled her eyes at him.

Once they'd placed their orders, Mason looked around the table. "So what's everyone been up to?" he asked.

Carter shrugged. "Business as usual for me. I'm going to be flat out for the next couple of months." He smiled at Cassidy. "I have some great new clients and some projects I'm really excited about working on."

Shane watched Cassidy smile back. Now that he knew it, he could see it—she wasn't interested in him. Not in the least.

"I can't wait for you to get started on my place," she said. "I love the plans you've drawn up."

"We can change whatever you like," said Carter.

"I don't think there's much I even want to change. There are a couple of touches I'd like to add, but nothing major."

"Well, I've got you on the schedule starting Monday. We can add in whatever you want."

"Where are you working this week?" asked Gina.

"I'm squeezing in a couple of Beau's rental properties, getting them spruced up before high season."

"When's he back again?" asked Cassidy. "I need to talk to him."

Shane groaned inwardly. He didn't want her showing interest in another of his brothers. "Next weekend, I think," said Carter.

"What do you want to talk to Beau for?" asked Shane.

She turned a cool gaze on him. He knew, just knew, that she wanted to say *none of your business,* but she didn't. "I want to ask him about a possible rental for a friend of mine."

The server came back with their food before Shane could ask any more.

Once they were done eating, Mason looked at Shane. "What do you say, little bro. Do you want to get your ass handed to you at pool?"

Shane grinned. "No thanks, but I'll be happy to kick yours." He looked at the others. "Want to make it doubles?"

"Go ahead, I'll watch," said Cassidy.

Shane grinned, she'd probably never played before. "You can play with me if you want to." He said with a wink. "I'll teach you."

She smirked at him. Maybe he was getting through to her? "Maybe later. I'd like to just watch first."

"Okay, later." He looked at Carter. "You and me?"

Carter nodded. "Sure."

~ ~ ~

Cassidy smiled to herself as she followed the others over to the pool tables. She wanted to sit back and watch, figure out how good they were before she played.

As she perched herself on one of the stools to watch, Gina shot her a knowing smile. This was going to be fun. She'd played pool for years and loved it. It was funny how guys always seemed to think they had a natural prowess and would automatically beat women. She loved proving them wrong!

She watched Mason break, putting down two colors straight away. Carter went next, but didn't put anything down. Gina looked as though she'd played a lot when she took her turn. Shane came to stand beside Cassidy as he chalked his cue. "I'll show you how it's done," he said with a grin. "When I finish these guys off you can play with me if you want to."

She met his gaze. "I have no intention of playing with you, Shane. In any sense of the word."

He grinned. "You'll change your mind once you know how good I am."

"Don't bet on it, Mister."

He grinned. "Maybe that's what we should do?"

"What is?" she asked.

"Come on, Shane," called Mason. "Take your shot!"

"Bet on it," said Shane with a wink as he walked away.

Cassidy watched him put three stripes down before missing and coming back to stand beside her. "I really am that good," he said, keeping his voice low so the others couldn't hear.

"You don't know how good *I* am." Cassidy couldn't resist replying.

"I told you on the day I met you that I wanted to find out."

"At pool, Shane. I'm talking about pool."

He feigned innocence. "So am I, sweet Cassidy. What did you think I was talking about?"

She narrowed her eyes at him. "Oh, sorry. I thought *you* meant something else when you said you wanted to play with me. My bad." She knew she'd scored points when his eyes widened in surprise. "And here I was ready to bet on it." She had to hold back a laugh at the gleeful look on his face.

"What do you want to bet on?"

She shrugged. "Never mind. I had the wrong end of the stick, sorry."

"No, go on. What are we betting?"

She shrugged. "We should probably play each other."

He grinned. "Want to get out of here then?"

"Play pool, Shane!"

He gave an exaggerated sigh. "Okay, we play pool, we make a bet. I win, I get you."

She laughed. There was no way he was going to win and she knew it. "You get me? Get me how?"

He looked over his shoulder at the others then looked back at her. "Get you naked," he said in a low voice. "We've spent enough time teasing each other."

She nodded slowly, then laughed out loud as an idea struck her. "And if I win?"

Shane shrugged. "You're not going to, but I'll humor you. What do you want?"

She held his gaze and slowly ran her tongue over her lips. "I get you naked and doing whatever I tell you to." The goose bumps ran down her spine under the heat of the look he gave her.

"Seriously?"

She nodded. "Seriously."

He held out his big hand and sent a tingly current of excitement zapping through her when she shook with him. "You've got yourself a bet. And I win either way."

Cassidy smiled inwardly. He was too cocky for his own good, and she was about to prove it.

Chapter Five

Cassidy couldn't help smiling to herself as she watched them finish playing doubles. The game went all the way to the eight ball. She watched as Shane stepped up to take what should be an easy shot to win. She shook her head when he named the most difficult pocket to get to.

"Thanks," said Mason. "I thought it was over, but you just gave us another chance."

Shane gave him that cocky grin of his. "Oh, you of little faith. Don't count your chickens, big brother." He caught Cassidy's eye. "I'm going to win, and I'm going to enjoy every second of my victory." He took the shot and bounced the white ball off two cushions before it hit the eight ball and sent it straight into the pocket he'd named. He straightened up with a grin and high fived Carter.

Gina laughed. "You're good when you want to be, Shane."

He turned to Cassidy. "I'm *great* when I want to be. So, what do you say, Cassidy? Do you want to play me?"

She laughed. And slid down from her stool. "I'm pretty damned sure you want to play me!"

Carter looked at her. "Do you want to play doubles? I can help you beat him."

He was so sweet. She touched his arm, and said, "Thanks Carter, but this is something of a grudge match. I think I can kick his butt all by myself."

Mason laughed and looked at Shane. "Sounds like you might have met your match and you don't even know it."

Shane eyed her suspiciously. "She may think she can take me, but she doesn't know what she's in for." He raised an eyebrow suggestively. "She can't even imagine how good I am."

"*You're* the one who doesn't know what he's in for, Shane," she said with a laugh, knowing he would interpret her words in a whole different way than she meant them. "You have no idea, but I cannot wait for you to find out." She chuckled to herself at the look on his face. He totally believed that she meant the same thing he did. That she was going along with his innuendo. Yet, she had something else in mind completely.

"Me neither," he said. "So let's get on with it. Ladies first, you can break."

She selected a cue from the rack and smiled at him as she chalked it. "Are you sure?"

"It wouldn't be very gentlemanly of me to beat you before you even get to take a shot, now, would it?"

She laughed. "No. That's not something a gentleman would do, but you're not one anyway." She held his gaze as she blew the excess chalk off the tip of her cue. This was going to be fun.

She stepped up to the table and broke. She didn't put anything down, but spread the balls well.

"Nice shot," said Shane.

Cassidy turned and rolled her eyes at the others. "He's going to patronize me?"

Mason laughed. “He’s going to try, but I have the feeling you’re going to be able to shut him up?”

She grinned at them and nodded.

Shane smiled as he lined up his shot. “I’m not patronizing, I’m encouraging. I want you to relax and enjoy yourself.”

He put down two striped balls and then missed an easy shot on the third. Cassidy was pretty sure it was a deliberate miss. She smirked at him as she walked around the table weighing up her options. “You can go straight at it you know. You don’t have to go slow and take it easy on me.”

He smirked back. “I’d rather we take our time and make it last. I don’t want it to be over too soon. Especially if I get there before you even get warmed up.”

She laughed out loud. “Don’t you worry your pretty little head, Shane. I’m all warmed up.” She bent over the table right beside him and wiggled her ass to nudge him out of her way. She put down three colored balls before looking up. She smiled at him and deliberately missed the next, leaving the white tucked against the cushion behind the eight ball. “Oops!” she grinned at him. “Sorry.”

He shook his head at her. “No problem.” He managed to get the white ball out and at least hit one of his stripes.

“Nice shot,” she said and couldn’t resist patting his shoulder in as motherly fashion as she could manage. “Well done, you.”

He narrowed his eyes at her. “Now who’s patronizing?”

She laughed. “I thought it was encouraging!”

“Okay. You made your point. Game on.”

She rolled her sleeves up as she eyed the lay of the balls, weighing up her next shot. Shane followed her and she shot a look back over her shoulder at him. “You wouldn’t be trying to put me off, would you?”

"Not at all."

She bent over the table and looked down her cue, making sure she could get the angle she wanted. She bit the inside of her lip when Shane came to stand right behind her and leaned in a little closer. She turned her head to meet his gaze. The laughter was gone from his eyes, replaced by an intensity she wouldn't have thought him capable of. He placed a hand on the small of her back sending the tingly shivers racing through her. All she could do for a moment was stare back into his eyes. He dropped his gaze to her lips, making her think he was going to kiss her. Her eyelids lowered, and her breath was coming low and shallow. She wasn't going to be able to resist. The feel of his hand on her back was making her want to throw the game and let him take his prize right here on the pool table. The moment seemed to last for minutes until he broke it by standing abruptly.

"It'll be a tough one to pull off, but I reckon if anyone can make it, you can."

She continued to hold his gaze. She had the crazy feeling he was talking about something more than the shot she was about to make. She shook her head. She was getting carried away. Her body was reacting to him and her brain was getting fuddled in the process. She turned back to take her shot. Cutting a sharp angle she sliced the ball into the middle pocket. "You'd better believe it," she said over her shoulder as she lined up the next shot.

He went to stand at the other side of the table. As the next ball rolled into the pocket she could have sworn she heard him say, "I'm afraid I'm starting to." Whatever the hell *that* might mean.

~ ~ ~

Shane watched the last colored ball roll into the pocket. Only the eight ball remained. Cassidy gave him a victorious grin as she walked around the table toward the white.

"Can you handle losing?"

He nodded. He didn't like the idea of losing, but given that she'd said that if she won she wanted him naked and doing whatever she said… He held her gaze for a moment.

"Be warned, Cassidy. He's a sore loser," called Mason.

She nodded without looking away from Shane. "I imagine he is. But you're also a man of your word, right, Shane? If you lose, you'll honor the bet?"

He nodded, relieved that *she* wasn't wanting to change the terms. "Yep. Whatever you say."

She pointed to the far corner pocket with her cue.

"Okay," he said.

She made pretty much the same shot he'd made to win the game of doubles. The white bounced off two cushions before hitting the eight ball squarely and sending it neatly into the pocket. She straightened up with what he could only describe as an evil grin on her face.

"Good game," he said.

She nodded. "It was."

"So, do you want to collect your winnings now?"

She shook her head. "Not yet. I was thinking of Thursday night. You can come to the gallery when I close up."

Shane knew he was grinning like an idiot, but he couldn't help it. "Great. I'll take you to the Valley Lodge for dinner if you like?"

There was something a little worrying about the mysterious smile she gave him, but her words were enough to make him ignore it. "Oh, that's okay. You don't need to buy me dinner. The gallery will do just fine for what I have in mind."

Shane swallowed and adjusted his pants. She wanted him naked, doing whatever she said—in the gallery? And she didn't want to bother with the niceties of dinner or a date first? He grinned. "Sounds great."

She chuckled. "It does, doesn't it?"

Carter came over and slapped him on the back. "It's nice to see you've learned how to lose graciously."

Shane laughed. He could hardly explain why he wasn't the least bit sorry to lose. "This may be a one off, bro. Don't expect me to be like this next time *you* beat me."

"Do you want to play again? I can give you a chance to practice being a good loser?"

Shane shook his head. "I need to get back to the ranch. I wasn't planning on staying out late tonight."

"Fair enough," said Carter. He looked at Cassidy. "How about you? Do you want to help me beat Mason and Gina?"

Shane scowled to himself. He'd said he didn't want to play because he was hoping to get Cassidy alone for a while. He was relieved when she shook her head. It seemed she had the same idea he did. "I should really get going, too. But give me a call? I want to go over the landscaping design with you before the weekend."

"Sure thing. I'll be down your way working on one of Beau's rental houses. I could stop by when I get finished?"

"That'll be great. Is the house available for rent?"

"Yeah, he had a lot of work done on it the last few months and didn't want to put it on the market until he was sure it would be ready."

"In that case would you give me a call before you leave there? I have a friend looking for a place. I'd love to come over and see it."

"Of course. In fact I can show you what I'm doing over there. You might want to use something similar at your place."

"Which place is it?" asked Shane.

"It's the old Handler place, the big cabin on the river, just a little further down from Cassidy."

Shane nodded. "It's a great house," he told Cassidy. "The perfect vacation spot."

She shook her head. "She's not coming on vacation. It'll be a few months at least by the sounds of it."

"Oh, how come?"

She looked a little uncomfortable.

"We're going to get going," interrupted Gina. It seemed to Shane as though she was covering for Cassidy for some reason. The surprised look on Mason's face confirmed it.

"Okay, thanks for a great night, guys." Carter tipped his hat and was gone.

Gina hugged Cassidy and then Shane. "See you tomorrow. We need to do this again soon. This was fun."

Shane hugged her and Mason punched his arm. "G'night, bro."

And then they were gone. He smiled at Cassidy. "Are you sure you don't want to collect your winnings tonight? We could go to the gallery now, if that's what you want?"

She shook her head. "No, I want to enjoy the anticipation."

Wow! She really was up for it.

"At least stay and have a quiet drink with me?"

He held his breath—she was considering it!

"Shane!"

He cursed under his breath and pretended not to hear or to see Katie Bell frantically waving at him from the bar.

"Shay-ane!"

Cassidy laughed and shook her head. "It doesn't look like it would be too quiet. Good night, Shane." She walked toward the door.

He started after her, but Katie stepped in front of him before he could catch up. "Where do you think you're going? Come buy me a drink."

"Not tonight."

"You keep saying that! I'm getting tired of waiting, Shane."

He looked her over. He used to think she was pretty and fun. Now he noticed the meanness around her eyes and the stubborn set of her jaw. "Then don't wait, Katie. Go find someone else." He shook her hand off his arm and hurried to the door. He opened it just in time to see Cassidy's little Beetle pull away. Dammit!

He walked down the block back to his truck, running the events of the evening through his head. He couldn't quite believe the way Cassidy had changed tack. She'd given him the brush-off in no uncertain terms since the very first time he'd met her. He had to wonder what had changed her mind. He reached his truck and climbed in with a grin. Had he finally worn down her resistance? He had to believe that was it. No woman had ever resisted him for this long, not when he set his mind to it. He was relieved that he'd had it all wrong about her and Carter, and thrilled to think that she'd made damned sure she won that game of pool—so she could get him naked no less! He was still grinning to himself as he left town and turned south, heading back down the valley. He couldn't wait for Thursday night.

~ ~ ~

Cassidy parked the Beetle in the garage and climbed the stairs into the house. She stopped in front of the mirror in the hallway and smiled. "You're not really going to, are you?" she asked herself. She laughed. Like hell she wasn't! He deserved it! He was a big boy. He could handle it. And if he couldn't, well that would just prove her point—that men's egos grew more brittle in proportion to their size!

She wandered into the kitchen and poured herself a glass of wine. Taking it through to the den she curled up on the sofa with her laptop. She had a reply from Summer.

Hey Chica!

Can't wait to see you either. It's been waaay too long. I need to hole up and hunker down. Your Paradise Valley sounds like, well… Paradise! Don't worry, I won't be a nuisance, I'll just be glad to see you now and then, when you have an hour to spare.

Love n hugs back atcha.

Xxx

Cassidy smiled. Summer was so sweet. She wouldn't impose on anyone—ever—but they'd be seeing each other for more than an hour here and there! Cassidy had thought she'd looked tired and drawn the last couple of times she'd seen her on TV. It would do her good to spend some time here. Take a break from her crazy schedule and just be for a while. She'd have all the peace she needed. Cassidy smiled. She hoped the place that Carter was working on was nice. It'd be great to have Summer just up the road.

She was pretty sure that she'd get along really well with Gina. She had a feeling Shane might take a shine to her, too! Well, if he did, she'd have to steer him away. She was surprised at the way her heart pounded at the thought. She hadn't realized she felt that protective toward Summer. That had to be the reason why she didn't want Shane showing an interest in her, right?

She picked up her wine and let herself out onto the deck above the river. She loved to come out here and listen to the sounds of the water and the night. She sat in one of the big rockers and leaned back to look up at the night sky. They weren't joking when they called this Big Sky country. With no light pollution, a million stars twinkled brightly against the inky blackness. It was beautiful, peaceful. It felt like maybe she'd found the place where she could finally settle. She shook her head at the thought—it was home. She smiled as a shooting star blazed a brief trail across the sky. Weren't they supposed to be a good omen?

Chapter Six

As Thursday afternoon drew on, Cassidy was starting to have a few niggling doubts. Should she really do it?

Gina gave her a puzzled look. "Are you okay?"

"Yeah, I'm fine."

"I have to ask. Shane said you're seeing him tonight, but I thought you were busy?"

Cassidy had to bite back a laugh. She certainly was planning to *see* Shane tonight. "I can do both can't I? I have the class, and I'll be seeing Shane. I'm surprised he told you."

Gina laughed. "You shouldn't be. He's been like a kid waiting for Christmas ever since we all went out the other night." She gave Cassidy an inquiring look. "*You*, on the other hand, haven't mentioned *him* at all."

She hadn't mentioned it because she didn't want to spoil the surprise. If he found out what she was planning, there was no way Shane would show up. She bit the inside of her lip. Was it also because she knew Gina might try to talk her out of it? Think it was a bad idea? Maybe it was? No, it would be fun. If he couldn't take it, he couldn't take it, that'd be his problem—not hers. She shrugged. "I just didn't need to hear you talking him up all week."

"Okay. Well, I hope you have fun. I'm going to head on home now. I want to catch the golden hour down by the river."

That made Cassidy laugh. "Every time you say that it sounds like you're hurrying home to catch a favorite TV show."

Gina laughed. "If I ever get to make a documentary, I think I should call it The Golden Hour. The light at dusk and at dawn is just so perfect."

"Well, you hurry on down there to catch it. I'll see you tomorrow."

Gina paused at the door. "I hope you and Shane have a good time."

"Thanks." Cassidy was pretty sure *she* would; she wasn't so sure how much Shane would enjoy it though.

~ ~ ~

Shane locked up his office and walked up to the house. He wanted to check in with his dad before he headed up to town for his big night with Cassidy. He hadn't been able to get her out of his head since he'd watched her drive away after their game of pool. He grinned. Tonight should take care of that! He was glad now that she hadn't wanted to take her prize straight away. He'd never seen the appeal of anticipation before, but, forced to endure it, he was quite enjoying it—he was even gladder that it was almost over though!

He let himself in through the back door and was surprised to not find his mom in the kitchen. His dad looked up from where he was sitting in one of the easy chairs working on his laptop. "You're out of luck if you're hoping to get fed. She's gone up to town. There's leftovers, but they're all mine."

Shane laughed. "Don't worry, Dad. I'm heading up to town myself. I just wanted to check in with you first."

"Hmph! If I'd known you were going I'd have made her ride with you. She wouldn't let me take her, and I hate her driving at this time in the evening. The deer are just lurking by the side of the road waiting to jump out in front of you."

"She'll be fine, Dad. She's never hit one yet. She's careful. What's she gone up for, anyway?"

"Some class or other. You know what she's like. Always wanting to learn something—beading class, art class, poetry class, salsa dancing class!" He shook his head with a rueful smile. "It's mostly just to hang out with her friends."

Shane nodded. As much as his mom loved the ranch, she liked to get away when she could, whether it was to catch up with the women in town or to head off to the warm sunshine whenever it was possible. "Is she doing okay?"

His Dad nodded. "She is, but she's getting itchy feet. I'm thinking this winter will be the one. I'm going to take her down to Arizona."

"You know you can. We've got everything covered here between us."

"I know. Mason's got the horses covered, you've got the dude ranch, Chance has got the cattle." He shrugged. "It's not that I doubt you boys. I just don't know what the hell I'm going to do with myself. I owe it to your mom. She's endured this life for me all these years, but…" he shrugged again. "This is all I know. All I've ever wanted to know."

Shane patted his shoulder. "You'll find fun stuff to do. Maybe Mom will teach you to dance salsa?"

His dad laughed at that. "Yeah, and maybe pigs will fly! They'd no doubt be more graceful. We'll work it out. Like I say, I owe it to your mom to get her out of the cold for the winter and take her somewhere she can enjoy herself."

"You owe it to yourself, too, Dad. So make sure you find somewhere that's going to be good for you as well."

"Thanks, Shane."

As his dad briefly squeezed his arm, it hit Shane for the first time how old he looked. He had to swallow hard and squeeze his eyes shut for a moment at the realization that he wouldn't always be around.

"Thank *you*, Dad. You've done so much for all of us. Worked your ass off your whole life. I just want to make sure that you have some fun." He swallowed even harder at his dad's reply.

"It's all been fun, son. Every backbreaking hour of it has been fun, because I was doing it all for you boys. I've been building on what my daddy left me, so that I can pass on something even better to all of you."

"Thanks, Dad." He didn't trust himself to say anything else.

His dad nodded, indicating that part of the conversation was closed. "So what did you want to check in with me about?

"I wanted to run an idea by you. I'd like to build some more cabins. We're fully booked with guests now through the end of the summer. We could take more—a lot more—if we had the accommodations. We have the horses, we can get the staff. We have all the extra capacity we need—except for a place for them to sleep."

"It's your business, Shane. Your decision."

"I know that, but I wouldn't do it without asking you first. It's still your land."

"I don't have a problem with it. You expand as much as you need to. And besides it's not going to be my land for too much longer. At some point soon I want to sit down with the five of you and figure out how best we divide it up."

Shane nodded. He knew that day was coming, but he really wasn't looking forward to it. He didn't want to see it happen. He'd rather nothing changed. He knew his parents would take even more of a backseat, and that was fine, but he wanted the ranch to stay whole.

"It'll be okay, son." His dad seemed to understand. "It has to be done that way. You don't see it yet, but someday you'll all have families of your own, and you'll need land that's just yours. No matter how well you all get along, you're all individuals. As the years go by, you'll all have different wants and needs."

"I know, Dad. I know it's necessary; it just makes me sad."

His dad held his gaze for a moment. "It does me, too. But there's no point clinging to the past when the future is calling. All we can do with the past is cherish it. We have to prepare for the future, adjust to the changes, and live life well." He smiled. "How are you planning on living well tonight? Where are you headed?"

Shane grinned. "I'm going to see Cassidy Lane."

His dad frowned. "The artist? The Moonstone Gallery girl?"

"That'd be her."

His dad gave him a puzzled look. "Oh. Okay."

"You don't like the idea?"

"No, it's not that at all. I just thought your mom…" He shook his head. "Never mind. You get on. Have a great evening. My memory's getting even worse than I thought. Say hi to Cassidy for me. She's a real firecracker that one. I like her. But I wouldn't go thinking you can get away with your usual tricks with her."

Shane laughed. "I don't think I can get away with a thing with Cassidy. I've been asking her out for ages, and I'm lucky she agreed to see me tonight. Don't worry, I'll be on my best behavior."

"You'll need to be, if you want a second date. And I have a feeling you will."

Shane took a deep breath. "So do I."

"Get going then. You don't want to blow it by being late."

~ ~ ~

Cassidy kept popping her head into the back room. She'd told Shane to park in the alley behind the gallery and come to the back door, but it was taking her longer than she'd expected to get everything set up out in the gallery. Once she had everything just as she wanted, she stood in the doorway between the two spaces so she could keep an eye on the front and an ear out for Shane in the back.

She heard him knock and pulled the gallery door closed behind her before going to let him in the back door.

She caught her breath at the sight of him. Damn, he was a good-looking guy. A denim shirt stretched across his broad shoulders, his muscular thighs were encased in work worn Wranglers, which she just knew would showcase his great ass perfectly.

"Evening, pretty lady."

He caught her off guard by presenting her with a bunch of flowers from behind his back. Roses! A dozen of them! She hadn't expected that. She felt a moment's hesitation. She didn't *have* to do this to him. She looked up at him. His sandy hair was perfectly tousled, making him look more like a surfer than a rancher. His strong jawline twitched as the corners of his mouth turned up in a smile. As she met his gaze his hazel eyes glimmered with amusement. He was gorgeous!

"Are you ready for this?"

Was she? Was she really going to do it to him?

His smile turned into that infuriatingly cocky grin of his as he stepped closer, crowding her, drowning her senses. His words sealed his fate. "Do you think you can handle this?"

She pulled herself together and stepped neatly aside as he tried to put his hands on her waist and draw her closer. Arrogant prick! She sure as hell could handle it. "Oh, I can Shane. We're going to find out if *you* can handle it. But, as per our bet, I need you naked first."

He seemed oblivious to any tension as he grinned and started to unbutton his shirt. "Anything you say, sweet Cassidy. Anything you say."

She nodded grimly. "That was the deal, and you *are* a man of your word, right, Shane?"

He shrugged out of his shirt and stepped toward her again. She took a step back. She couldn't afford to let him get too close. She was already covered in goosebumps. Her heart was pounding, and she could easily forget all her plans for this evening and go along with his instead. Before she realized it, she'd backed herself all the way up against the counter. He'd matched her step for step and now stood before her, his broad chest at her eye level taunting her to touch. Her fingers twitched to be allowed to do just that.

He placed a hand on the counter on either side of her hips and lowered his head to hers. Oh, God! If he tried to kiss her now, it would be game over, and she would not be the winner.

"So, what do you want me to do next?"

His cocky grin saved her again, giving her the strength to put a hand to his shoulder and push him back. "Get your pants off."

She picked up a towel and thrust it at him making him grasp it in surprise. "Then wrap that around your waist and come on through. I'll be in the front."

She fled for the door while she still could.

She managed to take her place in the middle just before he opened the door and came through. He was holding the towel around his waist with two fingers, about to whip it away with a flourish by the looks of him

"How long do you want me to keep this on for? I…?"

Oh, how she wished she had a camera! The look on his face was priceless as he stared around at the semicircle of ladies facing him, all of them smiling around their easels at him.

"You take it off whenever you're ready," said his mom. "I've seen it all before anyway."

Cassidy couldn't hold back a chuckle at the way both his hands now gripped the towel desperately, clinging to it—and his dignity.

She met his gaze. "Keep it for as long as you need it, Shane. We want you to feel totally comfortable before we begin." His eyes were narrow as he stared back at her. She was grateful for the presence of her seniors' art class. He looked as though he'd throttle her if he could. She pointed toward the chair she had set up on a platform. "Get yourself settled, and when you're ready, you can lose the towel."

He stared at her for a long moment. She was convinced he was about to turn around and storm out. She raised an eyebrow in challenge. It was only what she'd expect. To her surprise, a big grin spread across his face and he saluted her. "Whatever you say, Cassidy. That was the deal, right?" He turned and climbed up onto the chair. He shook his head at her with a rueful smile. "I'm at your mercy." Wow! She smiled at him. He was a much better sport than she'd given him credit for.

"Lose the towel already!" called one of the ladies.

Cassidy laughed out loud at the sight of Mrs. Dearborn, one of the most venerable townswomen, literally licking her lips. She picked up a brush and tapped rhythmically on her easel as she called, "Lose. The. Towel."

The other ladies laughed and joined her, the chant rising to a crescendo when Shane stood and smiled at them all. "This towel?" he asked.

The ladies cheered and wolf whistled. "Lose. The. Towel!"

Cassidy caught Monique Remington's eye. She'd talked to her yesterday about this, and Monique had happily gone along with it. She didn't have a problem and had assured Cassidy that Shane would survive. She winked at Cassidy now with a smile and a nod. Apparently she knew her son well. He'd turned around and was wiggling his butt behind the towel, working the crowd like a professional. Cassidy had to laugh when he turned back around and caught her eye.

He held her gaze as he raised a hand to the ladies. "Okay, playtime's over. Teacher says we need to get to work now." He sat down and waited while the ladies quieted, then slowly let the towel fall to the floor.

It took Cassidy everything she had not to lick her own lips at the sight of him. He smiled and winked at her. She smiled back and saluted him. She had to show her respect for the way he'd played it. She hadn't beaten him at all; he'd stepped up to the challenge.

"I think," he said, "that we're going to get this life drawing class going here in a minute or two—once teacher has had a chance to pull herself together."

She pursed her lips at him. "That's right, ladies. Tonight is our chance to put into practice everything we've learned over the last few weeks. I'd like to thank Shane for being so gracious in helping us."

The ladies all chattered and chuckled. "I'll be happy to give him a hand," called Edna Jenkins from the end of the row. That had them all howling with laughter, even Monique.

"Mom!" laughed Shane. "How can you let them do this to me?"

Monique shrugged and chuckled. "You're a big boy, Shane. You can stand up for yourself."

"A *very* big boy!" called one lady, setting them all off again.

He turned a mock pleading gaze on Cassidy. "Will you protect me from them?"

She nodded. "I'll call them to order. We need to get the class started."

"That's not good enough. I need you to promise me."

She held his gaze. "Promise you what?"

He grinned. "Promise me that you won't let any woman other than you come near me for the duration of the class. That you'll personally protect me. Then I'll relax and we can get started."

"Okay."

"No. You need to say it."

Cassidy sighed.

"Doesn't she ladies?"

They could all see what was going on and were happy to play along by the looks of them. "She does!"

Cassidy rolled her eyes. "I promise I won't let any woman other than me come near you."

"And?" He was enjoying this far too much!

"And I will personally protect you."

"For how long?"

"For the duration of the class."

"And you're a woman of your word?"

She narrowed her eyes at him. He was turning this all around on her! "I am."

"Great." He grinned around at the ladies. "How much longer does this class run for?"

Monique chuckled. "Another three weeks."

Cassidy scowled. "I meant *this* class—the next hour."

Shane gave her a victorious smile. "*We* didn't, did we ladies?"

They all laughed. "No!" called Mrs. Dearborn. "The duration of the class, Cassidy. You have to make sure you don't let any other woman near him for the next three weeks!"

What the…? How the hell had he managed to pull this one off? Cassidy glared at him. He shrugged with that infuriating grin of his. "*I* kept *my* word. Are you going to keep yours?"

She stared around at all the eagerly expectant faces smiling back at her. She heaved a big sigh. "It looks like I have no choice."

"It does, doesn't it?" Shane lay back on the chair. "Draw away, ladies. Draw away."

Chapter Seven

Shane dropped the towel once he was safely in the back room. He pulled his jeans back on and fastened them, then shrugged into his shirt. He shook his head as he reached for his boots. Cassidy had certainly put one over on him tonight. He couldn't help but chuckle to himself. She'd set him up and he'd walked straight into it. Hell he'd run headlong willingly into the trap she'd set for him. She hadn't lied. She'd said she wanted him naked and doing whatever she said. It was his assumption about what she might want that had led him into trouble. He couldn't blame her.

He listened as she said good night to the ladies. He'd given them a laugh at least. That he didn't mind at all. And though he'd lost the battle, he'd put himself at an advantage in the war of wills he was engaged in with Cassidy. He'd made her promise, in front of all those women, that she wouldn't let another woman near him for the next three weeks. He smiled. He intended to make the most of that one. He knew she'd keep her word, no matter how much she resented it. As long as he didn't push her too far, he cautioned himself as he pulled his boots on. She'd play along, but she wouldn't take too much crap. He'd have to push the line, but not cross it. He stood up, and listened. He heard her bidding good night to still-chattering women, and then closing the door behind them. He'd wait before he buttoned his shirt. It wouldn't do any harm to give her another good look at what she was missing out on. He'd noticed her reaction earlier. For all her fight, she wanted him. But not nearly as badly as he wanted her.

She knocked on the door. "Are you decent?"

He chuckled. "Never been accused of that in my life. But I am dressed."

She came in and stopped in the doorway eyeing him suspiciously. "I thought you were dressed!"

He held his shirt open with a grin. "You've seen it all, sweetheart. Don't tell me you're going to act shy about seeing my naked chest now?"

She smiled. "Yeah. I suppose you've got a point."

Hmm, it seemed she was less confrontational now. Maybe he should take advantage? "That was a dirty trick by the way."

She shrugged. "You deserved it."

He nodded. "Maybe I did. But you deserve what you've got coming, too."

Her head jerked up, and she met his gaze. "What do I have coming, Shane?"

Looking at her standing there, her eyes shining, her hands on her hips, her perky breasts jutting up at him as if in a challenge of their own, several replies flashed through his mind, but he bit them back. "Just you wait and see. Remember you made me a promise?"

She nodded reluctantly.

"I'm going to make you work to keep it."

She nodded again. "Oh, don't worry. I know it."

He stepped closer, smiling at the way she backed away from him. He knew damn well she wasn't scared of him. What had him smiling was the realization that she was scared of her own reaction to him. He kept coming, his smile—and his hard on—growing as she cornered herself against the counter. When he'd had her there earlier, it had taken every ounce of willpower he possessed not to kiss her, not to sit her up on the counter and spread her legs. He wasn't sure he had any willpower left now.

He placed his hands on the counter—on either side of her hips—and leaned forward. She leaned back, looking up into his eyes. Damn, she was beautiful! Her hands came up to his shoulders, clinging to him to keep her balance as he leaned further forward. He slid his arms around her and closed his hands around her ass. Her breath was low and shallow. She was his for the taking. He stepped his feet between hers and they both moaned as he thrust his hips, pressing his cock into her heat. Her gaze was locked with his as he brought one hand up to trace her cheek. He trailed it down over her throat and made her thrust her hips into him as he teased her breast with his fingertips.

They both sprang away from each other at the sound of banging on the gallery door. Cassidy looked around wildly and Shane instinctively stepped in front of her as she made to go out front. She glared at him.

"I'm not a damsel in distress, Shane. I need to see who it is. One of the ladies probably forgot something."

He scowled, more at himself than her. Why had he tried to protect her? Step between her and some perceived danger at the front door? He didn't have time to come up with any answers before they heard…

"Shane? Shay-ane?"
"Oh, for fuck's sake! What does she want now?" How in the hell had Katie found him here?
Cassidy laughed. "I think we both know what she wants. What I don't know is why she wants it now and knows to come here to get it. Did you have her lined up for after you'd done me?"
Shane glared at her. "Don't be crazy!"
Cassidy glared back. "You're the one who's crazy if you think you're going to fuck me and then run straight out and do her as well. Get out, Shane. Go do your sure thing."
She made for the door again, but he caught her shoulder. "Not so fast, princess."
She whirled around, eyes blazing. "What?"
Jesus! She was scary when she was mad. And damn, did it turn him on!
"Are you forgetting your promise? You're not going to let another woman near me for three weeks. You can't send me out there into her clutches. You have to protect me yourself."
He had to laugh at the struggle on her face. She wanted to send to him packing, no doubt about it. But, she had a sense of honor, too. Her word was her bond; he'd seen that about her, Gina had even told him as much. He grinned at her and shrugged. "Unless your word means nothing?"
She looked as though she might explode as she stood there glaring at him. He could see she was doing battle with herself. He held his breath; this could go either way. Maybe he was pushing her beyond her limits already? After a long moment she blew out a big sigh. "I'll keep my word, Shane, but be warned, you may live to regret it."
That sent a shiver down his spine. He didn't doubt she could be right, but for now he had this tiger by the tail, and he didn't

intend to let go. He smiled. "Then you'd best go get rid of her, huh? I'll wait here."

She pushed the door to the gallery open and stormed through it. He listened to her heels tap across the hardwood floor to the front door. He heard it open and then her and Katie talking. He couldn't make out the words, but there was none of the yelling or screaming he'd half expected. He thought about buttoning up his shirt while he waited, but then thought better of it. It had been working for him just the way it was—until Katie had turned up and killed the moment.

It was a good five minutes before Cassidy returned. She gave him that mysterious smile, the one he now knew to be wary of—very wary!

"What did you tell her?"

The smile grew bigger—more worrying. "Don't you worry your pretty head, Shane. You're safe."

"I am?" He had to wonder what she'd said that made her so sure. *He'd* had no success in shaking Katie off.

"You are—for the next three weeks," she added with a chuckle. "Then you're not my problem anymore."

He didn't like the sounds of that, but he wasn't going to let Cassidy know. He shrugged. "We'll see."

She shook her head. "You're such a cocky bastard!"

He laughed. "I like to think that I know my worth. I thought that was a trait we shared?"

"Oh, I know my worth, Shane. It seems you overestimate yours."

He laughed. "How can you say that when you don't even know me? Won't take the chance to get to know me. What are you afraid of, Cassidy?"

Her eyes blazed. "I am not *afraid* of anything!"

He held a hand up "Whoa! Calm down. You're a badass, I know. You're not afraid of anything or anyone. So why not let your guard down?"

She stared at him for a long moment. "I don't have my guard up. You just piss me off, that's all."

Shane dared to take a step closer. Maybe he could get her back to where they'd been before they were interrupted. The way she laughed quickly set him straight on that one though.

"Don't even think about it. I admit I'm attracted to you. You're attracted to me. We could very easily get to screwing each other's brains out right there on the counter."

Shane grinned. "So why don't we? You know you want to."

She glared at him then slowly relaxed and laughed. "You are unbelievable, you know?"

He nodded. "I've heard that before. Why don't you try me and you can judge for yourself?"

She laughed again. "Because, Shane, it would only end badly. It's not worth it."

"It'd be well worth it. You can't say that till you try it." He took another step closer, but she shook her head.

"You run along home. It's not going to happen." She really meant it.

Shane reluctantly started buttoning up his shirt. "Do me a favor?"

"What's that?"

"Tell me why?"

She thought about it.

"You already said you're attracted to me. You know I'm attracted to you. What's the harm? Why don't you want to?"

"Because…" She was so cute, the way she chewed on her bottom lip as she pondered how best to answer. "Because, I'm a ball buster, Shane. I hurt men. I make a mess anytime I get involved with a guy. I don't want to hurt you."

He didn't get it. He'd never been hurt by a woman in his life! He'd broken a few hearts himself. He felt bad about it, but he'd never done it intentionally. "I don't get hurt, Cassidy. I play for fun, not for keeps."

She sighed. "That's what they all say. You men want someone small and sweet to feed your ego. I look like I fit the bill. Trouble is, I'm also strong and smart, and that is not something the male ego deals with too well."

Shane thought about it. "I won't argue that small and sweet is sexy, but it's also available. Strong and smart doesn't usually come in a very attractive package. You…" How could he put it? "You're like…the ultimate challenge, the ultimate prize. You're strong and smart, packaged in small and sweet. It doesn't get any sexier than that."

"I know, Shane. I've heard it all before. It's a very appealing proposition for a guy. But the reality turns out to be tougher than you expect. Then your ego suffers, then I get painted as the wicked bitch of the west. That's what guys do. When you realize I'm too strong, you can't admit that it's because *you're* too weak. So you demonize me in order to feel better about yourself. I'm not up for that. I'd rather keep our banter going, have a laugh, be a friend even, but I don't want to go down the same old road again. It sucks."

Wow! She was laying it all out for him.

"So now you know. If all you're after is a quick roll in the hay, you're not going to get it, and if you're after something more than that, you're not going to get *that* either." She shrugged. "I guess I'll see you around."

Shane held her gaze for a long moment, trying to choose the right words.
She pointed to the door. "If you don't mind? I've got work to do. Good night."
He nodded and grabbed his jacket. "Good night Cassidy." He was surprised by the force with which the door slammed behind him. He grinned and made his way back to his truck.

~ ~ ~

Cassidy slammed the door and then folded her arms across her chest. "Asshole!" she stalked over to the cupboard and pulled out a fresh canvas. She needed to paint when she was this angry—oils! No wishy-washy watercolor tonight. Her hand flew across the canvas with bold, bright strokes. Soon she was lost. Forty minutes later she sat back. Why had she been so angry anyway? Shane had only done exactly as she'd asked him to. She'd told him there was no hope and asked him to leave. Why should she be mad that he'd gone? She stared at her work. He was beautiful. Why the hell had she painted him? She'd captured his cocky-ass smile perfectly. She shook her head. She'd captured him perfectly—at least in oils—at least in outline. So maybe he'd gotten to her a little more than she cared to admit. She never painted anything she wasn't passionate about. Hate was a passion, too, though, right? No. She wasn't going to try to lie to herself. She liked the guy. Liked him far too much. She was angry that he'd left, because somewhere down deep inside, she'd hoped he'd fight for a chance. She'd hoped he'd try to convince her that he wasn't like other guys—that he was strong enough to deal with her. She shrugged. He hadn't even bothered. He'd just gone as soon as she'd asked. It wasn't fair of her to be angry with him for respecting her wishes. He had plenty of options, he was probably pursuing one of them right now.

She packed up her things and locked up the gallery. It was time to head home. She felt oddly deflated. Her prank on Shane hadn't been the fun she'd thought it would be, and his ready acceptance of her rejection had left her feeling flat. She'd done herself out of the one male interest she'd had in a long time. She'd been dumb to lay it out so clearly for him. Now their sparring days would be over, and he wouldn't flirt with her anymore. She should be glad; instead, she had a ball of disappointment lodged in her stomach. When she reached her Beetle she saw a note tucked under the wiper. She pulled it out, a smile spreading across her face as she read it.

I don't give up that easy, Princess. You're having dinner with me tomorrow—even if it's only for banter and friendship. You can't let another woman near me, so you have to take care of me remember?:0) Oh, and go back for the roses. They'll need water!

She laughed. How did he know she'd forget the roses? She hurried back to the gallery and picked them up, telling herself it was only because she didn't want Gina to see them in the morning. As she locked the door a second time, a big hand came down on her shoulder. She turned around with a smile.

"What are you still doing here?" she asked.

Shane smiled. "I had to know if you cared enough to go back for the flowers."

She looked down at them and then back up at him. "I'd hate to let them die."

His smile was gentle, his eyes questioning. "You care?"

She chewed the inside of her lip. He was asking about more than the flowers. Part of her wanted to brush him off. Just because she'd been disappointed that he'd left, that didn't mean anything could happen between the two of them. But something—the genuine concern in his eyes?—the way her own heart was pounding? Whatever it was, something made her bite back the snappy retort. She searched his face and nodded. She couldn't say it out loud.

The way his eyes softened made her so glad she hadn't beaten him down. He offered her his arm and she took it. "Good, let me walk you to your car then."

When they reached the Beetle he smiled down at her. "Dinner tomorrow?"

She nodded again. She felt as though she was admitting defeat in some way, but she didn't want to fight for the win. Losing to him like this felt like a different kind of victory.

He held her gaze as he brushed two fingers over her lips. "Thank you."

She waited, surely he was going to kiss her? He didn't! Damn him. He just kept on smiling that sweet and very un-Shane-like smile. She wanted to kiss him! But no. She unlocked the car and he held the door open for her as she climbed in.

He closed the door and watched her pull her seatbelt on. "See you tomorrow, Princess."

"Why do you keep calling me that?"

He shrugged. "It suits you."

Was that a compliment or an insult? She had no idea, and she couldn't stick around to get him to explain. She turned the ignition and pulled away. If she stayed a moment longer, she'd be begging him to come with her!

Chapter Eight

At lunchtime Shane headed back up to the cabin; he needed to get away from the guests for a while. Lena had stayed back at the ranch today, apparently determined to get him to take her in the barn. He would never have done that, not a guest right here on the ranch. He did have some boundaries. He had no interest whatsoever in her now anyways. His head was filled with thoughts of Cassidy. He couldn't stop smiling—or whistling. He stopped in his tracks as he rounded the corner of the barn. He was surprised to see Carter out here.

His brother laughed. "What's going on, littlest bro? You look like a cartoon stereotype of happiness!"

"What do you mean?"

"Strolling along with your hands in your pockets, whistling a happy little tune. That's what I mean."

Shane shrugged. "I'm a happy guy. Little Mr. Sunshine. You know that."

"I do, but even you aren't this happy for no reason. Come on, tell your big brother what's going on?"

Shane grinned. He couldn't help it. "I finally talked Cassidy into having dinner with me tonight." His heart started pounding at the way Carter's face fell. Did that mean he really was interested in her himself? "What's wrong?"

"Nothing. It's just that I said I'd get with her before the weekend about her landscaping plans. I haven't had a chance yet, and I was going to call her to see if I could stop by this evening when I get finished on Beau's rental house. She wanted to look that place over, remember?"

"Is that all?"

Carter gave him a puzzled look. "All? That's my business, Shane. If I tell a client I will get with them before the weekend, I get with them before the weekend. I just don't want to hold her up if she has plans with you."

Shane smiled. He was being overly sensitive. Carter's only interest in Cassidy was, as he had said, in her landscaping. "I'm sure she can do both. I was going to pick her up early and go for a walk by the river before we head out, but we could kill two birds with one stone. We could walk up to Beau's place and meet you there."

"What, and you're going to sit around twiddling your thumbs while she and I talk about landscaping?"

Shane grinned. "It might win me some brownie points."

Carter laughed. "Okay, then. You talk to her first. I'll give her a call later to confirm it's okay."

"Will do. What are you doing out here anyway?"

"Since I'm working on Beau's place I said I'd come have lunch with the folks."

Shane smiled. Carter was good at hanging the family together in a way the rest of them weren't. "Has Dad said anything more to you about dividing the place up?"

"Not in a while," Carter looked sad. "I know we have to do it, and he wants to do it soon, but I just wish everything could stay as it is." He met Shane's gaze. "I'm dreading it, if I'm honest. I want Chance to get his fair share, but Beau doesn't like the idea. I know he's going to make it difficult."

Shane nodded. "I wish I could argue with you, but he's had a problem with it ever since Dad first mentioned it. To me, Chance is just another brother. It's only right that he should get his share. I know Mason feels the same way. You…" He punched Carter's arm. "You're too laid back to kick up a fuss about anything. But Beau's always resented Chance. I just don't know why."

"Come on, Shane. You don't know why? It's plain as day! He feels as though Chance stole his place. Mason's the eldest, you're the baby. It's easy for the two of you. Me…" He grinned. "Like you say, I'm just a big old chump who doesn't let much of anything bother him. But Beau always felt the need to compete, as though if he didn't excel, he wouldn't get Dad's love or attention or…something. When we were kids he was always trying to outdo Mason. It's why he studied so hard, played every sport so hard, had to be captain. When Dad took Chance in, made him part of the family in the way he did, Beau took it personally. Chance and Mason became so close so fast, it was like Beau was knocked out of second place and down to third, when he'd spent his whole life trying to compete for first."

Shane stared at him. "Jesus!"

"What?"

"You! You've got it all figured out haven't you?"

Carter shrugged. "It's hard to miss if you watch and listen to what's going on around you."

Shane thought about it. He never really had watched or listened to what was going on around him when they were growing up. As Carter had said, he was the baby—and he'd made the most of it. He loved the attention and the extra leeway that being the youngest had given him. He was naturally happy and upbeat. When others weren't, he tended to stay out of their way—which was why, of all his brothers, he was least close to Beau. "Now you put it like that, I kinda feel bad for Beau. I've always thought he was just being an asshole about Chance."

Carter shook his head, "Never dismiss anyone as an asshole before you know their story—their motivation, their pain. Everyone has reasons for the way they behave, the way they think. You can't judge them from where you sit. Well, you can, but if you do, it makes you the asshole, not them."

Shane laughed. "Good point, though I'd never thought of it that way before."

"It might do you some good to start thinking that way." Carter gave him a sly smile. "Especially if you're finally going to attempt a real relationship."

Shane raised an eyebrow. "And what makes you think I'm going to do that?"

"Ah, nothing much. Just the way you were tootling along whistling to yourself and the fact that it's because you're seeing Cassidy tonight." He smiled. "I think you two might be good for each other."

"Don't get carried away. I'm taking her out for dinner, that's all. She says she's not interested in going out with me." He shrugged. "Or even just sleeping with me."

Carter laughed. "But you think you can change her mind?"

"I don't know. But I'm going to have fun trying."

~ ~ ~

Cassidy checked herself over in the hallway mirror. She looked good. She always did! But she'd made an extra effort to this evening. That was weird. But it felt good, so she wasn't going to question it. She was just going to head out onto the deck and wait for Shane to arrive. She had no clue yet how she wanted to play this evening. She'd been wrestling with the options all day; as far as she could see, she had three. She could stick to what she'd told him last night—friendship and banter. She could revert to where they had been—sparring while determined not to let things devolve into anything more than that. Or, and this was the scary option, she could just keep being honest with him and see where it went. She kept coming back to that third one. But she didn't know why. Was Shane really worth it? Was the obvious attraction between them so undeniable that he was worth taking the risk? Or was she just doing what she did—amusing herself, like a cat with a curious mouse? No! It wasn't that at all. Was it?

She smiled at the sound of the buzzer letting her know a car had entered the driveway. Here he was. She went out onto the front porch to greet him. When he jumped down from his truck and grinned up at her, he helped her make the call. She was going to keep being honest with him and see where it went.

"Are you ready to go?" he called.

"Sure. Just let me grab my purse." She went back and grabbed it from the island in the kitchen and then ran down the steps. She stopped before him when she reached the bottom.

"Hey."

He really was gorgeous. "Hi." She realized that they had never started up a normal conversation. Shane usually hit her with some inappropriate comment and she came back with a put down. She had to wonder if they'd have anything left to say to each other once that was taken away.

He offered her his arm. "Shall we?"

She laughed and linked him. "Lead on. I don't even know where this house is."

He led her down the path toward the river. "You mean you haven't even explored your own property yet?"

She frowned. "I guess I haven't. I've been down by the river, but I haven't wandered too far." She looked up at him, wondering if she should share. The look on his face encouraged her to risk it. Now he wasn't hitting on her the whole time, he was warm and sunny. "Okay, you have to promise not to laugh at me."

He raised an eyebrow. "I don't like to make promises I can't keep."

"Then I'm not telling you. I feel pretty stupid as it is, and, if you laugh, I'll be mortified."

He nodded. "Okay. I won't laugh."

"It's just, well…I'm a bit scared."

"Of what?"

She laughed herself. It felt a little ridiculous, but she was also aware that her fear could be totally justified. "Of everything! I mean, I love it here. I love that I get to see the deer and the eagles and the bunnies in the morning, but there have to be other creatures around, too—less friendly ones?"

Shane nodded.

"Every time I've asked about hiking trails, the first thing people tell me is to never hike alone. So, how can I come down here by myself? I wouldn't have a clue what to do if a bear jumped out at me. I hear the coyotes every night, and it sounds cool—but what would I do if I ran into them? What would *they* do? And everyone is always arguing about the wolves. Where are they? And what do they eat?"

Shane smiled, but he didn't look as though he was about to laugh at her. "It must be strange for you. Not so long ago, I would have laughed at everything you just said. But that's because I grew up here. It's all so familiar to me. That isn't the case for you. It's all new, and I can see how it would be scary." He squeezed her arm with his as they reached the bottom of the path. "Stick with me; I'll keep you safe."

She smiled. He was back to his flirting, but this time it felt good. She was looking for more than protection though. She wanted knowledge, wanted to know how to protect herself. She chewed the inside of her lip, wondering how to tell him that without it coming across as another put down.

She didn't need to figure it out though. He surprised her. "Knowing you though, you want to know how to handle it by yourself."

She nodded. "I don't like not knowing what to do. I don't like not even knowing what's a valid fear and what's just ignorance."

"Then I'll help you learn the difference…if you like?"

"Yes, please. I would like that."

"It'll take a while though. You'll have to come out in the backcountry with me…hiking." He gave her a saucy grin. "Maybe even camping?"

She laughed. "Are you just trying to get me alone out in the wilderness?"

He winked. "Not *just* that, no. But I promise you'll enjoy it if you come."

"And you think you can make me come?" She chuckled. She couldn't help it.

"I believe I can. If you're interested?"

She shook her head. "Sorry. I shouldn't have said that. We're not going to go there."

He stopped walking and turned to face her, resting both hands on her shoulders as he looked down into her eyes. "Why not though, Cassidy?"

Her mind was screaming the same question as her body reacted to his touch. *Why not?* She blew out a sigh. "You're testing my willpower, Shane."

That made him grin. "Good." He lowered his face to hers. "Tell me you don't want me. Tell me you don't think I can make you come."

She searched his face as he brushed his fingers over her lips. "I'm not a liar."

"So what's the problem?" He stepped closer sliding one hand into her hair and tilting her head back so she was looking up at him.

Her willpower was packing its bags, about to admit defeat and abandon her, leave her at the mercy of her desire. She made one last attempt. "I just don't want to make a mess. I don't want to end up hating you or having you hate me. You're a guy, you have an ego. I tend to bruise those…or shatter them. I'd hate for that to happen with you."

"I don't know what happened in your past, but he was an asshole. I'm not like that. I'm happy-go-lucky, easy come easy go. Have some fun with me. We can make a deal that when we're done, we'll walk away as friends."

She considered it. "That sounds all well and good, Shane, but what happens when I piss you off, just by being me. What happens when you piss me off, by wanting me to be less than I am?"

"Less than you are?"

"Yeah, less strong, less intelligent." She gave him a rueful smile. "Less stubborn. Less independent, less confident. I could go on."

"Please do, because I don't want you to be less of any of those things. They're what makes you different, they're what I like about you. And if you think I'm some insecure prick who can't handle you, you're wrong…very wrong."

She looked into his eyes. He wasn't defending himself or making a point; he was just stating his truth. What the hell, here she went again. "Then kiss me."

She saw the smile in the moment before his lips met hers. He closed his arms around her and she reached hers up around his neck. God he felt good. She pressed herself against his hard chest, loving the feeling of being all wrapped up in him. He nibbled her bottom lip, then thrust his tongue into her mouth. His kiss wasn't like any she'd known before. It wasn't demanding, but it was assertive, confident. She willingly kissed him back, opening up to him as he explored her mouth. It was the sexiest kiss—she moaned into his mouth as he stepped it up, unwilling and unable to deny him. She loved the way his arms felt around her, pressing her to him and at the same time enveloping her in his warmth. Damn, she wanted him! Eventually, he lifted his head and smiled.

She smiled back. "Wow!" was all she could say.

"You ain't seen nothing yet." He took her hand and led her on down a path she hadn't seen before that followed the bank of the river.

She followed, unable to wipe the big smile from her face. She might be about to make one hell of a man-mess, but she was determined now that she was going to enjoy the hell out of him before disaster struck.

Chapter Nine

It was a beautiful walk along the river to Beau's rental property. Cassidy was really hoping that the house would be suitable for Summer. It would be awesome to have her friend living this close, awesome to be able to make this walk to visit each other. She shuddered—once she had a handle on what she might have to expect along the way in terms of creatures that might want to eat her! She hadn't given that a thought as she walked with Shane. She felt totally safe. That realization was quite something in itself. Normally being around a guy made her feel less safe in her environment. Normally a guy presented some kind of threat she needed to defend herself against. Why? And why didn't Shane?

He turned to smile at her. "We're almost there. When we come out of the cottonwoods on the bend there you'll see the house. It's a great place. What's the story with you friend?"

Hmm, she really didn't want Shane taking a liking to Summer, and she was prepared to admit to herself now that it wasn't out of protectiveness toward her friend! "She's a singer. She needs to get away for a while and rest her voice."

"Anyone I might have heard of?"

"Depends if you like country music."

"I love it."

"Well then yes, I'm sure you've heard of Summer Breese."

"Really?"

She had to laugh at the expression on his face. "Good grief, Shane, your tongue's hanging out! Put it away and calm down, would you?"

He laughed. "She's awesome. I love her voice."

Cassidy was surprised at the little pang of jealousy she felt. It wasn't a familiar feeling to her. Jealousy was something other people did—insecure people. That wasn't her. "I'm sure you'll love *her* when you meet her. She's a real sweetheart."

"She's not one of those people who's a bitch in real life, but acts all sweet for the cameras?"

"No!" Cassidy hated it when people thought that about her friend. "She is genuinely one of the nicest, kindest, most beautiful people you will ever meet!"

Shane grinned. "And beware, she has the ferocious Cassidy to defend her."

Cassidy smiled. "She does." They rounded the bend and her smile grew when she saw the cabin. She turned to Shane. "Is this the place?"

He nodded. "What do you think?"

"I think it's perfect! I'll have to look around inside, but I think Summer will love it."

"Can I tell Carter that it's her?"

Cassidy raised an eyebrow at him. "Of course, but please don't go telling everyone else. She wants to come here for some peace and quiet, to rest."

"Oh, I didn't mean like that. I wouldn't say a word, it's none of my business and none of anyone else's, it's just Carter." He grinned. "He has a crush on her. He doesn't date or anything, but he goes all goofy whenever she's on the radio. If he sees her on TV he just sits and stares with a big daffy smile on his face."

"Aww! He's such a sweetheart."

"He is." Shane's smile faded. "Does she have a boyfriend?"

"No. She never has time for one." Cassidy grinned. "Wouldn't it be something if we could get the two of the together?"

Shane gave her a worried look. "Maybe."

"But?"

"But Carter's been hurt before. I don't want him finally opening up to someone who will walk all over him and then leave him behind and never look back."

Wow! That was a side of Shane she hadn't seen before. She loved that he was protective toward his brother. "I'd hate to see him get hurt, although Summer isn't like that. It's probably best that we stay out of it, huh? Tell him she's coming and leave it at that."

"Yeah, but also take them both for a night out here and there?"

"If she'll go out. It might be easier for her not to." Cassidy knew what he meant though. "Don't worry we can make sure he gets the chance to meet her properly. I'll have everyone over for dinner." She caught his eye. "And a game of pool."

He narrowed his eyes at her. "You have a pool table?"

She laughed. "I do."

"You're a little hustler!"

"Why, thank you."

"I'm going to need a rematch you know. I need to beat you and claim my prize."

His look sent shivers racing down her spine. She couldn't wait!

"Hey guys!" called Carter. He was building a rockery in the little side yard. Cassidy couldn't help but admire the way his muscles rippled as he hefted a huge rock into place. He was a little too bulky for her taste. She smiled to herself as she thought about it. Even when they were kids, Summer had always gone gaga over big, built guys. Cassidy had a feeling she would swoon at the sight of Carter. That would be awesome. They were two of the sweetest people on earth. But she was a little concerned too; she'd hate for either of them to get hurt.

"Yo bro!" called Shane. "It would appear that Cassidy has been rendered speechless by the sight of your physique."

Cassidy slapped his arm, and Carter looked uncomfortable. She hated that Shane would embarrass him like that. "He's just jealous, Carter. I was actually thinking about how much my friend is going to like you."

Shane pouted at her. "I thought you were going to let me tell him?"

"I was, but I didn't think you were going to embarrass us both!"

He hung his head. "Sorry, you're right. I am jealous of my big brother. I mean what guy wouldn't be? He's big and buff and…" Cassidy had to laugh as Shane flexed his own muscles. "And my girl isn't noticing me because she's ogling him!"

The corners of Carter's mouth turned up in the hint of a smile. He raised an eyebrow at Cassidy.

She looked at Shane. "*Your* girl?"

He shrugged and gave her his cocky grin, which was much more appealing now. "I'm working on it."

"Will one of you tell me?" asked Carter.

"Oh, yeah. Sorry." Shane looked at Cassidy. "Can I?"

She laughed and nodded. "Go ahead."

Shane went over and put an arm around Carter's shoulders. "Cassidy's friend, the one who is going to be staying right here in this house…"

"If she likes it," said Cassidy. "I haven't even seen inside yet."

Shane waved a hand at her. "She'll love it. She's going to be staying right here."

"*Who* is?" asked Carter with a laugh.

"None other than the beautiful, the angel voiced, the sweetest of the sweet…"

"Who?"

"Shane just tell him, or I will!"

"The one and only, Summer Breese!"

The corners of Carter's mouth turned up at the same time his head went down. He looked so embarrassed, Cassidy felt for him. Though she couldn't help smiling at the touch of color on his cheeks.

"The singer?" he asked without looking up.

"Yes, the singer, dumbass!" Shane punched his arm. "The very same Summer Breese who you moon over whenever she's on TV. The one you sing along with in your truck."

Carter's cheeks turned even redder as he shot a look at Cassidy.

She smiled. She didn't want him to feel bad. "I sing along with her, too. I love her voice and all her songs. Did you know she writes them all herself?"

Carter nodded.

Shane laughed. "Of course he does! He knows everything there is to know about her; well, everything that's in the public realm. And now he'll get to know what she's really like, too!"

Carter shook his head. "Oh no. I wouldn't want to intrude on her privacy. She doesn't like the spotlight." He met Cassidy's gaze and shook his head again. "Don't worry. I do think she's awesome, but I'll stay away. She must want some peace if she's coming all the way out here."

"She does, but she wants to spend time with me, too. I'd like her to meet my friends. She's not coming to be a hermit or anything."

Carter gave her a shy smile. "I would like to meet her, and I won't embarrass you."

She laughed. "I know that!" She looked at Shane. "I'm not so sure about *him*, but I'm not worried about you at all."

Shane laughed. "No worries here. I've already got my hands full with you."

Carter looked from her to Shane and back again, seemingly surprised at that. It wasn't enough to distract him though. "How do you know her?"

"We grew up together. I went to school with her and her sister."

"Autumn? Is she coming, too?"

"I'm not sure. She may come to help Summer get settled in, but I can't see her staying for long. This place will suit Summer, but Autumn's a big city girl."

Carter nodded. "That was the impression I got."

"Well, once her sister's gone, I'm sure you can help Summer settle right in. It'll be your pleasure, right?" asked Shane.

Carter looked at Cassidy again. "I'll be on hand for anything she needs, but I wouldn't want to impose."

Cassidy touched his arm; he was so sweet. She was starting to wonder if anything might happen between him and Summer. They would make an adorable couple—but she mustn't get carried away. "Thanks, Carter. I think we'd better take a look inside the house first, don't you? I'd love to call her tonight and tell her we've found somewhere for her."

He nodded. "Come on in then. It's a great place."

~ ~ ~

Shane smiled at Cassidy across the table. They'd spent a good hour with Carter while they went over his landscaping plans for her house. Shane was glad to finally have her to himself. "What made you want to come here?"

She laughed. "The Valley Lodge is the only place I've eaten outside of town. Everyone says this place has the best burgers. I haven't had a burger in ages."

Shane nodded. He was a little disappointed. He'd wanted to take her to the Valley Lodge as it was one of the best restaurants in the Mountain West. It made sense that she would be familiar with it though. To her that was the norm and somewhere like this, the Riverside, just a regular burger joint to him, was somewhere new and different. It didn't really matter where they ate though. What mattered was that he was on a real date with her—hopefully the first.

She raised an eyebrow at him. "You weren't hoping to impress me were you?"

He met her gaze. She was blunt, no doubt about it, but that was one of the things he liked about her. She didn't give him any room to put on a façade to impress her. He liked that because it gave him no choice but to be completely honest and, therefore, transparent. He was used to maintaining a certain distance from women—mentally if not physically. He gave them the front, and they loved it. They gave him the sex, and he loved that! He couldn't wait to get Cassidy into bed. "Of course I was hoping to impress you, Princess." He gave her a wink and caught hold of her hand across the table. "How else am I supposed to schmooze you into the sack?"

She threw back her head and laughed. "You're such an asshole, Shane!"

He gave her a hurt look, but couldn't hide his smile. "I try to be. I know it's what you like best about me."

She shook her head. "No, I think it works pretty well for you with most women. But you have to remember that I'm not like most women."

"How could I forget?"

"What does that mean?"

He smiled. He wanted to play with her, not piss her off. "I mean I'm here, aren't I? With most women, I would have given up weeks ago. You've not exactly been nice to me, have you?"

"You've not exactly deserved it, have you?"

He laughed. "With most women, I don't need to be. My charm and dashing good looks are all it takes."

She laughed. "It'll take more than your normal with me."

"Exactly." He squeezed her hand and looked into her laughing, honey-colored eyes for a long moment. "I want more than my normal *from* you."

The laughter faded from her face as she looked back at him. They stared into each other's eyes until she broke the moment. "Ha! Nice one, Shane. I almost fell for that!"

His heart sank. Her words felt like a slap in the face. He'd meant it! He didn't want to *just* screw her, he wanted to spend time with her, get to know her. He recovered quickly.

"I can see you're going to keep me on my toes," she said.

He laughed as the server approached the table. “I’d rather get you on your back.” He smirked at her as the server looked from him to her.

She gave him the evil eye before turning to the girl to place her order.

Once the server had gone she gave him a cool look. “So what are we doing here? Are you just taking a roundabout route to the inevitable?”

He raised an eyebrow. He thought he knew what she meant, but he wanted her to spell it out.

“The inevitable screwing each other’s brains out,” she clarified.

“I hope not. I mean yeah, I hope that part is inevitable, but I hope it’s not all we’re going to do together.” Her face relaxed a little. He hoped it was because she wanted to get to know him too. He rushed on while it seemed her defenses were down. “Since you have to keep other women away from me for the next three weeks, I was thinking we should spend some time together actually getting to know each other.”

She gave him a wary look. “Doing what?”

“Teaching you all those things you were asking about down by the river. I’ll take you out in the backcountry if you like?”

She looked suspicious. “If you just want to screw, I’d rather do it at my place.”

He laughed. “You, Cassidy Lane, are a cynic. Has anyone ever told you that?”

Her face was hard as she nodded. “Oh, yes. I’ve heard that one before. I prefer to think of myself as a realist.”

He shook his head, “No, reality is a lot less harsh than you give it credit for. I’m a nice guy. Yes, I want to sleep with you, but I also want to have fun with you outside of the sack, too. So I dare you.”

She smiled at that. "What do you dare me?"

He'd been right, she wasn't the kind to refuse a dare. "To spend the weekend with me. We'll head out into the backcountry. We'll camp, I'll teach you what it's like out there." He met her gaze, you'll have to depend on me to keep you safe." He watched the struggle on her face. He already knew her well enough to know that the thought of depending on anyone was alien to her. The thought of depending on him was probably even worse, but if she was too much of a hardass to do it, then there really wasn't much point in him pursuing her. He liked that she was strong, liked her spunk, but he was a guy after all. He wanted to feel that she wanted him—maybe even needed him—for something.

She pursed her lips. "I accept."

He laughed, "But you don't like it, do you?"

"Not one bit, no. However, I am intrigued. You're not the big goofball you make yourself out to be, are you?"

He smiled, she knew what he was doing. "Not many people see beyond the pretty face."

She shrugged. "That's a problem—or a blessing—we share. I see beyond yours; you see beyond mine. You think we may as well find out straight off the bat if we're going to be able to handle each other."

He smiled. "You know I want to handle you." He let his gaze rest on her breasts and was rewarded when her nipples hardened.

She narrowed her eyes at him. "You know damn well what I mean!"

He smirked, "And you know what I mean."

She let out an exasperated laugh. "I do. And I guess this weekend we're both going to find out just how much we can handle!"

"In every sense."

~ ~ ~

Cassidy watched Shane as he drove back down the valley after dinner. It had been a great evening. They'd laughed a lot. He was great company when he wasn't being a cocky asshole. That wasn't fair, she enjoyed it even when he was. Sparring with him was fun. She just hadn't realized what a decent guy was lurking behind the banter. Looking at him now, the moonlight shining on his relaxed face as he drove, he was gorgeous. His strong jawline twitched as he smiled.

"Do you like what you see?"

She'd thought he was concentrating on driving. "You caught me," she said.

He laughed. "I forgive you, I know it's hard not to stare." He turned and shot her his cocky grin making her laugh, too.

"You are so damned full of yourself."

He shrugged. "It's hard not to be. You want to be, too. Admit it."

She cocked her head to one side not understanding.

He turned and gave her that look that set her heart racing and the shivers racing down her spine. "Full of me."

"Damn you, Shane!"

He laughed. "Come on, Princess. Be honest. That's where we're headed. I'll take you home, we'll chat a little until we can't wait any longer, then, finally, we're going to…"

"No we are not!" She couldn't believe she was saying it. She wanted him so badly she was wet for him already. She was desperate to get naked with him, be full of him, as he put it.

But…no way was she going to let him dictate it on his terms, in his time, like she was some sure thing, that he'd play with and then take when he was ready.

He glanced across at her. "You don't mean that. You want it as much as I do."

"I do mean it, Shane. No!"

He drove on in silence, leaving her to wonder whether he was angry. Whether he'd lost all interest because he wasn't going to get what he wanted.

He pulled onto Mill Lane and drove up the long driveway. Once he brought the truck to a stop, he cut the ignition and turned to look at her. She couldn't decipher the look on his face.

"No?"

She shook her head.

He unbuckled his seatbelt and leaned toward her. Damn her traitorous fingers, they were reaching up to his shoulders, pulling him closer. He stopped with his lips inches from hers.

"Why not?"

"Because you expect it."

He chuckled. "You're right there." He brushed his lips over hers and traced her cheek with his fingertips. "You want to though."

She nodded and let out a little sigh when he slid his hand down to cover her breast, his fingers teasing her taut nipple. She looked up into his eyes and his lips came down on hers. She clung to his shoulders as he kissed her deeply. His hand left her breast, stealthily making its way down between her legs. She was so glad she'd worn a short skirt. If she was honest, this was exactly why she'd worn it. She moaned into his mouth as his fingers traced her inner thigh until they reached her panties. He lifted his head a moment and gave her a questioning look. Damn him he was seeking permission now. She nodded and reclaimed his lips, kissing him hungrily as she opened her legs wider. He pulled her panties aside and traced her opening with his fingertips, then circled her clit, making her gasp. She was utterly defenseless as he teased her there, circling and squeezing until her hips were bucking. As she thrust them up, he slid two fingers deep inside her making her moan and thrust harder—wanting, needing more. He stilled his hand, not withdrawing his fingers, just letting her move around him. She rubbed herself against him, frustrated now.

He lifted his head and smiled down at her, removing his hand and straightening her panties and skirt. He brought his fingers to his lips and licked each one, tantalizing her with the way he trailed then flicked his tongue, making her wish he was using it on her. She squirmed wanting to feel it on her where his fingers had been.

"Mmm, sweet," he murmured. She stared at him as he sat back. "Goodnight, Princess. You tell me when you're ready. Until then I'll just enjoy the anticipation."

Damn him! She couldn't go back on her word now. She'd told him no. But she was desperate for him now.

He gave her that aggravating smile. "I'll come get you in the morning."

She let out a frustrated sigh. "I'm not going to give in you know."

He shrugged. "So I gathered. But if I'm not going to be able to sleep tonight because I'm so damned frustrated, then I thought it was only fair to leave you in the same state."

She had to laugh. She reached across and cupped his impressive erection in her hand, holding his gaze as she did. “I’ll see you tomorrow then.”

He narrowed his eyes at her and shook his head before drawing a deep breath. “You will.”

Chapter Ten

The next morning Cassidy woke to the grey light of the predawn. She'd tossed and turned all night. At three o'clock she'd almost called him. She'd sat there with the phone in her hand seriously considering calling and asking him to come back and finish what he'd started. She hadn't though. Despite feeling more horny and frustrated than she'd have believed possible, she had way too much pride. She also knew that she wouldn't have to wait too long. She doubted they'd get very far into their little camping expedition before they both had to give in. Instead, she'd texted Summer the photos of Beau's house. It was just as great inside as it was out. She was hoping her friend would soon be her neighbor. At least for a few months.

She got up and went downstairs to make coffee. Even aside from what she knew she and Shane would be doing, she was looking forward to going camping. She'd been thinking for a while that she needed to get out and explore. She hadn't known where to start by herself though. Now she would have a guide, a very hot and horny for her guide, thrown in! She shook her head; it had been a long time. Maybe that was why

Shane got to her so much? He was hot, and she hadn't had sex in way too long. That was all.

She took her coffee to sit out on the deck. It was still chilly, but she loved to sit out here. Her robe was thick; it'd keep her warm. She listened to the morning sounds—the river burbling by, the birds waking, chirping their greeting to a new day. She tensed as she heard something moving in the shrubbery. She went to lean on the railing to see if she could spot what it was. It sounded big enough to be a bear, but surely it couldn't get to her up here? She could see the bushes moving. What on earth was it? She heard another sound and then a chuckle. Shane popped out onto the walkway.

She had to laugh. "What the hell are you doing?"

He grinned up at her. "I didn't know if you were awake yet."

"So you went crawling around in the bushes?"

He laughed, "I was going to try to surprise you. Show you that you never know what might be lurking out here." He made his way to the stairs and came up, holding her gaze the whole way. When he reached her, he wrapped his arms around her and held her against him. If anything his hard-on felt even more impressive than it had last night. He looked down at her. "Or what they might do to you."

She reached her arms up around his neck and rubbed herself against him. "You'd better come in then, and show me." She took his hand and led him into her bedroom. She couldn't have asked for better than this. Her bed was still warm and now she had Shane in it! She stopped in front of it and unfastened her robe, letting it slide from her shoulders and fall to the floor. She loved the look on his face as he watched, the way he smiled as he looked at her naked body. He pulled his own shirt up and off over his head before pulling her to him.

She reached up and buried her fingers in his hair, pulling his head down to kiss her as she pressed her breasts against his hard chest. As his tongue explored her mouth he walked her backwards until her legs hit the bed and she lay back. He smiled as he unbuckled his jeans and pushed them down. He was naked underneath. She'd seen him naked before, in the gallery the other night, but that hadn't prepared her for how he looked now—fully erect, his cock standing proud. She licked her lips and went to sit up, reaching to touch him. He surprised her by putting a hand to her shoulder, pushing her back down. He dropped to his knees with a smile.

"I've wanted to taste you since the first time I saw you."

She gasped as he spread her thighs, pinning them to the bed with his big hands. She squirmed to get away, but he held her firm, his face hovering above her.

"Let me taste you." He lowered his head, holding her gaze as he breathed her in. "So sweet," he murmured.

Her hands came down to tangle in his hair as he dipped his head and flicked her clit with his tongue. She yelped as he took it between his lips and sucked. Oh, God. He was going to make her come in no time if he kept that up. He trailed his tongue slowly down over her, then back up. She moaned as he thrust it inside making her buck underneath him. It felt so good, but she didn't want to come like this. She felt too vulnerable. She sat up, and as he looked up at her in surprise, she closed her fingers around him and began to work her hand up and down the length of him. She smiled as he closed his eyes and let out a long sigh. She pulled him down onto the bed beside her and nibbled her way down over his abs. She knelt on the floor, reversing their positions as she spread his muscular thighs and held them open. She trailed her tongue up and down the length of him, loving the way his thighs quivered under her touch. She opened her mouth and breathed on him, making his cock twitch, eager to be inside the source of the hot wet air. She closed her lips around him and sucked, then bobbed her head to take him deep. He caught a fistful of her hair, and just as she tensed, thinking he was about to control her, move her mouth as *he* wanted, he pulled her head back. She looked up at him, his breath was coming hard. He shook his head.

"I won't last." He worked his way up the bed and lay back against the pillows. She crawled after him, dipping her head to flick him with her tongue one more time.

"Cassidy!" He grasped her shoulders and pulled her up face-to-face with him. "Don't tease. Fuck me! Please!"

She smiled and sat back on her heels, looking down at his cock throbbing between her legs. "Oh, okay then. If you insist." She cupped her breasts in her hands, loving the dazed look on his face as he watched, his hips moving rhythmically underneath her. She didn't get time to torment him for long. He grasped her hips, lifting her slightly, making her gasp at the way his hot head pushed at her. Her fingers involuntarily tightened around her nipples, heightening the pleasure as he thrust up deep and hard at the same time pulling her down to receive him.

"Oh, God!" he cried as he buried himself to the hilt. "Ride me."

It was like riding a bucking bronco. His hips thrust wildly, stretching her, filling her. She didn't fear falling though as he gripped her hips tight. She continued to caress her breasts, rolling her nipples between her finger and thumb as Shane watched transfixed. He slowed his thrusting and moved back until he was sitting up against the pillows. He brought his knees up behind her, making her lean forward to grasp the headboard. The feel of his warm breath where moments before her fingers had been squeezing made her moan and thrust her own hips to take him deeper. He filled his hands with her breasts, bringing them to his mouth so he could lick and nip. She moved desperately over him, her inner muscles clenching around him tighter each time he closed his lips around her nipple. He latched on and sucked hard as he grabbed her hips again and pounded into her relentlessly. Each thrust took her closer to the edge. All she could do was cling to the headboard for dear life as he grew bigger and harder, hurtling them both toward release. She screamed as her orgasm took her, his voice joining hers as he tensed. Wave after wave of pleasure went crashing through her, as their bodies heaved together. Shane clung to her, filling her over and over as he gasped his way through his climax. Eventually she collapsed onto his chest, still panting.

His arms came up around her and instead of trying to wriggle away, she nuzzled into his neck, once again loving the feeling of being all wrapped up in him. It was such a strange reaction for her. She didn't have the energy to question it though, her brain was too fuzzy right now. Eventually she rolled off him. He turned to face her, his usual grin replaced by a very genuine smile.

"Wow!"

She smiled back. "Wow yourself."

He laughed. "I knew *I* was that good; I just wasn't so sure about *you*."

"Ditto!"

"I think there's room for improvement though."

"You do?"

He nodded. "I think if we practice hard and often, we can take great to even greater. What do you say? Think we should try?"

She laughed. "I could be persuaded."

He propped himself up on his elbow and smiled down at her. "Hmm, and what will it take to persuade you?"

"It'd be no fun if I tell you. I'd rather see you running around trying to figure it out."

"I'll bet you would. Tell you what, how about we start out in the shower? We need to get going if we're going to get to camp by nightfall, and maybe I can do a spot of persuading while we're in there."

She got up from the bed and held her hand out to him. "That works for me."

~ ~ ~

Shane grinned as he came around and opened the truck door for her. She didn't get down immediately, but sat there eyeing the three horses, two saddled, one packed.

She looked down at him. "You're kidding me, right?"

He shook his head. "I'm deadly serious. You said you wanted to learn what it's like out there, this is how you learn."

"I was thinking more along the lines of sitting in a truck with binoculars."

He laughed. "That's what tourists do. You're not a tourist. You live here." He had to smile at the little crease that formed between her brows. For the first time since he'd known her she looked unsure of herself. He liked it, but he knew he'd better not push it. "Seriously, I do this all the time." He waved his arm out over the lodge and the cabins, the horses grazing and minibuses waiting to take ranch guests down to Yellowstone for the day. "People come from far and wide and pay good money to get the opportunity to ride out and camp in the backcountry. I know what I'm doing. You're safe with me."

She looked into his eyes and smiled. "I'm out of my element, uncomfortable I guess, that's all."

"I know, but you're going to love it." He held out a hand to her and she jumped down. "Life begins at the edge of your comfort zone, Princess. Come live a little."

She laughed and waited while he pulled their bags from the back of the truck. He'd taken an extra bag with him when he went back to her place this morning. After they were done in the shower—an experience he intended to repeat as soon as possible—he'd supervised her packing, laughing and offering her the spare backpack when she'd pulled out a small suitcase with a questioning look.

He carried the packs over and strapped them to the third horse who turned to give him a gentle head-butt. Shane laughed and rubbed his ears. "Hey, Teddy. How you doin', old fella? Meet Cassidy." He beckoned to her and she came a little closer. Teddy nuzzled her hand, and Shane was relieved to see her smile and rub his nose.

"Nice to meet you, Teddy."

Shane smiled. "Teddy's a good friend. He'll be carrying our stuff." He turned to the two saddled horses. "This," he pointed at the gray mare, "is Lady." He patted her neck. "She's a sweetheart." He led Cassidy over to the third horse, a dun gelding who watched them patiently. "And this guy is Cookie, your mount for the weekend."

Cassidy approached him cautiously. "Hi, Cookie."

Shane couldn't resist. "Cookie is a lover. Give her a kiss, boy." He laughed at the look on Cassidy's face as Cookie sniffed her cheek ever so gently and then moved his lips against hers.

She reached up and patted his cheek then turned to Shane. "Let me guess, he's yours?"
Shane nodded. "He's my boy. We grew up together. How can you tell?"
"Because he's a charmer." She laughed. "He kisses like you do, too."
Shane feigned a hurt look. "You're saying I kiss like a horse?"
"No! I'm saying he's good at it. Take a compliment would you!"
"Well excuse me. That's the first compliment you've ever given me. You can't blame me that I didn't recognize it."
She laughed. "I'll give you that." She looked up at Cookie again. "He's so big."
"That's another thing we have in common." Shane winked, "Now, if you're saying he's hung like me—*that* I will take as a compliment!"
Cassidy slapped his arm. "Get over yourself!"
"Okay, sorry. He's tall, like me." He held her gaze. "He's also very good-natured and kind. He knows what he's doing. You're riding him because he'll take very, very good care of you."
She stared back into his eyes. "Are you still talking about Cookie?"
Shane didn't reply. He was talking about himself, and the words surprised him. He felt incredibly protective toward her and pretty dumb about it at the same time. She'd hate it if she knew what he was feeling. She was Miss Independence—and that was what attracted him to her—but damn if she didn't bring out all his male instincts to protect the little lady! He shrugged and decided to turn it around on her. "You decide."
He loved the shadow of a smile that crossed her face. Maybe he was bringing out her female instincts? Maybe she liked the

idea of having a guy look out for her? And maybe he was kidding himself!

"We'd better get going. I want to take it easy to start with, give you chance to get used to being in the saddle before we pick it up."

She looked wary as she eyed Cookie again. "And just how am I supposed to get up there?"

Shane untethered him and started to lead him across the yard to the mounting block. "We have beginners use this." He had to bite back a smirk at the stubborn set of her chin.

"If I'm going to do this, I need to learn to do it properly. Show me. You get on him, and then I'll do what you do."

"Whatever you say." He brought Cookie to a halt. "You do it like this. Hold the reins and a handful of his mane in this hand—make sure you're not pulling on him though. Then one foot in the stirrup." He brought his foot up and swung his other leg over to sit. He smiled down at her. Cookie was a big boy, but so was Shane, it was easy for him. Cassidy was much shorter, he hoped she'd manage it. He swung his leg back over and dismounted. "Do you want to try?"

She nodded, a determined look on her face. Shane handed her the reins and waited. He loved that she took a moment to talk to Cookie first.

"Okay, Mister. He says you're kind, so please be kind to me? If I mess it up, I'm sorry, okay?"

Shane had to laugh at her expression when Cookie nodded his head and then sniffed her cheek.

She looked at Shane. "He really gets it, doesn't he?"

"He sure does. Told you he's a smart guy."

"Okay, I can do this." She held the reins and grasped the front of the saddle as she brought her foot up to the stirrup. She looked thrilled as she swung her leg up and over and landed lightly in the saddle. "I did it! Did I do it right?"

Shane smiled. "You did great. Just one question. Why did you hold the saddle instead of his mane?"

"You noticed?" She hung her head. "I didn't want to hurt him."

Shane could have kissed her for that. So many beginners yanked on the horse's mane in an attempt to scramble onto their back. Cassidy was already thinking about the animal ahead of herself. "Don't worry. You won't hurt him. The reason we don't hold the saddle when we mount is that if the cinch isn't tight enough you could pull the whole thing down and land yourself on your ass in the dirt and your horse with a saddle under his belly."

"Oh. Sorry." She looked so crestfallen he felt bad,

"No need to be. You did great. And it wasn't a concern this time. I just wanted you to know why I asked you to do it that way."

She nodded. "Thank you." She did that lip chewing thing that was so cute. "I'm afraid I tend to like to think I know better."

Wow, that was an admission and a half coming from her. "And I'm sure in a lot of cases you do. But this weekend, I'm going to need you to trust me. If I tell you to do something a certain way, there's a reason. I'll explain it if I can—if there's time—but if there's any danger, I need you to do as I say, as fast as I say."

"Okay."

"I'm not trying to be an asshole, Cassidy. I…"

She shook her head rapidly. "I was thinking that I was being an asshole." She gave him meek smile, it was so unlike her it was almost comical. "I'll do whatever you say."

He winked at her. "Anything at all?"

She narrowed her eyes at him, but she was laughing. "No! If I'm going to give you my trust in the things that matter, you can't abuse it in the things that don't."

"Fair point." Joking aside, she was right. "Let's get this show on the road then."

Once he'd made sure she was all set and comfortable on Cookie, he mounted Lady and brought Teddy around. "Are we set?"

She nodded eagerly. "I think I'm going to enjoy this."

Shane smiled. He knew he was.

Chapter Eleven

Cassidy was enjoying herself. She sat by the fire watching Shane tend to the horses. On the ride up here both he and Cookie had been everything he'd said they were—kind, good-natured and they'd taken very good care of her. When they'd arrived at the barn this morning she'd wanted to back out. She didn't like to be outside of her comfort zone. At least not anymore. She pondered that. She used to thrive in a new environment, rise to any challenge, what had changed? She realized that she'd gotten used to feeling accomplished. She excelled at her work, she managed social situations well—even though she didn't enjoy them. She'd set up a safe, if small, world and was used to being queen bee within it.

Coming on this camping trip with Shane put her in a very different situation. She was out of her depth, a clueless novice about everything she was experiencing, and yet she was loving every moment of it. She sighed, admitting to herself that it was all down to him. He was a great teacher—patient and open to all her questions. More than that though, he seemed to understand her. He could see that she was uncomfortable being the follower rather than the leader, and he was doing his best to set her at ease.

He returned to the fire and sat down beside her with a grin. “How are you doing, Princess?”

She scowled at him. “I wish you wouldn’t call me that.”

He looked genuinely surprised. “I mean it in the nicest possible way.”

She laughed. “Yeah right. Every time you say it I think you’re calling me a stuck-up drama queen!”

“Hell no! I guess it all depends on how you think a princess behaves though, doesn’t it?”

She nodded. “To me they’re stuck-up drama queens in pretty pink dresses who’d cry over a broken nail. That’s not who I am, and I don’t want you to think of me like that.”

He laughed. “I guess I’d better find another name for you then. See to me a princess is a beautiful woman who knows how to carry herself with grace. She handles whatever is thrown at her and makes people comfortable. Everyone wants to know her, everyone wants to be around her.” He smiled. “And for this weekend at least, I’m the lucky SOB who gets to be around her.”

Wow! She would never in a million years have guessed that was what he meant. “You’re shitting me, right?”

He laughed. “I’m not. Although that isn’t a very princess-like response!”

“Well, you shouldn’t expect one from me. I like to think I fit the description you just gave, but that’s not all I am. I’m also the hard-nosed, tell it like it is woman. I’m confident, some would say to the point of arrogance.”

He raised an eyebrow.

"And I know you don't disagree. I just like who I am, and I won't dial myself down just so other people don't feel threatened."

"I know that, but why?"

She shrugged. "Why should I? Why should anyone?"

Shane thought about it. "No one should have to, but most people tend to. Just in order to get along with others."

"Exactly. I refuse to be less of me just because other people are insecure about themselves."

He held her gaze. "I'm not insecure."

"Maybe I just haven't pushed the right buttons yet, haven't threatened your male dominance."

"Or maybe we're two of a kind?"

She stared at him, thinking about it.

He smirked. "What? You don't think I'm good-looking or confident or good at what I do?"

"Hmm."

He laughed.

"I guess you are. But you're a guy. It doesn't threaten people in the same way. People expect a guy to be all those things and to be unapologetic for them. A woman is supposed to be more modest, more accommodating, more…I don't know what, just more of everything I'm not."

"Well, I'm glad you're not. I like you just the way you are."

She relaxed a little. "Thank you. I like you, too. Much as I hate to admit it."

He pulled a bottle from one of the bags and poured two tin cups. "Here."

She took it and sniffed it. "What the hell is that? It smells like apple pie!"

He laughed. "It's apple pie moonshine; try it."

She took a sip and then looked up at him. "It *tastes* like apple pie! I love it!"
"Just don't get too carried away. It tastes innocent enough, and it'll go down real easy while you sit there. It's when you try to stand up that you'll realize just how potent it is!"
She took another sip. "Hmm, warning heeded,"
He brought his own cup and came to sit closer, wrapping an arm around her shoulders. She leaned against him with a smile. He felt so good, such a big reassuring presence. She stared suspiciously down into her cup. Was this stuff working already? Since when had *she* ever wanted reassurance from a guy in any form? She turned to look up at him. The way he smiled down at her made her relax. *Sunny*—that was the word for him. He was warm and pleasant, he made you feel good. He was bright and funny and straightforward.
He gave her a questioning look. "What's up?"
"Tell me about you? What makes you the way you are? I feel as though I might be being unfair to you. Painting you with someone else's brush. I see a big guy, confident—with reason to be. A good-looking guy who knows it, and I guess happy-go-lucky is the right word for you. What makes you like that?" Part of her also wanted to know what would rattle him, what would cause the thunder clouds to roll across his usually sunny disposition.
He shrugged. "I'm just a natural born sweetheart, I guess."
She laughed. "And modest, too!"
"Hey! You're the one who says no one should have to deny who they are—how good they are. It's funny. I was talking to Carter the other day and he said it's because I'm the baby of the family. I hadn't thought about it like that, but I think he's right. I always got lots of attention as a kid—from everyone.

My parents love all of us, but they especially seemed to look out for me. I thought it was because I'm special, but I can see now they were teaching my brothers about how to look out for people younger and smaller than themselves. My brothers took it on board and they've always made a fuss of me, too."
She loved the way his jawline twitched as he smiled to himself.
"I'm lucky that I'm big and cute looking. My parents taught all of us to be kind, generous, and polite, and that makes everyone love you even more." He shrugged. "I don't know. I guess I've just lived a charmed life. I've never had anything horrible happen to me. Nothing has ever made me question the fact that life is inherently good or that I am inherently good." He stopped and looked at her. "That's why it's so strange to me—such a challenge—that you seem to think I'm an asshole."
She chuckled. "I can see that. It's not that I think you're an asshole so much as I know your sort."
"Hmm. And here I was thinking that I'm a special snowflake, no one else like me on earth."
"Maybe you are, but maybe you're not, too. In my experience, guys like you—all big and strong and confident—crumble in the face of adversity and blame those around them because they can't face the realization that they're not nearly as strong as they thought."
Shane gave her a puzzled look. "Are we talking one guy in particular?"
She shook her head. "I wish. But no, I'm talking about time and time again. You are my type, physically and everything else. I've made the same mistake over and over, that's why I'm not prepared to do it again. Something within me apparently longs to be the little woman. Even now, sitting like this with

your arm around me, part of me wants to melt into you and let you take care of me, surrender myself to your strength and protection."

He grinned. "You want to surrender?"

She slapped his arm. "Be serious for a minute, would you? It's my biggest flaw. I want to feel that way, even though I don't *need* to. So I end up with guys like you. You have to be big and strong. But sooner or later—usually sooner—it turns out that *I'm* the one who's too strong. I'm seen as a threat. Like I said, guys want small and sweet and don't know what to do with strong and smart, especially when it turns out to be stronger and smarter than they are."

"I do feel as though you're painting me with someone else's brush. I don't need to be smarter, I don't need to be stronger—at least not emotionally. I'm not sure I could handle a woman who's physically stronger than me." He laughed. "She'd have to be a really big girl, and I'd probably be scared of her! But I'm happy enough with me, I don't need a woman to feed my ego by making me look better than she is." He thought about it for a minute. "If anything you feed my ego by being *so* smart and *so* strong and still being interested in little ole me."

She shook her head at him. "Don't mock me, Shane. I'm just trying to be honest about why I don't want to get involved with you."

His face fell. "You don't? I thought that's what we were doing?"

She shook her head. "Nah, we're just having some fun." Her heart sank as she said it, but the more time she spent with him, the clearer it became that this was a friendship she didn't want to risk. She'd rather keep him as a friend—hopefully with benefits when it suited them both—than try for something more than that and end up hating each other.

His arm tightened around her shoulders. "Just fun, huh?"

She looked up into his eyes. Yes, it was for the best. She could fall for him way too easily otherwise. "Just fun."

He laid her back on the blanket and kneeled above her. "Starting now?"

She laughed as he caught her hands and pinned them above her head with one of his own. "Starting now." She closed her eyes wondering what his free hand was about to do. Whatever it was she was willing. She parted her legs. She kept her eyes closed as his breath came closer, was he going to kiss her? In one swift movement his fingers found their target—under her armpit tickling like crazy! She squirmed to get away, laughing uncontrollably. "Let me go!"

"No way!" he laughed. "This is what you want. This is fun!"

"It's not going to be much fun for you when I get free." She managed to say between her giggles. "Shane!"

"Yes?" He carried on tickling mercilessly.

"You're going to pay for this!"

He laughed. "Not until you prove that you really are stronger and smarter than me. That's the only way you're going to be able to escape."

"You…!" She couldn't get any more words out, she was laughing too hard. She wasn't going to let him win though. She began to move her hips underneath him and soon felt him respond. He tried to remain focused on keeping her hands pinned and tickling her, but his body was paying more attention to her movements than her hands. She smiled as he thrust his hips against her; he felt hot and hard between her legs. His tickling slowed and he looked down into her eyes. She made the most of his distraction and pulled her hands free, ready to push him off her and roll on top. He was faster than she gave him credit for though. He caught her hands again and smiled at her as he pinned them back above her head.

"Sorry, Princess. I didn't realize you meant that kind of fun." He clamped both of her hands in one of his and smiled as he knelt between her legs, spreading them with his knees. With his free hand he unfastened her jeans and pulled them down along with her panties. The feel of the cool night air between her legs heightened her arousal. She watched as he deftly unbuckled his own jeans and pushed them down over his hips. She found it incredibly sexy the way he took himself in hand as he smiled down at her. "Is this the kind of fun you had in mind?"

She nodded. Longing to feel him inside her. She struggled to free her hands, wanting to touch him, to guide him to her entrance and let him take her. He didn't let go of her though. Instead he surprised her by grasping her wrists tighter and lowering himself onto her. Her breath was coming fast as she felt him pushing to be inside her. She struggled again to free her hands but he only grasped tighter still. This *was* fun! She tried to bring her legs together, fighting him in a different way. He shook his head and used his knees to keep her thighs spread. His fingers joined his cock, pressing at her, teasing her clit and then dipping inside. She struggled harder and almost got a hand free. That had the effect she'd hoped for. He brought both hands up and pinned her wrists on either side of her head. Now neither of them could delay his impatient cock from thrusting its way in to where it wanted to be. She gasped as he filled her. He was so hard, so hot. He moved with such determination. He was carrying her away and there was nothing she could do to stop him—physically or emotionally. He was taking possession of her body, and while he did so, something inside her wanted so badly to let him take all of her.

She wanted him to carry her along, take her where he wanted to go and fill her with pleasure as he did. Her hips bucked underneath him as he drove into her over and over. He showed no mercy, and she didn't want any! She tried one more time to free her hands, but he tightened his grip, spread her legs wider and thrust harder, making her scream. The tension in every cell in her body was building and building. His movements quickened, and then he tensed.

"Cassidy!" the way he breathed her name took her over the edge. His orgasm triggered her hers, their bodies melding frantically together giving and seeking more and more pleasure as they reached a crescendo. He freed her hands and she reached up, pulling his head down to kiss her, their tongues coupling in the same way as their bodies, intensifying the connection.

When they finally lay still, Shane lifted his head. "Was that fun?"

She held his gaze. That had been so much more than fun! How could she tell him what it was though? She nodded. "Great fun!"

He smiled, but it didn't reach his eyes. Maybe he felt it, too? But even if he did, what did it matter?

~ ~ ~

Shane rolled off her and pulled her into his arms. She was the most fun he'd ever had, but she was doing something strange to him. She was making him want more than just fun. Lying here under the big starry sky with her, he didn't want to let go. He wanted her to be his girl. Normally after sex he was in a hurry to get his boots on and be gone. Right now all he want to do was hold her, talk some more. What the hell was she doing to him? Why was he disappointed that all she wanted was to have some fun with him? He should be thrilled! He was used to dodging women who wanted anything more than that.

She looked up into his eyes. He couldn't help dropping a kiss on her lips. She looked so small and sweet. She had this hang-up about also being smart and strong, but he didn't know why. Lots of women were small and sweet—and it got old really fast. It usually translated into needy and clingy too. Both of which made Shane's skin crawl. Cassidy was the perfect package, she embodied the softness that a guy sought in a girl, while at the same time possessing a mind and a spirit that he respected and admired.

"You look way too serious for a guy who just got laid."

He laughed. "Not serious. Just thinking."

"Thinking what?"

He held her gaze for a moment. There was no point. She'd made it clear where she stood. He knew how it felt when someone pushed for more than you wanted to give. He shrugged. "About what we're going to do tomorrow."

She smiled. He wanted to think she looked disappointed. But that was just his imagination.

"What are we going to do?"

"Teach you what to look out for when you're hiking." He didn't want her hiking by herself, but more than that, he didn't want her hiking with anyone but him. "For now though, we should probably get some sleep."

"Oh, we're not going to sit up a while and drink that moonshine?"

He laughed. "Nope. We'll be up early and you're going to need a clear head." He was pleased to see how disappointed she looked. "Maybe, if you're nice to me, I'll come over to your place one night and bring a bottle."

She snuggled closer. "That sounds like fun."

"It does, doesn't it? So come on. Let's get inside the tent and you can practice being nice to me, if you want."

She laughed. "I've already been nicer to you than I have to any guy in a long time."

He hated the thought of her being nice to any other guy…in any sense. He stood and held out a hand. "We'd better get you some practice then, hadn't we?"

Chapter Twelve

When she opened her eyes, it took Cassidy a few moments to figure out where she was—it was early, it was very chilly, and she was in a sleeping bag…in a tent…in the middle of nowhere. And no Shane in sight! She pulled her clothes on and stuck her head through the tent flap. He wasn't by the fire. He wasn't with the horses. For a moment her heart pounded. Was this some kind of revenge for her trick on him at the gallery? What the hell would she do if he'd abandoned her out here in the wilderness? She took a deep breath. She'd figure it out, that's what she'd do. She'd take Cookie and no doubt he'd help her find her way back to the ranch. He was a smart horse! Looking over at him she chuckled and made herself get a grip. Shane would hardly have left Lady and Teddy here if he'd taken off. At that moment she saw him emerge from a stand of cottonwoods. He cocked his head to one side.

"What's so funny?"

She didn't want to tell him what she'd thought. "I just gave myself a scare, then realized I was being an idiot. Where did you go?"

"To do what comes naturally."

"Oh!" She frowned. She'd peed behind a bush a couple of times yesterday, she was hoping they'd make it back to civilization before she needed to do anything else. She was curious though. "When you take ranch guests out do you have a camp place that you take them to?"

He laughed. "You mean some place with bathrooms and hot and cold running water? No ma'am. They come out here to experience what it's really like."

She nodded. "I guess they do."

Shane reached in his back pocket for his phone. His face looked troubled as he read a text. "Sorry, Princess, but we're going to have to head back."

"Oh no. Is everything okay?"

"Yeah. Nothing serious, but something I have to take care of back at the ranch."

She couldn't believe how disappointed she felt.

"I'm sorry."

"No problem."

Shane went to get the horses ready. Cassidy felt a little useless; she didn't know what to do to help. She went into the tent and got her things together then rolled up the sleeping bags as best she could. She kind of had them fastened like they had been…kind of. Shane popped his head in through the flap. The way he smiled made her feel proud of herself. "Hey, thanks. That's great."

"Did I do it right?" She held one out to show him.

"Perfect. Now if you'll bring them out you can help me take the tent down, and I'll show you how we pack Teddy. So you'll know for next time."

"Next time?" She scrambled out of the tent to join him, unable to repress a smile.

He smiled back. "Of course. I owe you a weekend, since we're losing out on this one."

"Oh. We're missing out on the whole weekend?"

He nodded. "We have to get back as fast as we can."

"And you'll be busy for the rest of the weekend?"

"No, but we won't have time to come back out."

"So how about you bring that moonshine over to my place later?" She was surprised she was being so pushy. She should just leave it. She didn't want to get involved with him, so why was she after more time with him? Because she'd thought she was getting the whole weekend, she reasoned. Why miss out on it just because of a slight change of plan?

He grinned. "I'd be more than happy to. Come on, let's pack up. The sooner we get back, the sooner I'll be done."

By lunchtime, Cassidy was back at her place. Their ride back had been much faster and via a much shorter route than they'd taken yesterday. She was grateful that Cookie took such good care of her. She'd spent most of the time holding onto the saddle as he made his own way. Once they were back at the ranch, Shane had bid her the briefest of farewells and disappeared into the lodge as soon as one of the hands had taken the horses. She'd felt a little lost standing there staring after him, but he'd reappeared moments later. He came to her and handed her the keys to his truck. "I'm sorry about this. I'll call you when I get done here. See if you still want to get together tonight."

She could have told him right then and there that she did.

Now she was home with an afternoon stretching ahead of her and unsure what to do with it. She wandered into her office and turned on her laptop. She had an email from Summer.

Why aren't you answering texts??? I love the pictures! I want the place! How soon can I come? Call me!!!!

She dug out her phone. She had three new texts, but no notification that they'd come in. They were all from Summer in response to the pictures of Beau's rental house. She loved it. Cassidy dialed her number.

"Cassidy Lane! Get me that house!" Summer's voice was quiet, but still full of laughter.

"Hey, chica. I'll get right on it. Sorry I only just got your messages. Isn't it awesome? And it's just a short and beautiful walk along the river from where I am. I can't wait to have you here."

"I can't wait to be there! I want to come now. Do you have the guy's number? I want to find out how soon I can move in. I'm going nuts here."

"Well then get your ass on a plane and come! If there's any problem you can stay with me until it's available."

"I can?" Summer's voice sounded scratchy now.

"You can. And I bet you're not supposed to be talking are you?"

"What was I supposed to do when you wouldn't answer my messages?" Summer laughed, but she sounded really hoarse.

It worried Cassidy to hear her like that. "Listen. Just hang up, and we can text each other. You get a flight booked and I'll try to get hold of Beau."

"Perfect. Bye." Her voice was barely a whisper now. She was worse off than Cassidy had realized.

She dialed Beau's number and got no reply. She paced her office, looking out the window. It was going to be so cool to have Summer here. She wanted to get it all organized right now. She picked her phone back up. Carter might know what was going on with the house. And she had a feeling he'd be pleased to hear that Summer was on her way. She dialed him.

"This is Carter."

"Hi Carter. It's Cassidy."

"Oh, hi. Is everything okay?"

She smiled to herself. He was always making sure that everyone was okay. "Yes, great, thanks. I just talked to Summer, and she wants Beau's house. I can't get hold of him though. Do you know when it's available or how much he wants or anything?" The line was so quiet she thought she might have lost him. "Carter?"

"Yeah, sorry. She's really coming?"

Cassidy laughed. "She's really coming. And soon. I've told her she can come stay with me until the house is available."

"Oh. I. Um."

The poor guy! She had to hope he'd relax when he actually met Summer, or it could be really awkward—for all of them.

"Sorry. I did talk to him about it yesterday. He said it's ready as soon as he finds a renter. I told him you might have someone. I didn't tell him who it was though."

"Thanks, Carter. Do you know when he'll be back?"

"Not for another few days. He decided to stay on. But I'll get hold of him and put him in touch with you."

"Great. I told Summer to go ahead and book a flight. She sounds eager to get here, so I'm sure it will be in the next couple of days."

"Do you want me to hold off on the landscaping while she's with you?"

"No! I want you to meet her. She won't be very talkative because she has to rest her voice, but she's a lot of fun. You'll love her."

"I'm sure. I just don't want to intrude."

"Will you quit with that? You're both my friends. It's not an intrusion, okay?"

"Okay. I'm going to try to get hold of Beau. I'll let you know what he says."

"Thanks, Carter. Bye."

After she hung up, she wandered around the house. She was pleased at the ways her life was changing. Her first few months here in Montana had been very quiet. She'd set up the gallery, done a lot of painting, and mostly hibernated through the winter. Things had started to change the day she met Shane. He'd come into the gallery asking whether she worked with local artists. He'd flirted with her shamelessly and it had really pissed her off. Yes, he was a good-looking guy—really good-looking, but it had made her mad that he would flirt with her while trying to find work for his girlfriend. Of course, it had turned out that it wasn't a girlfriend, but Gina that he'd be trying to help. Gina had gotten in touch of her own accord and the two of them were now working together, creating a new line of art, mixing her paintings with Gina's photography. And since she'd been working with Gina her social life had expanded, too, or better said, she had one now. Again, Shane was an integral part of that, seeing as he was Gina's best friend, and Carter's brother. Now Summer was going to be here, too. It just kept getting better and better! Whenever she'd talked to her dad over the winter, he'd told her he was worried that she was hiding and hibernating. Last time they'd talked he'd said it sounded as though she was coming back to life with the spring. He was right, too.

He phone buzzed in her hand. A text from Shane.

Sorry. Not going to make it tonight. Rain check?

She made a face. Why should she feel disappointed? She should hardly expect anything else from him. He'd probably had a more convenient offer from one of his ranch guests. She could buy some of that apple moonshine stuff for herself anyway.

Sure.

Was all she typed in reply. She sure as hell wasn't going to ask him when. If he wanted another round, he'd have to work for it.

~ ~ ~

It was late by the time Shane made it back to his cabin. He was tired and hungry, and he needed a shower. More than any of that he was pissed that he'd had to miss out on going to see Cassidy tonight. He knew from her one word reply that he might not get another chance. Maybe he should have called her and explained. He shrugged. He hadn't had the time. He'd been running like crazy ever since they got back to the ranch at lunchtime.

Brandon had texted him to say that the minibus full of guests had broken down in the park. While at the same time they'd had a complete mix-up with bookings and a group of twelve guests had arrived to check in—one week early! After he'd dealt with those issues, one of the hands had found a mare down in the bottom pasture with her hoof caught in a gopher hole. That had taken the rest of the afternoon to take care of. She was lucky; he'd once seen a horse break a leg so badly in a gopher hole that he'd had to be euthanized. The vet had assured Shane that this girl would make a full recovery, but she'd be lame and off the roster for a while. That had left him reworking guest to horse assignments for a good hour, too.

He pushed open the door to the cabin ready to take a hot shower, find some food, and maybe watch a movie. If Cassidy's reply had been anything more than a curt, *Sure,* he would have called her, hoping to still go see her. But he was too beat to handle one of her put downs or rejections tonight.
He sat on the bench in the hallway and pulled his boots off.
"How's it going?"
"Chance! I didn't see your truck. Man am I glad to see you back."
Chance smiled and ran a hand through his unruly black hair. "I left the truck at the shop. It needs an oil change and a good look over after that trip."
"How was it? How did April do?"
Chance nodded. "She's settling in just fine. I think she's going to do great. I swear she relaxed more with every mile farther away we got from this place. Even the kid. He was a little wimp about being in the truck at first, but by the time we made it to the lake he'd come out of himself. I even let him sit in my lap and have a drive down the backroads before I left."
Shane smiled. Chance might come across as tough and unyielding, but he had a heart of gold underneath it all. "You're not such a badass really, are you? Saving damsels in distress, helping little kids come out of their shell. Hell, next thing we know you'll be falling in love and living happily ever after."
Chance's smile was gone in an instant; his eyes narrowed and lips pressed into a thin line. "Not much chance of that."
Shit! Shane could have kicked himself. What had he been thinking? "Sorry, dude. I wasn't thinking."

Chance shook his head. "Nah, it's okay. I guess I'm even more testy than usual on that subject. Just being back at the lake, you know?"

Shane nodded. He knew what had happened in Summer Lake before Chance had come to Montana. "Does it still hurt as bad?" he asked.

Chance heaved a big sigh. "I think I made some kind of peace with it this time. Chloe's sister is back there. I always thought she blamed me. Turns out she always thought I blamed her. We were able to talk things through. It did us both some good." He stared out the window for a long moment, then looked back at Shane. "I dunno. I think talking to Renee helped me realize a lot of things. I gave her shit for not getting on with her life—for clinging to Chloe's memory."

Shane raised an eyebrow, not wanting to voice his thoughts.

Chance gave him a rueful smile. "I know. I give her shit for doing the very thing I've been doing. It's so much easier to see it when it's someone else doing it."

Shane nodded and grasped his shoulder. "I'm not going to claim to understand how you feel. All I know is I'd love to see you living life to the fullest. You deserve it. And I don't think you have to let go of Chloe's memory to do that."

Chance stared at him, but didn't say anything. His eyes shone with what Shane couldn't quite believe were tears. He stood abruptly. "When did you get so smart? Anyway, I've got the grill going out back. Want me to throw on a burger for you?"

"Please. I'm just going to jump in the shower. I'll be right out."

A little while later the two of them sat out back. The burgers and the beers were gone. Chance held up his bottle. "Want another?"

"Yeah. Let's take it inside, shall we?"

They settled in the living room. "It's weird with Mason gone," Chance said.

"It's been even weirder for me with both of you gone."

"I'm surprised you even noticed," said Chance with a laugh. "In fact, what are you doing here tonight? I thought you'd be out at Chico or up in town with some chick or other."

Shane made a face.

"What does that look mean?"

He shrugged. "I haven't been going out as much."

"How come?"

"Cassidy."

Chance shook his head. "Is she still giving you the cold shoulder? When are you going to do something about it?"

Shane laughed. "No. As a matter of fact, I thought I was getting somewhere with her."

Chance raised an eyebrow.

"Well, yeah. I got *there*."

"And let me guess, it isn't enough?"

Shane nodded. "You know me. Once I've slept with 'em it's on to the next."

Chance shook his head. "Not with Cassidy. That was obvious from the get-go. She's got your head turned right around and I can see why."

"Why?" It was the question Shane kept asking himself. Why did he want more from her? He didn't even know *what* he wanted. But he wanted more than to just sleep with her and move on.

"She's hot, she's funny, she's talented, she's confident. She's got it going on and she knows it. *And* the kicker for *you* is that she's not falling at your feet like most women do."

"Do you think that's it?" Shane wondered himself. Was it simply that she was the only woman he was really interested in who'd ever knocked him back repeatedly?

Chance shook his head. "I don't. Sorry. It'd be easy if she were just a challenge. It's more than that though. She's gotten to you in a big way. That much was obvious at your mom's birthday party."

Shane cringed a little remembering what a fool he'd made of himself the first few times he'd tried to hit on Cassidy. She'd put him down in no uncertain terms. "But what am I supposed to do about it? *I* don't know what it means to want anything more than a good time with a woman, and *she* insists that there's nothing more than that in the cards for us anyway." After today he wasn't sure she'd even be open to that.

Chance's brows drew together in a puzzled look. "What's her reasoning for that? She doesn't strike me as a chick who just wants a booty call when it suits her."

Shane hated the thought of being her booty call! "I don't know. She's got this weird hang-up that big guys have big egos and that she's too much of a challenge. She reckons at some point she'll piss me off by being too strong and we'll end up hating each other."

"She's definitely smart, then."

"What's that supposed to mean?"

Chance laughed. "It wasn't aimed at you. You're the exception, not the rule. You're just a big puppy dog. But haven't you noticed that big guys do tend to be that way? They're the life of the party while they're the center of attention, but when they're challenged—especially if they're outsmarted by a woman—they get mean. They blame other people for their own shortcomings."

Shane shook his head. "Seems as though everyone has something to teach me about how people work. Cassidy, Carter, now you. I like to think everyone is just straight forward, what you see is what you get."

Chance laughed. "That's because it's how you are. You're as straightforward as they come. But not everyone else is. Once you learn that the hard way, you tend to look out for it down the line. Sounds like that's what Cassidy's got going on."

Shane sighed. "So where does that leave me? What am I supposed to do?"

"Whatever you want to do. As I see it, you have two choices. You can either give up and move on, or you can put the effort in to prove her wrong. Show her who you really are and..." he trailed off.

"And what?"

Chance shrugged. "And hope that she's not right. Hope that when she does piss you off that it isn't so much of a blow to your ego that you blame her."

Shane considered that. "I just don't see how that could be. I really don't."

"You'll never know till you get there." He laughed. "I'd say your first challenge is going to be getting to the stage where you have the opportunity to find out. Last I saw she was pretty damn good at slapping you down. You're going to have to up your game."

"I know. I know. Anyways. Enough of all this. Do you want a watch a movie?"

Chance smiled. "That was my plan for the evening before you showed up."

Chapter Thirteen

Cassidy checked her watch and then looked a Gina. "You're sure you don't mind holding down the fort?"

"Not at all. I was planning on spending the afternoon here anyway. If anyone comes in I can take care of them. Don't worry about it. Get going."

Cassidy grabbed her purse. "Thanks. I'll be back as soon as I can."

"You don't need to rush. I've told you, I'll close up if you want."

"No, I'll just take Summer to my place and then come back in."

Gina shrugged. "If you want, but you don't need to. I'm perfectly capable of closing up the gallery. I thought it'd be nice for you to spend the afternoon with Summer."

Cassidy thought about it. It would. They had a lot of catching up to do.

Gina laughed. "Just get going or you're going to be late. Call me if you decide to stay home."

"Thanks. See you later."

As she waited at the stoplight to turn onto I-90, she noticed a big, red Tundra waiting to come the other way. Was it…? Yep.

Shane blew her a kiss as the light changed and he passed her. She had to laugh. He didn't give up. She took the on ramp and pointed the Beetle toward Bozeman and the airport. That was the first time she'd seen Shane since she'd left the ranch on Sunday. He'd left her a voicemail on Monday to say he'd come pick his truck up after work. She texted him back to tell him she wouldn't be around but would leave the keys in the glovebox. She'd sat on the floor in the hallway and watched on the screen as a big black pickup came up the driveway. Shane had got out and spoken to the driver—it might have been Chance. The black truck had left and Shane had wandered around looking up at the house before getting in the Tundra and driving away. She'd felt like a fool after he'd gone. Why hadn't she just invited him in? She sighed. Because she didn't need another man-mess, that was why. And the time she'd spent with him this weekend had made her realize that she and Shane could make a bigger mess than any she'd known before. She could fall for him way too easily and end up getting hurt.

She put her foot down, urging the Beetle to make it to the top of the big hill. She'd do better to leave well enough alone. She needed to put Shane out of her mind. She had Summer arriving, she and Gina had a lot of work to do at the gallery, and she had Carter hard at work getting her property into shape. She didn't have time to get entangled with Shane anyway. She needed to stop thinking about what she'd do if they were out together with the others—as she knew they would be. She needed to stop scheming up ways she could get him to come home with her. She needed to stop thinking about him at all, and go back to the way they'd been before. That had been fun in its own way—Shane giving her all his come-ons, her giving him all her put downs. She needed to be satisfied with that.

She did manage to put him out of her mind as she drove over the pass toward Bozeman. That took all her attention. She loved her Beetle, but it wasn't the best vehicle to have out here. She kept thinking about getting an SUV of some kind, but she didn't know what. She was clueless about cars. Hell, she'd bought the Beetle because it had a flower vase in the dash and daisy rims on the wheels! They didn't bring her much comfort when the wind was blowing as hard as it was today though. They hadn't done much for her through the winter either when she'd really needed four-wheel drive. She felt a little better as she got closer to Bozeman. She and her car felt less out of place in Boze Angeles as the locals called it. She took the exit for the airport. She could not wait to see Summer. Everything had come together perfectly. Carter had managed to get hold of Beau. He was going to meet them at the house tomorrow, and, as long as it suited Summer, she'd sign a month-to-month lease. Summer hadn't been able to find a flight with less than three changes, so Autumn had fixed her up with a jet charter. She should be landing at two o'clock. Checking her watch, Cassidy realized that she would only just make it.

She parked up, smiling at how different the Bozeman airport was. She loved it. It was so small and civilized. The parking lot was right outside the terminal building. All she needed to do was find a spot and walk fifty yards and she was inside the big lodge-like building. She knew Summer wouldn't be coming down the escalators from the commercial gates, but she wasn't sure where she would be. She walked over to the information desk.

"Can I help you ma'am?" asked the old gentleman sitting there.

"Can you tell me where a passenger from a private jet charter would come through?"

The man smiled. "That'd be general aviation. Just down the road."

Oh no! "You mean I'm in the wrong building?" Crap! She didn't want to leave Summer stranded by herself open to the possibility of being recognized and having to talk!

The man patted her hand. "It's only down the road a little ways. It won't take you but five minutes." He pointed through the window. "You see the gray building? It's right in there."

"Thank you." Cassidy scrambled for her phone in her purse as she headed for the doors. She dialed Summer.

"Hello?"

"Summer, it's me. I'm so sorry, sweetie. I'll be there in five minutes; I came to the wrong building."

"That's okay. No rush. I'll be right here waiting."

Cassidy frowned. "You sound far too relaxed. You normally panic if you're left to fend for yourself in public. What's going on?"

Summer's laugh sounded flirty. "I told you, I'm okay. Take your time."

"Are you with a guy?" Cassidy could hear the nagging mom tone in her own voice, but she couldn't help it. She was way too protective of Summer.

"Yes, mom. I'm going to hang up to rest my voice. I'll see you when you get here, but don't worry I'm in good hands."

Cassidy stared at her phone. She'd hung up! The little minx! She smiled and headed for the car. It seemed as though Summer was open to having some fun, then. Well good.

Cassidy had just the guy in mind for her—and it wasn't some asshole hitting on her at the airport.

A few minutes later she pulled up outside the Jet Center and went marching inside. She spotted Summer sitting on one of the big couches—with a pilot! She let out a little laugh. The guy was gorgeous! And the uniform helped of course. He was flirting with Summer and she was going right along with it, in her own sweet way. Cassidy stood for a moment and watched. She didn't want to be a party pooper and Summer *had* told her to take her time. She was wondering whether to go back out and wait in the car for a while when Summer spotted her. She stood up and flew toward Cassidy, wrapping her in a hug.

"Chica! I've missed you!"

Cassidy hugged her back gently. She felt so small and frail, like a little bird. Cassidy was almost afraid to crush her. "I've missed you, too. It's been way too long. But we're going to make up for it now."

Summer smiled. "We are. We're going to have all kinds of fun over the next few months." She shot a look back at the pilot who was standing by the couches. "*He* seems like a lot of fun. Come on let me introduce you."

Cassidy scowled. She wanted to get Summer out of here and she did not want this guy latching on to her. Summer was already back at his side though. "Cassidy, meet Carl. Carl flew me here today. Carl, this is my dear friend, Cassidy."

Carl extended a hand and Cassidy shook it briefly. She could see what Summer saw in him as he smiled. "It's a pleasure to meet you, Cassidy." He turned and beckoned to another uniformed guy who was just coming in from the ramp. "Let me introduce you to my co-pilot Justin."

Cassidy eyed him. He was hot! He came over to join them. Once the introductions were complete, Carl looked at Summer. "Are you sure you can't join us for dinner?"

"Sorry," said Cassidy, before Summer had chance to speak. "We need to get going. We have a long drive back."

Summer nodded. Cassidy guessed she'd worn her voice out and was happy to let her do the talking for both of them. "It was very kind of you to wait until I got here. Nice to meet you. Bye." She turned, hoping Summer would follow. After a few steps she turned back to see not Summer, but Justin following her.

He grinned and held up Summer's bags. "I thought I'd help you load up while they say good-bye."

Cassidy rolled her eyes. Carl had his hands on Summer's shoulders looking down into her smiling face. She huffed. It was up to Summer, she supposed. "Okay. Thanks."

Once he'd loaded the bags into the back of the Beetle, Justin smiled. It was all white teeth and twinkling eyes. He could have stepped out of a commercial! "Are you sure I can't persuade you to have dinner with us?"

"Absolutely positive," she replied.

"I know you want to get your friend settled in, but we've got a couple of days' turnaround. We'll be here for the next few nights, if you want to change your mind." He held her gaze, his eyes were bright blue. He really was hot! Why was she turning him down so quickly?

She smiled back. "Thanks, but the next few days are going to be crazy getting Summer settled in."

He nodded. "Maybe next time then? We're usually out here a couple of times a month. If you give me your number I could call you."

Cassidy started to shake her head, then thought better of it. Why shouldn't she? She could hardly make a man-mess with a guy who was only in town a couple of days a month. She handed him her card with a smile. "Call me, leave a message. I'm not promising I'll call you back though."

"Thanks. I'll take my chances." His smile was gorgeous. He was hot, uniformed, and would only be looking to get together every now and again. What was her problem? The answer to that stunned her—he wasn't Shane. *That* was her problem!

She turned as Summer emerged from the building with Carl at her side. He walked her to the car and looked genuinely sad to see her go. Cassidy checked herself. She shouldn't be dismissing him so quickly. He might be something special for Summer? Maybe they were in the middle of that brief moment of fate when they met *the one?* She hurried around to the driver's side and got in. And maybe *she* was going nuts! *She,* Cassidy Lane, did not believe in any of that horseshit! Or at least she never used to, said a snide little voice in the back of her head. If she still didn't believe in it, why wasn't she speeding away? She scowled to herself. She was erring on the side of caution—for her friend's sake, that was all. She didn't want to be the one responsible for killing off a once-in-a-lifetime love before it had chance to get started. And yes, she was still thinking about Summer. Not Shane. Not Shane at all!

Just over an hour later they pulled up in front of Cassidy's house. Summer climbed out of the Beetle and looked around her with a huge smile on her face.

"Oh my God, Cass! It's beautiful". She waved her arms out across the river on one side and toward the mountains on the other. "I can see why they call it Paradise Valley. You've found your very own slice of paradise." She looked up at the house.

"And this! This is the most beautiful house I've ever seen." She ran back to the car and started pulling her bags out of the back.

Cassidy took the bigger cases and left Summer the smaller bags. "You know I'm never modest. This place really is paradise. And I can't wait to show you the house."

She showed Summer to her room and then gave her the grand tour, smiling the whole time at her friend's enthusiastic response. When they were done, they settled out on the deck with a glass of wine.

"It's awesome!" said Summer. "I want to say you are sooo lucky. But I know with you it's never luck. It's always by design. So, well done. You've outdone yourself this time. I…I…" Her voice was a barely a whisper. She shook her head with an apologetic smile.

"You've done too much talking," said Cassidy. "Autumn would kill me if she could hear you right now."

Summer smiled and nodded. She reached into her huge purse and pulled out a legal pad and pen. She scribbled on it for a few moments and then held it up.

Autumn would bust both our butts! But she's not here :0) I'd better be good. So tell me about you. How are you? How's the gallery? Tell me about your new friends…Any new men? :0)

Cassidy smiled. "I'm doing great. I love living here, and I think I might finally have found home."

Summer beamed and nodded enthusiastically. She scribbled on the pad and held it up.

It's love at first sight for me with this valley. If the house is as good as the pictures you sent I might want to buy it not just rent it!

Cassidy squealed. "Oh, Summer! That would be amazing! I love this place. And I'd love it even more if I had you here as a neighbor! Okay, let me tell you more. New friends....oh shit! I'd better call her! Gina is looking after the gallery for me while I came to pick you up."

She dialed Gina's number.

"Hi. Did you pick her up okay?"

"I did, and I'm really sorry, but would you mind if I don't come back?"

Gina laughed. "I already told you the answer to that. I'll see you tomorrow."

"Thanks, G. You're the best."

"I know. See ya."

Cassidy hung up and smiled at Summer. "Gina really is the best. You're going to love her."

"What's her story?" croaked Summer. She gave Cassidy a shamefaced grin and covered her mouth.

Cassidy laughed. "Don't be so impatient and I'll tell you. She's a photographer who worked in New York for years. She just came back here and got engaged to her long lost love. We're working together, putting together a line of Montana-themed art. I think it's going to be big."

Summer scribbled.

Knowing you, it will be. When do I get to meet her? I want to meet all your friends.

"Patience! You will. You'll get to meet Gina tomorrow at the gallery, and maybe her fiancé, Mason. He's is gorgeous! He's like the quintessential broody cowboy!

And he's taken? ☹ Does he have any brothers???

Cassidy had to laugh. "Actually he has three. You should meet two of them tomorrow. Carter will be here working on the landscaping. Summer, I think you're going to love him. He's gorgeous! He's big and built, spends all his time in the gym, and yet he's such a sweet guy, all caring and thoughtful."

Summer beamed and nodded, then scribbled.

Sounds lovely, but I already met one like that—my pilot!

Cassidy scowled. "That Carl guy was good-looking, but he's got nothing on Carter. And I know the uniform is a turn on, but come on, you can't beat cowboy boots and a hat—or Wranglers on a great butt!"

Summer waggled her eyebrows. "Sorry, but I can't stay quiet on that one! Sounds like I really have found paradise and I'm spoiled for choice!"

"There's no better choice than Carter. He's an absolute sweetheart."

Summer scribbled.

Sounds as though you like him yourself. What about the other two?

"No, I think Carter is perfect for you, that's why I'm talking him up and that's why I didn't like your Carl guy today! Wait till you meet him, you'll see. As for the other two brothers, Beau is one of them, you'll meet him tomorrow. He's a nice guy, good-looking, I just don't know him as well as the others." She wondered what she should say about Shane. She knew him better than any of them, but she shouldn't spend any more time with him. Not if she didn't want to make a mess.

Summer held up her pad.

So tell me what you've got going on with the brother you're not talking about?

Cassidy laughed. "You don't miss a trick do you?"

Summer shook her head. "So tell me."

"Shane," said Cassidy with a sigh. "I don't know what to do with Shane. I don't know what to do about Shane. He's gorgeous. He's totally my type, big, like six-four big. Muscled, tanned, fun, funny, life and soul of the party kind of guy." She held Summer's gaze and shrugged. "And you know how that usually ends for me. I avoided him for a long while, but I spent some time with him last weekend and I like him. I like him a lot. But I don't think I should go there. I mean it'll only end in disaster. I'd rather keep him as a friend than get involved with him and end up hating each other."

Summer looked sad.

"What? What's the matter?" asked Cassidy.

"That's not my friend Cassidy talking," she croaked. She had to scribble the rest.

My Cassidy goes for it, whatever it is, and to hell with the consequences.

Cassidy shook her head. "I know. It's not like me, is it? It's never mattered before. I don't know what's happening to me. Am I growing up? Am I just becoming a coward in my old age?"

Summer smiled. "Or have you finally met the one who makes it matter?"

Cassidy swallowed…hard. That couldn't be it, could it?

Chapter Fourteen

Shane stared out the window of his office. No matter how hard he tried he could not concentrate on his book work. His thoughts kept drifting back to Cassidy. He'd even dreamed about her last night. It was getting ridiculous. No matter what he did to take his mind off her, she'd taken up residence in his head.

It didn't help that all of his brothers had seen her this week. And each of them had had some comment about how great she was. Beau had stopped by after showing the rental property to her and her friend, Summer. He was thrilled to have a longer term tenant, especially considering who that tenant was. He'd rattled on about Summer being such a sweet and genuine person. He'd also gone on about how cool Cassidy was. Mason had been by the gallery to see Gina, and he was all enthusiastic about what the two women were doing with their art. He'd sung Cassidy's praises long and loud about how talented she was in both art and business. Poor old Carter had been slinking around at Cassidy's place working on the landscaping while avoiding Summer. Shane had to smile at that. Carter had delayed starting work until Summer had moved into Beau's place. Now that he had gotten started, he kept running down here to the ranch whenever Summer was at Cassidy's. It wasn't like him to be away from a job when he started—he never usually noticed who or what was around, he got so involved in his work. But he was so nervous about meeting Summer he'd left his guys to get on with it without him. Of course it hadn't helped Shane, because every time Carter showed up here, he talked about Cassidy and how understanding she was being.

Unlike his brothers, Shane still hadn't seen her or talked to her since their camping trip got cut short. Well, if you didn't count crossing paths at the stoplight up in town. He grinned. She'd looked pretty pleased when he blew her a kiss. But she hadn't answered his texts. He shrugged. Maybe he should stop by to see her? He could go up to the gallery. Or he could stop by her place. If Summer hadn't arrived he would have done that already, but he didn't want to impose. He sure as hell didn't want Cassidy thinking that he was there to meet her famous friend. Damn. He didn't know what to do. All he knew was that he wanted to see her.

As he stared out the window he had to smile as Carter's truck came into view yet again. He went out to meet him.

"What's up, Big C?" he called as Carter got out looking around furtively, as though worried he might have been followed.

Carter gave him a sheepish grin. "Hey, Shane. How you doing?"

"I'd be doing better if my brother didn't keep hightailing it over here every five minutes disturbing my work time."

Carter hung his head. "Sorry. I…Umm…"

Shane laughed. "You're running away from Summer again, aren't you?"

Carter nodded. "I am! I'm a big dumbass, but I get all tongue-tied just seeing Cassidy's car, knowing that Summer Breese is inside it, all beautiful and sweet and…I'm an idiot. Sorry, I don't want to mess up your work time. I'm wreaking havoc on my own."

Shane grasped his shoulder. "So, what, have they just showed up again?"

"Yeah, evidently Cassidy hired someone to help out in the gallery so she can spend time with Summer, show her around and that. Now they're coming and going all the time, I have to keep running out of there at a moment's notice."

Shane shook his head. "Carter, Carter, Carter. You're neglecting your work?"

Carter looked mortified. "No! I…I'm…"

Shane gave him a stern look.

"I guess I am, aren't I?"

Shane nodded. "And that's not like you. You love your work, you're conscientious. We need to put a stop to this craziness right now."

"How though?"

"We're going to take the bull by the horns and go over there and meet her."

"We?"

"Yes, we. I'll come with you for moral support."

Carter laughed. "You mean you're such an opportunist you'll use my misery for your own benefit?"

"Aw, that's not nice. How can you say that?"

"Because I know you! And because you haven't met her yet yourself."

Shane shook his head. "And I'm not worried about meeting Summer."

"Oh. Yeah. Right. How long has it been since you saw Cassidy?"
Shane held his gaze for a moment. "Far too long. So let's go kill two birds with one stone, can we? We can do each other a favor here."
Carter scuffed the ground with his toe. "I suppose."
"Come on, big guy. You're not really scared of meeting that little tiny lady are you?"
"Scared? Hell no. I'm petrified. I just know I'm going to make a fool of myself somehow."
"You are not. I've got your back, and you know Cassidy will do everything she can to make it easy for you. Let's go, before you chicken out."
"Okay." Carter headed for his truck. "Are you going to ride with me?"
Shane thought about it. "No, I'll follow you up there. I don't want to give you the excuse to run out of there again to bring me back."
"Okay. I'll see you there."
Shane climbed into his own truck with a grin on his face. Going up with Carter made him feel better about going. He wasn't just crumbling and crawling to Cassidy for another shot; he was going to help his brother get over his nerves. Honest!
He pulled into Cassidy's driveway behind Carter, wondering as he did if she'd be watching on that little monitor she had. He grinned and waved through the windscreen just in case.

~ ~ ~

Cassidy smiled as Summer came back into the kitchen. "So do you feel up to having everyone over tomorrow night?"
Summer looked worried. "Two trucks coming," she croaked.

Cassidy stood. Who might that be? She walked over to the window and had to smile when she saw Shane and Carter pulling up out front. "Well, it looks like you'll finally get to meet the two remaining Remington boys.

Summer came to stand beside her and then looked up at Cassidy with a big smile on her face. "Please tell me the muscly one isn't yours?"

Cassidy laughed. "Neither of them are mine! But the muscly one, as you put it, is the elusive Carter. The one I've been wanting you to meet. I told you he's a bit shy. My guess is that's why he keeps disappearing." As she watched them start up the stairs, she also guessed that this little visit was Shane's idea. Left to his own devices, Carter would have kept running and hiding. She looked at Summer who waggled her eyebrows.

"He looks like he worth waiting for!"

"Come on then." She made her way to the front door. "Let's introduce you finally."

She opened the door and caught her breath at the sight of Shane. The tingly shivers went racing down her back. For a moment she had nothing to say. She just stared into his eyes. He stared back, his smile more questioning than cocky.

"Hi. I hope you don't mind us stopping by." He grinned at Summer. "I confess, I twisted Carter's arm into bringing me over."

Summer smiled at Shane. "I'm glad he did." She looked back at Carter. "I'm so pleased to finally meet you."

The touch of pink on Carter's neck turned a deep red as Summer held out her hand. "You're quite the mystery man."

"Pleasure's all mine," he mumbled as he wrapped her little hand in his big paw.

~ ~ ~

Shane shot Cassidy a conspiratorial smile and was thrilled when she winked back at him. He didn't want to extend his own hand as it seemed neither Summer nor Carter were ready to let go. They just stood there smiling at one another. He looked at Cassidy again and she lifted a shoulder.

"Come on in," she said. "We don't need to be standing out here."

"Oh," said Carter. "I should be getting back to work." He looked over to where his men were laying pavers for the patio.

Summer still hadn't let go of his hand. "Please?"

Shane grinned at the look on Carter's face as he nodded. "Okay."

He was like a big puppy dog following her inside.

Cassidy led them all through to the big living room. "Lemonade?" she asked.

Carter and Summer both nodded.

"I'll give you a hand," said Shane. Carter shot him a panicked look as he followed Cassidy through to the kitchen. Shane gave him a reassuring smile. He was giving him time alone with his dream girl; he was hardly going to stay and supervise. Besides, he had business of his own to take care of.

"Close the door," said Cassidy in a low voice.

He closed it behind him and turned to her with a grin. "Don't you think it's a bit risky?"

She narrowed her eyes at him, but he could see the laughter lurking. "I mean to give *them* some privacy, not us!"

"Aw. And here I was thinking you were desperate to make up for lost time! You can't tell me you haven't missed me?"

She shook her head. "I don't think I've ever known a guy who was as full of himself as you are."

He shrugged. "Not so long ago someone told me that false modesty is a bad thing. And I'd never want to lie to you. I've missed you. I figured you missed me, too." She was so damned beautiful! Her eyes shone as she smiled back at him. He could tell she was chewing the inside of her lip again, and, by now, he knew that that meant she was doing battle with herself. He decided to see if he could sway her in his direction. "I'm hoping that you're as bowled over by whatever's going on between us as I am."

Her eyes widened in shock. "You are?"

He nodded. "You can take the win on this one. I openly admit it. You've gotten to me, okay? I don't know what to do about it. I hate not knowing whether you feel same." That knocked her sideways, he could tell.

She nodded slowly. "You've gotten to me, too. I have missed you, you aggravating, cocky…" she laughed. "I don't know what to do about it either." She held his gaze. "I think we should do *something* though. If we end up hating each other, so be it."

"I keep telling you, we won't." Shane was determined to cease the moment. "So, when can we have dinner?"

Cassidy shook her head. "Not tonight. Summer is cooking for me at her place."

"Tomorrow?" he asked hopefully.

She shook her head. "I was going to invite everyone over here tomorrow."

"And does *everyone* include me?"

She nodded. "I could hardly leave you out, could I?"

He smiled through pursed lips. "So if I'd just waited a little longer, *you* would have come crawling to *me*?"

She laughed. "I don't crawl, Shane."

He shrugged. "I never have before either. I seem to be making an exception for you."

She gave him a sassy smile. "I'm worth it."

"Don't I know it."

She quickly fixed a tray with glasses and a pitcher of lemonade. "Do you think we should make sure they're okay?"

Shane shrugged. "They'll figure it out." She looked so concerned, he went and peeked his head around the door. He couldn't see them, so he went out into the living room. No sign of them. Cassidy brought the tray out. He gave her a puzzled look.

"Where the hell did they get to?" she asked.

She went to the big windows overlooking the deck and smiled back over her shoulder at him. "Come see this."

Shane went to join her and smiled at the sight of them down in one of the new flower beds. Carter was squatting before Summer, pointing at a pretty blue flower and explaining something. Summer had her hands clasped in front of her, and a big smile on her face as she listened intently.

"Seems like Carter found his tongue," he said with a smile.

"I'm glad. One of them needs to do the talking and Summer can't."

"I think she might," said Shane as he watched the petite beauty squat down in the dirt beside Carter and ask him something. The smile on his big brother's face as he replied made Shane happy and wary at the same time. He'd never seen Carter smile like that since his wife had cheated on him and left town over ten years ago. Shane had hoped that he would find another woman to make him happy someday, but it scared him that Summer could break his heart all over again without even trying.

Cassidy looked up at him. "What do you reckon?"

He shrugged. "I like it, but it worries me."

"Me, too."

He slung an arm around her shoulders. "But they're both grown-ups, and we've got some making up of our own to do.

She shrugged his arm off and gave him that teasing smile of hers. "You certainly have!"

"*I have?* You're the one who's been neglecting her duties!"

He loved the way her eyes flashed at that. "Duties? What duties do I have?"

"You were supposed to protect me from all other women remember? And for almost a week you've left me alone—prey to all the wicked women out there."

This time he was pretty sure there was a fleck of green in the way her eyes flashed. She was jealous? Wow! He wouldn't have expected that.

"I'm good, Shane, but I'm not Wonder Woman. It'd take superhuman effort to keep you away from all the women out there—wicked or not."

Ouch! "That's not fair. You haven't even tried." She was mad. He knew he shouldn't, but it made him smile.

"So what are you saying, that you couldn't resist and fell prey while I wasn't around to protect you?"

There was an edge to her voice that said she really didn't like that idea. "Hell no! I'm saying I had to fend 'em off all by myself." He slid his arm around her shoulders again. "And I like it much better when you do it for me."

She relaxed as she smiled up at him, and this time didn't shrug him off. "Okay then. If you really managed not to succumb, then I suppose I can keep my word and protect you for a couple of weeks."

"Only a couple of weeks?" he raised an eyebrow.

"That was the deal, don't push it."

He grinned. "Okay, but I'm going to ask for an extension when the time's up."

She smiled and shook her head. "You're exhausting, do you know this?"

He pulled her to him and dropped a kiss on her lips. "I'd like to think I will be—tomorrow night."

She pressed herself to him as he closed his arms around her. It seemed as though she really had missed him too as she rubbed her hips against his, making him hard. "We'll have to see about that, won't we?" She gave him an evil grin as she pulled away from him and headed for the door. "For now, I think we'd better go join those two."

He groaned. "You're going to drag me out there before I've had chance to calm down?" He looked down at the bulge in his pants. He got no sympathy from Cassidy though.

"You started it; you'll have to deal with the consequences." She picked up the tray and pushed through the door to the deck. "Lemonade's ready guys," she called.

Shane shoved his hands in his pockets as he followed her out. He needed to remember that she was as good at this as he was—if not better!

Chapter Fifteen

Cassidy looked around. The others should be arriving soon. She was looking forward to this evening. This would be the first time that she'd entertained in this house, and it was perfect for it. She'd thought about cooking. She used to have a lot of dinner parties when she lived in San Francisco, and she loved to cook, but it hadn't felt right tonight. Instead she'd had the little catering company up in town prepare everything, and all she had to do was warm it. She knew that with everyone's unpredictable work schedules she'd do much better to wait until they all arrived before she threw it all in the oven.

She went back up to the bedroom and smiled. She was looking forward to bringing Shane back here later. If she was honest, that was what she was most excited about. If he hadn't come over with Carter yesterday, she would have called him to invite him this evening. She hadn't been able to get him out of her head, and Summer's assessment that maybe she was holding back—because she was scared he might be someone important—had rung true. If there was even a possibility it was true, she needed to find out either way. And the only way to do that was to jump in with both feet. She couldn't help thinking that maybe she was just in lust with him and she was twisting things around so she could sleep with him again. She shook her head as she straightened the pillows. Who was she kidding? She liked him too much; that was the problem. If it was just lust she wouldn't have a problem at all!

The sound of the buzzer had her scurrying back to the hallway to check the monitor. She was hoping that he'd be the first to arrive. She was a little disappointed to see Mason's truck making its way up the drive. She needed to get a grip. She shouldn't be disappointed to see them! She really liked Gina and Mason. She went out onto the front porch to greet them.

"Are we early?" asked Mason looking around.

"Not at all, but you are the first, come on in."

Gina grinned and held out two bottles of wine.

Cassidy took them with a grin as they took their coats off. "Are we planning on drinking a lot?"

Gina laughed. "No, this is that Malbec I was telling you about. One bottle is for tonight, the other is for your cellar so that you've got it on hand for our girls' night. I'm still waiting, you know, and getting less patient all the time.

"Ah. Yeah. We need to make that happen."

Mason nodded. "You do. Only can you include me in the scheduling?" He put an arm around Gina. "I don't want this one driving home after a night of wine and girl talk. I'll be chauffeur."

Gina huffed. "I can easily stay here if I have too many."

"And I can come get you. Just as easy."

Cassidy laughed. Those two were still trying to figure out the balance of being a couple. Mason was definitely a Montana man in the way he wanted to look after his woman, and Gina was a little on the stubborn side to say the least. Cassidy looked at Mason. "Maybe you should organize a guys' night out, then everyone can fend for themselves."

He grinned. "Now that's a good idea. How soon are we talking? I need to catch up with Chance and my brothers."

Gina huffed. "See, he's all over-protective toward me, until he's got something better to do."

He shrugged. "I have to respect your independence, right?"

She laughed. "You do, but I'd rather it wasn't only when it suits you."

Cassidy listened to them as she hung their coats. They were finding their way. They were both strong, smart, and stubborn. Mason wasn't exactly a pushover, yet they were happy together. His ego wasn't threatened by Gina's stubborn independence. Maybe it was a Remington thing? Maybe Shane *was* just as comfortable in his own skin as he seemed to be? She closed the closet and smiled at them. And maybe she was just getting carried away, wondering if she and Shane could be like Gina and Mason—that was just plain ridiculous!

"Looks like they're all arriving at once." Mason jerked his head toward the driveway where three sets of headlights were approaching. He caught Cassidy's eye. "Do you have any idea what Carter was like about picking Summer up?"

"Do you have any idea what *she* was like about it?"

Gina laughed. "They are just so cute together. It's obvious they really like each other, but they're both doing this 'we're just friends' thing."

Cassidy nodded. "They are cute, but I'm starting to get a bit worried. Summer is totally smitten, but she doesn't think they should do anything about it." She looked at Mason. "I told her about Carter's ex-wife. I thought she should know how badly he's been hurt." She didn't add that Summer was such a sweetie that she'd cried for Carter, she was so sad for him. "She says he's just such a nice guy that she wants to spend time with him as a friend. I'm guessing she'd like a lot more than that, but she doesn't want to risk him getting hurt when she has to leave."

Mason nodded. "I went up to see him this morning. He's like a dog with two…"

"Tails!" Gina finished for him.

Mason grinned, "Yeah. Two *tails*. Right. Let's just say he's got his head in the clouds. But he says he's just going to make the most of her friendship for the short time she's here."

Cassidy hoped that neither of them would end up getting hurt. But at the end of the day, they were both their own people and would handle it however they saw fit. She wasn't one to say what anyone should do. And certainly not in this situation. Especially not when she herself had been swinging like a crazy pendulum over what she should do about Shane. As she watched him climb out of his truck she was very glad that she'd finally decided to go for it. He was gorgeous, and he was giving her that cocky smile of his that infuriated her, and at the same time made her want to send the others home and drag him into her bedroom. She was surprised to see Chance get out the passenger side of Shane's truck. She had invited him, but hadn't thought he would show. She was so bad—her mind immediately went to how he would get home! She hadn't thought Shane would be driving back.

The next truck pulled up and Beau got out. He'd asked if he could bring a date. Cassidy had been uncomfortable with it. She'd checked with Summer before she'd said yes, and of course Summer had said it would be fine. She wouldn't put anyone else out for her own sake—no matter what. She watched as Beau walked around to open the passenger door and a pretty girl with short dark hair got out.

Mason groaned. "What the hell did he bring *her* for?"

Cassidy shot him an inquiring look. He shook his head.

"Mase thinks Angie is trouble," said Gina. "I think she's okay."

Mason shook his head. "That's because you like to see the best in people. She's trouble I tell you." He looked at Cassidy. "You might want to warn your friend to watch what she says around that one. I don't trust her."

"Oh, Mase," said Gina. "Don't be mean."

"Just trying to be practical."

Cassidy nodded. "Thank you." She trusted his judgment.

Soon they were all inside and had a drink in their hand. Cassidy noticed that Angie kept trying to corner Summer. She had to smile at the way Carter never left her side. He was like a bodyguard. He could be one, too, with his build and protective instincts.

She spun around at the feel of Shane's hand on her shoulder. "Can we send them all home now and get the party started?"

She laughed. "No. We have to wait. Enjoy the anticipation."

His eyes shone as he smiled back. "I like anticipation when you're the reward for waiting." There went those goose bumps again as he placed a hand in the small of her back and pulled her a little closer. He leaned down to whisper in her ear. "I like fucking you better though!"

Damn him! She tried to move away, but he slid his hand down over her ass. "Don't tell me you don't want to."

She met his gaze. "I told you, I'm not a liar. I'm not moving away from you because I don't want to. You've got me all hot and wet and needy. I'm moving away because what I really want to do right now is unbuckle you, close my fingers around you, and then bend my naked ass over this counter in front of you." She loved the way his eyes glazed over at her words. She looked around to check no one was watching, then covered the hand that he still had on her ass with her own. She moved it around. "See, I took a leaf out of your book. I'm commando under here. Figured it would help with ease of access. And if you keep talking about fucking me, we may have to make our excuses for a minute and go upstairs so you can."

His hand grasped her ass hard. "You think you can call my bluff? Let's go."

She *had* been hoping to call his bluff, but now she was tempted to go. "And leave my guests and your family standing around here waiting for dinner?"

He grinned. "They know what I'm like."

Hmm. Cassidy didn't want them to think that was what she was like. And she certainly didn't want them thinking she was just another of Shane's conquests. "I think I'll stick with anticipation."

He nodded. "We can make up for it later."

She smiled. "We can. Now, do you want to make yourself useful in the meantime?"

He grinned and pressed her against the island, grinding his hips against hers. "Sure. Is this useful enough?" She couldn't help it. Her eyelids drooped and she let out a low, deep breath as her hands came up to his shoulders. He grasped her waist and pressed into her.

Her eyes flew open and she pushed him off. "Okay, you can take the win on that one. I want you. I can't wait for them all to leave, so you can make good on what you just promised, but for now, that wasn't the kind of useful I had in mind."

He smiled. "Okay. I'll behave. What do you want me to do?"
She showed him around the kitchen. "I'm going to pull everything out soon. Can you help me serve?"
He nodded. "I'd be glad to."

~ ~ ~

When he finally took his seat, it took a moment for Shane to realize that she'd sat him at the head of the table. He smiled to himself and looked up in time to catch Mason watching him. His brother gave him the slightest of nods. It seemed that he'd noticed, too. He'd watched as Shane had helped Cassidy get everyone served. It was weird. He'd felt as though they were a real couple and they were hosting their friends and family—and he'd loved it! Him! Shane! The guy who ran a mile if a chick suggested so much as a night out with a group of friends. Yet here he was, playing the man of the house and loving the idea of it. What the hell was she doing to him? And why didn't he mind?
Beau looked down the table at him. "Have you decided what you're doing about the cabins yet?"
Why did he want to talk about that right now? He shrugged. "Yeah. I talked to Dad last week. I'm going to build."
Beau nodded and looked from him to Chance. "And whose land will that be on?"
Oh shit. Why was he going there? That was family business, something to be talked about at home, not aired in front of other people like this. He smiled. Hoping to change the subject. "On Dad's land, of course." He knew damn well what Beau meant, but he didn't want to get into it tonight.
Beau scowled.
Shane was surprised that it was Summer who stepped in to avert the awkward moment. She was sitting between Beau and

Carter. She turned to touch Beau's sleeve. "Speaking of what land belongs to whom, I've been wanting to ask you. Do you own the place I'm renting, or do you manage it for someone?"
Shane did his best not to chuckle. Beau was evidently spoiling for a fight, but he was too polite to ignore Summer. He shot Shane another scowl and then turned to her. "I own it. Most of the properties I rent are managed, but I own several and that's one of them."
Summer had such a sweet smile. Shane wanted to ask Cassidy where she was from. She had a southern twang, but not a very pronounced one. He had a feeling she was one of those southern belles though. Softness and sweetness on the outside with a will of steel underneath. He was taking a liking to her, and it surprised him to realize that he liked her as person, not as a female to pursue, but just as a fellow human being.
"Why, are you interested in buying it?" asked Angie.
Shane did not like that girl. She was one of Katie's cronies. He'd hung out with them often enough to know the way they gossiped, how bitchy they were. He didn't want her getting her claws into Summer.
He had to laugh at the reactions around the table.
In the same moment, he looked at Angie and said, "Don't be so nosey."
Cassidy stood and asked, "So who wants dessert?"
Mason looked at Angie and asked. "How about you, do you want to tell us what you're planning to buy?"
And Carter glared at her and said. "That's none of your business."
After a few moments of stunned silence, Summer started to laugh. Everyone joined her and the tension was gone.

Angie looked around the table. "Sorry. That was really rude of me, wasn't it?"

Cassidy nodded. "I'm afraid so. But you didn't deserve that response. I'm just on edge trying to take care of my friend here." She smiled around at the brothers. "And it seems I have quite a lot of backup in protecting her."

Mason and Carter grinned at her. Then she met Shane's eye. He tried to convey to her without words that it was *her* he was most concerned with. She gave him a grateful smile. He hoped she understood.

Once they'd finished eating, Cassidy shooed everyone out of the dining room and into the living room, assuring them she'd join them very shortly.

Shane hung back to help her. Between them they made short work of clearing the table and loading the dishwasher. The kitchen was cleaned up in no time. Shane was struck again by how much he was enjoying this—enjoying feeling that they were a couple and in this together. "We make a good team, huh?" He held out his fist and she bumped hers against it.

She gave him an odd look. "We do. Scary, huh?"

He laughed. "Scary? I was thinking it was kind of cool."

"You were?"

"You weren't?" Maybe she was feeling the way he normally did at the very idea of shared domesticity?

She gave him a puzzled look. "Actually I was. I was thinking it was really cool! And I was wondering why it doesn't freak me the fuck out!"

He laughed out loud at that. "See we are the same kind of animal. You stole my thoughts. I was really enjoying playing house with you until I realized I'm the guy who runs a mile from all that shit."

"And I'm the girl who does it all by herself or doesn't do it at all."

They stared at each other for a moment. She looked a little scared, and he *felt* a little scared. He held his fist out again. "Okay, let's just go back to good job, partner, and leave it at that, shall we?"

She laughed and bumped her fist against his. "Gladly. And let's go get a drink. We deserve it."

Just as they made their way to join the others, Chance held up a hand to catch Shane's attention. He came over. "Thanks for a great dinner, Cassidy."

"Thanks for coming. Do you want to play pool? I'm going to see if everyone wants to head down to the basement to play?"

He shook his head. "Thanks, but I'm going to head home." He looked at Shane. "Could I have a word?"

Cassidy laughed. "Yes, he's staying, yes you can have his keys."

Shane burst out laughing. "Don't you just love my shrinking violet?" He put an arm around her shoulders and grinned at Chance as he dug his car keys out of his pocket and handed them over.

Chance grinned. "And there I was worrying how I could be subtle about it."

"I have many strengths, Chance," said Cassidy. "Subtlety is not one of them. So, I'll be blunt again. Why are you leaving?"

Shane knew that Chance warmed to Cassidy in that moment. She could see something was bothering him. He shrugged. "I'm the odd man out on couples' night."

"You knew that before you came. What's really the problem?"

Chance held her gaze for a moment. Shane knew he was weighing it up and deciding to be straight with her. "Beau and I don't see eye to eye. Mostly we let it ride, but something's eating at him. I can tell he's working his way up to a showdown, and I don't want to spoil your evening by letting it happen here."

Cassidy nodded. "Thank you. I appreciate it, even though I don't want you to leave."

He shrugged.

"Will you come over another time and just hang with us?"

Shane was pleased at the genuine smile on Chance's face. "Thanks. I'd like that."

Cassidy leaned in and pecked his cheek. "Me too. I'll say goodnight now, because I'm guessing you're going to slide out the door before anyone notices."

Chance nodded. "You got it." He looked at Shane. "You've got yourself a good 'un here."

Shane nodded. He knew it. Now all he had to do was figure out how to make it last.

Chapter Sixteen

The next morning Cassidy opened her eyes to find Shane propped up on one elbow smiling down at her.

"Good morning, Princess."

She shook her head. "You're still calling me that?"

"I still see you that way, the way *I* described it, not the way you did."

She shrugged.

"You'd better get used to it, and you'd better change the way you look at things."

"What things?" she mumbled. Her brain wasn't fully awake yet.

"What you think a Princess is like." He trailed a finger down her cheek. "What you think I'm like. You're wrong about me, you know."

She smiled. "I was right about one thing."

"Oh yeah? And what was that?"

"You *are* exhausting." They'd had quite a night!

He grinned. "I'm glad you think so. I didn't want to disappoint."

She reached her arms up around his neck. "Oh, you didn't disappoint at all. I'm impressed, very impressed." She winced as she moved to pull him down to her. "And maybe a little sore too."

He lay his head on the pillow next to hers and looked into her eyes. "I'm sorry. Do you want a massage to help you feel better?"

She shook her head. "Maybe tonight? I have to get a move on this morning. I'm supposed to pick Summer up, and we're heading into Bozeman." She'd love nothing more than to stay here in bed with him, but she couldn't.

He pouted. "I'm supposed to be back at the ranch by now, but I'll stay here if you want me?"

"That's not fair. You know I want you. I've told you enough times. But I've got things to do." She scrambled out of bed before her willpower deserted her. "Come on. We've got time for a quick shower, but the rest will have to wait until tonight."

He hopped out of bed and started pulling her toward the bathroom. "You already know what happens in the shower."

She grinned and let him lead her in—that was what she'd been hoping for.

Half an hour later they were both dressed and ready to go. "Do you want me to drop you off?" she asked.

"I can get Carter to take me, if you're in a hurry."

She checked her watch. "I've got time."

He grinned. "Then yes. I'd love you to give me a ride, and I'll do the same for you tonight."

"You're just one of those guys who can't get enough, aren't you?"

"Not when it comes to you, I can't." He pulled her to him and kissed her. She loved his kisses. They were so confident, so adventurous. He didn't dominate her, take possession of her. It felt more like he was inviting her to join him, to go someplace with him and to have fun. She kissed him back, hoping that her kiss could tell him that she accepted the invitation, was up for the adventure—wherever it might lead.

By lunchtime she was exhausted. She and Summer had spent the morning shopping. Now they sat in a café on Main in Bozeman. Summer smiled at her. "I take it you and Shane had a good time last night?"

Cassidy grinned. "One hell of a good time! And what about you? What's really going on with you and Carter? I can tell you like him."

"I do. He's wonderful, Cass. It's like someone upstairs listened to everything I wanted in a man—physically and in personality—and went away and made Carter just for me." Her smile faded. "But we lead such different lives. He lives for his work as much as I live for mine." Her voice cracked as she finished the sentence and she shook her head.

Cassidy nodded. "He does, and I don't see him getting involved with anyone unless it's for keeps."

Summer scrabbled in her purse and pulled her pad out.

I would love to keep him! He's my ideal man in every sense. But it couldn't work. Neither of us is talking about it. It's like we have this silent agreement that we'll just be friends. He always jokes that he's a dumbass, but he's really smart. He understands. He knows.

It made Cassidy sad, but she knew her friend was right. There was no point in the two of them starting something they wouldn't be able to finish. Summer's stay here was temporary. Carter's entire life was here. He wouldn't get involved lightly, neither would she for that matter. They were doing the smart thing, the best thing. That made her wonder, was she doing the dumb thing by getting involved with Shane after she'd promised herself no more man-messes? Only time would tell. Dumb or smart, she was doing it. He was coming back for dinner tonight, he'd no doubt stay over again. They were on the fast track to somewhere—disaster or delight, they'd find out soon enough.

Summer was scribbling away on her pad again. She held it up.

You and Shane are made for each other. He's not like your other guys. Yes, he's big and strong and sexy ;0) BUT he's not a control freak.

Cassidy frowned. "I never thought of him as a control freak!"

Summer smiled and scribbled again.

You didn't think Al was either. Or Adam.

Cassidy shuddered. "You know, I don't think I knew they were until right now. I've always thought it was about ego, with both of them."

Summer shook her head. "Control," she croaked. With a look of frustration, she started to scribble again.

Damn this is annoying! So much I want to say and my voice just won't keep up! You're like this wild, beautiful, free spirit. You attract guys who only want the best – you ARE the best. BUT they want you on their terms, and can't handle that you have your own terms and you live by them. It seems to me that Shane likes that about you. He doesn't want to control you, he wants to run alongside you, because he's another wild, free, beautiful, spirit.

Cassidy read the words and then reread them before looking up.

Summer nodded. "It's true."

It was. Shane had never tried to make her do or be anything that…well, anything at all. He just waited for her to be her and, as Summer put it, ran alongside. Maybe he *was* different.

She smiled at the thought. Maybe he was as special as she was secretly hoping he might be.

"Your smile says it all," whispered Summer.

Cassidy met her gaze. "Maybe. But that's enough talk about men for now. I want to talk about you. How long are you thinking you're going to stay here? Do you really think you might want to buy the house from Beau? How would it work if you did? Would this be your escape place?"

Two little lines creased Summer's forehead as she bent over her pad once more.

I'm trying not to think about it all. I would love to buy the house. I already feel more at home there than I've felt anywhere for years. I don't know how long I'm going to be here though. The doctor's say rest, rest, rest the voice and I should get it back without surgery—I don't want surgery!

She stared off out the window before she continued to scribble.

Part of me wants to use it as an excuse. An excuse to give it all up. I don't enjoy it anymore.

Cassidy read that last line and looked up. "I thought that might be the case."

"You did?" Summer looked pale and uncertain. "Don't tell Autumn!"

"You mean you haven't talked to her about it?"

Summer shook her head.

"She only wants what's best for you know."

"I know, but she thinks the career is what's best for me. What would I do otherwise?" She hung her head. "What would Autumn do?"

Wow. Cassidy hadn't thought about it like that. She thought of both sisters as being the perfect team. Summer was the face—

the voice—while Autumn was the business brain, working tirelessly in the background. If Summer were to give up her career, what *would* Autumn do? She patted her friend's hand. "Well, you've got plenty of time to figure it all out while you rest your voice. And you need to have some fun, too."

Summer nodded. "Resting *is* fun for me right now—it's such a novelty!"

"Is that your way of saying you want to go home?"

She nodded. "Yes, please. I hear a hot tub calling."

Cassidy grinned. "I can just picture you sitting in your hot tub out on that deck, listening to the river, watching the stars."

"My idea of heaven. Want to join me tonight? I'll supply the wine."

"Sorry, I can't. And will you get your pad out? You're talking too much."

Summer made a face and scribbled, then waggled her eyebrows as she held up the pad.

Don't be sorry. You're seeing Shane. Just wish I could ask Carter to join me!

Cassidy laughed. "You should!"

Summer shook her head sadly.

Cassidy wished the two of them could figure something out. They were so cute together. "Come on then. Let's get you home." She looked around for the server to ask for the check. She frowned when she saw two familiar faces sitting at the counter. It took her a minute to place them. It was the two pilots who had brought Summer in. She looked away, hoping they could make a quick exit without having to stop and talk to them. No such luck!

"Summer!" called the one who had been hitting on her. Carl? Was that his name?

Summer smiled when she spotted them and gave a little wave. They made their way over.

Justin, the one who had asked for Cassidy's number, smiled at her. "We meet again."

She nodded. "We do. However, we're just leaving."

"No," said Carl as he sat down next to Summer. "Don't go just yet."

Summer looked at Cassidy. It seemed she wasn't as interested in the guy as she had been. Her eyes pleaded for help.

"Sorry," said Cassidy. "We really have to run. We're late."

She stood and Summer joined her.

"Maybe next time, then?" asked Justin.

"Maybe," said Cassidy.

He took her by surprise as he leaned in for a hug. She was so surprised that she hugged him back. She rolled her eyes at Summer over his shoulder. Summer winked and gave Carl a quick hug. "Bye then."

As they pushed their way out through the door, Cassidy shook her head. "They don't give up too easily do they?"

Summer smiled. "If you'd never heard the name Remington, you wouldn't want them to—would *we*?"

Cassidy laughed. That was probably true. She frowned as she thought she recognized another guy standing outside looking at the menu board in the window. Her memory was terrible. She knew she knew him, but she couldn't place him. He was kind of good-looking, but he had a mean air about him.

He tipped his hat and smiled. He reminded Cassidy of a wolf. Handsome, but predatory. She nodded.

"Good afternoon. I see you're making friends everywhere you go."

She gave him a puzzled look. Who the hell was he? She didn't have time to figure it out before he turned and walked away.

"Creepy!" breathed Summer. "Who's he?"

Cassidy shrugged. "I don't know. I've seen him around before, but I don't remember where." She shuddered and set off at a brisk pace back to the parking lot. She slowed a little when she realized Summer was having to trot along to keep up. "Sorry, I guess that guy creeped me out."

Summer nodded. "Let's go home. Bozeman was fun, but I want to get home to Paradise." She grinned. "Also known as Remington land."

Cassidy laughed and unlocked the Beetle. She was starting to think of the valley the same way herself.

~ ~ ~

Shane pulled up outside Cassidy's place with a smile. He'd been looking forward to getting back here all day. He was a little disappointed to see that Carter's truck was still here and a few of his guys were still around, too. He wanted Cassidy and the place to himself.

"Hey bro," he called when he saw Carter coming around the corner.

Carter smiled. "Back again, huh? Though I shouldn't be surprised. At dinner last night it felt as though you and Cassidy were hosting, not just Cassidy."

Shane nodded. It wasn't just him who had noticed it then. "I know. It's weird, isn't it? But I'll tell you what. It felt like the most natural thing in the world."

Carter didn't seem in the least surprised. "It looked like it. It wouldn't surprise me if it happens sooner rather than later."

"What do you mean?"

Carter smiled. "You two getting together. Living together. I dunno, maybe even getting married and having a bunch of kids."

Shane stared at him. He didn't know what to say. Mostly because the idea didn't sound nearly as ridiculous as it should.

"I say go for it, Shane."

Shane didn't know how to respond, so instead he chose to deflect. "What about you and Summer? You're telling me to go for it, while you won't go for anything. Insisting that you two are just friends, that you're just looking out for her." He regretted the words as soon as they were out. Carter looked so down.

He shrugged. "It's different for me. You're a first-timer.. I had my shot and got screwed over. Yes, I like Summer. I like her a lot. But it's different. She's only going to be here for a while. I know how it feels to have my heart broken, and I never want to go there again. That little lady could destroy me."

"Aw, Carter." Shane grasped his shoulder. "I'm sorry."

Carter shrugged. "It is what it is. I choose to look at it that I'm a lucky SOB. How many guys would give their right arm to be able to spend time with her like I'm doing? I'm happy enough with that. It'd be greedy to ask for anything more." He smiled at Shane. "So stop feeling sorry for me, would you? Get your ass in there and have a great evening with Cassidy. I'm going home."

Shane paused on the steps to watch him drive away. He wished there was something he could do, but he knew there wasn't.

Cassidy appeared at the front door. "If you're thinking about turning around and leaving, go ahead and do it would you. I turned down another offer to be here with you tonight, I can still go."

His head jerked up to check her face. His heart was pounding. Was she serious?

She laughed. "What's up? You don't like that idea?"

He ran up the steps and closed his arms around her, backing her against the wall as he did so. "I don't just not like that idea. I *hate* it!" He smiled as he spoke. But the words were true and the look in her eyes told him she knew it.

She looped her arms up around his neck. "I didn't know you had a jealous streak."

He nibbled her bottom lip. "Neither did I till just now." He gave her his cocky grin, the one he knew infuriated her. "Don't go thinking it's about insecurity though. I'm just greedy. I want all of you, all for me."

"You do, do you?"

He nodded. "I do." A thought struck him and he smiled. "You know you're supposed to be protecting me from all other women?"

She laughed. "Supposed to be? I am. I'm keeping you here every night. Out of harm's way. In the one place where I know no other woman can get to you." She rubbed her hips against him, making him ache for her. "In my bed."

He smiled. "Well, it only seems fair to me that we should be equal in all things."

She raised an eyebrow.

He didn't know where it had come from, but now he had the thought it felt really important to share it—and that she should agree to it. "I think I should protect you from all other men."

Her eyes widened. He wasn't sure whether she was pleased, shocked, or annoyed. "What do you mean?"

He tried to keep it light. "Do you want to do the E-word with me?"

"The E-word?"

"Exclusive." It was a word he'd shied away from ever since high school. He'd often joked that it wasn't in his vocabulary, yet here he was the one saying it—asking for it, no less. And his heart was hammering while he waited for her answer.

She still looked slightly puzzled. "That's what you want? To be exclusive? With each other?"

He nodded, holding his breath.

A big smile spread across her face. "You think you can handle it?"

He nodded rapidly. "I can. Can you?"

She thought about it for a long moment. "I think I might." She smiled up at him. "In fact, I think I'd quite like it."

He let out his breath and dropped a kiss on her lips. "Thank you."

She took him by the hand and led him inside. He took a seat at the kitchen island while she poured two glasses of wine. When she handed him one he smiled and raised his glass. "To us."

She looked uncertain. "Us?"

He nodded. "I feel it, you feel it. We both like winning points off each other, but I think our biggest win is going to be when we admit what we have going on between us is something pretty special."

She grinned. "I've already admitted that to myself; I just wasn't ready to admit it to you."

Shane felt his heart expand in his chest. It *wasn't* just him then! "Well, I'm glad I was brave enough to go first and risk rejection." He winked at her. "I know you're just a weak little lady, but I'm strong enough to put myself out there for the sake of *us*."

Her eyes flashed, just as he'd known they would. She slapped his arm. "You are not braver than I am."

"Oh no?" he teased. "You knew we were special but you weren't ready to admit it to me, because you're *scared* of getting hurt."

"I am not!" she laughed.

"Don't worry. I'll be gentle with you and take good care of you. I won't rush you."

She laughed. "You're just pushing all my buttons on purpose aren't you?"

Shane nodded. "And it's working, isn't it?"

"It is! I have to outdo you! You think you're braver than me? No way. I'm braver than you. I'm brave enough to say—if we're going to do this, let's do it. Dive right in. You're here, you're going to stay the night again. Why don't you just stay?"

"Stay?" he thought he knew what she meant, but he couldn't quite believe it.

She had her hands on her hips as she nodded. "Move in with me."

Wow! Was he ready for that? The hint of a smile playing on her lips told him she didn't think he was. She thought she'd won? Hell no! "Perfect! Thank you. I will. I'd love to."

She laughed. "Can you stammer out anymore?"

He laughed with her. "Apparently not."

They stared at each other, both realizing what they'd just done. Shane swallowed. He could back out—if he wanted. He raised an eyebrow at her. So could she. She grinned back at him and shook her head. Okay! So they were going to do this.

He raised his glass again. "To us."

This time she chinked her glass against his. "To us."

Chapter Seventeen

Cassidy walked into the gallery and grinned at Gina. "Here again?" she asked.

"I love having this place as a base. I spend so much time roaming with my camera and I love it, but it's nice to have a home base, too." She smiled. "And besides, I feel like one of us should come in every now and then. And you seem to be otherwise engaged these days."

Cassidy had been feeling a little guilty that between spending so much time with Summer and with Shane, she was neglecting the business and Gina. "I'm sorry. Don't worry though, I won't let us get off schedule."

Gina laughed. "I'm not criticizing. I'm just hoping you'll open up and tell me what's going on with you and Shane. You keep putting me off whenever I ask about a girls' night, so I figure I'll just have to start asking whenever I get chance. I can't get anything out of Shane because he's always at your place."

Cassidy grinned. She couldn't wait to see Gina's reaction. "Well, anything you want to ask him, you just come on over to my place. As of last night, he's moved in with me!"

Gina's mouth fell open. For a moment she just stared at Cassidy in disbelief, then she jumped to her feet and came to wrap her in a hug. "Oh. My. God!! That's awesome!"

"You're not shocked?"

"I'm shocked. I'm stunned. I'm going to need all the details! But I'm so happy for you both!" She stood back. "Let's go back to shocked and stunned a minute though. I mean, this is really fast for anyone. But for two people who aren't interested in committed relationships? And you especially! No man-messes in general and no Shane in particular. How did you get from there to here—and how did it happen so fast?"

Cassidy shrugged. "I'm not sure I know. You were right though. We do have something going on between us." She smiled. "It's something pretty special. We just figure we may as well dive in and get on with it. If we're going to be good together, then why waste time getting there? And if we're going to go down in flames, it's better to find out sooner rather than later, isn't it?"

Gina nodded. "I guess it is. And neither of you like to waste time, so it kind of makes sense. But what happened? Did he just come right out and ask if you wanted to move in together?"

Cassidy smiled through pursed lips.

"What? Did you ask him?"

"Not exactly."

"Oh, come on!" Gina said with a laugh. "Fill me in. I'm dying of curiosity here!"

"I kind of dared him to."

Gina threw her head back and laughed. "You *dared* him?"

"Yeah. I suppose. See, he was telling me that he was braver than I am, because he'd come out and revealed his feelings for me first. I said I was braver because I was prepared to ask him to move in with me."

"Ugh, you are a pair together. Neither of you will be outdone. Tell me it's not just about one-upmanship though?"

Cassidy shook her head. "I tried to convince myself that it was. But it isn't. It's what we both want to do anyway. This has just sped up the process."

Gina nodded. "Well, however you got there, I'm glad you did. I just hope you're both prepared to put the effort in to make it work."

Cassidy nodded. So did she.

She followed Gina's gaze as she looked out the gallery window and shuddered. "Who is that, guy?" she asked. "Summer and I saw him in Bozeman. I recognize him, but I can't place him."

Gina made a face. "Well, make a note, he's one to be wary of. That's Guy Preston."

"Oh! He's the guy that caused all the trouble for you and Mason?"

Gina nodded. "He's also mad at all of us right now. I think he got wind somehow that it was Mason and Chance who helped his wife April to skip town. He's a piece of work. He's got it in for all the Remingtons. Once he knows you're with Shane you'll be on his radar, too."

Cassidy shook her head. "He gives me the creeps."

"Then you've got good instincts. Trust them! He'll cause trouble for you if he can."

Cassidy couldn't see how Guy might cause her any trouble, but maybe Shane. She'd have to stay on her toes if she saw him around again.

Guy waved at them and smiled that wolf smile before carrying on down the street.

"Asshole!" muttered Gina.

~ ~ ~

Shane headed back to the cabin at lunchtime. He was still stunned that he'd agreed to move in with Cassidy—but he didn't regret it. He went into his room and pulled his pack from under the bed. He started throwing clothes in, all the while wondering what the hell he was doing. He started at the sound of the front door closing.

"Are you home?" called Mason.

"Yeah. In here."

Mason came and stood in the doorway. He leaned against the frame and folded his arms across his chest. Did he know?

"What?" asked Shane as he continued throwing clothes into his bag.

"Do you know what you're doing?"

Shane grinned. "I'm pretty sure I'm packing a bag, but if you see something else going on here, do tell."

Mason chuckled. "I see my littlest brother about to make one of the biggest moves of his life. And I'm wondering if he knows what he's doing. How about that?"

At least he'd said *move* not *mistake.* That was a good start. Shane straightened up and met Mason's gaze. "I'm not sure I know what I'm doing either, Mase. But I do know it feels right."

"That's good enough then."

"Does that mean I have your approval?" Shane was surprised to realize that the only thing bothering him about moving in with Cassidy was what his family's reaction might be.

"I'm not about approval. You don't need it."

Shane tried to figure out the look on his face.

Mason smiled. "I'm here for support—if you want it."

Shane relaxed. "I do. I mean it's no big deal really, is it? I move in with her, and if we don't get on I move back here."

Mason gave him a stern look. "So you're not serious about it, then?"

"Of course I am! I'm just trying to downplay it before I scare myself stupid. It's not a big deal—it's a *huge* deal!"

Mason grinned. "That's more like it. Take it seriously and you might make something good of it."

"How do you even know?"

"Gina."

"Of course." So that meant Cassidy had told her. Had she told her because she was happy or because she thought it was some big joke?

Mason put a hand on his shoulder. "I think it's great. I think the two of you will do great together. I've been thinking that since we all had dinner over there the other night. You two just stepped right into the roles of host couple, as though you were natural together, as though you'd been together for years." He smiled. "Apart from the way you kept mauling her when you thought no one was looking."

Shane smirked. "Yeah, well. I can't help that. And hopefully I'll still be doing it when we *have* been together for years."

"Talk like that makes me think you're going to be fine. I just wanted to stop by, because I know you. I know you'd worry about how to tell us. You don't need to worry, because I know, and if you want I'll tell the others, too."

Shane nodded. "Thanks. I think I should go see Mom and Dad and talk to them myself though."

Mason nodded his agreement. "That was the other thing I was wondering about. If you're all in, then you go tell them. I wasn't sure if you'd wait before talking to them about it."

Shane knew what he meant. "No. I'm not hedging my bets. I'm going with the intention of making it work."

"Good. You go talk to them then."

Shane nodded. "As soon as I've packed."

As he made his way up to the main house, Shane had to wonder what his parents would think. They knew and liked Cassidy, but still. Even he knew this was pretty fast for him to be moving in with her. Especially considering he'd always said he stayed here on the ranch so he could be on hand for anything he was needed for at the guest ranch. Nothing ever came up, and he knew he didn't *need* to be here, but he liked living here and had used that as his excuse to not ever go off and buy or build a place of his own.

His mom was in the kitchen when he let himself in. She smiled. "Did you smell cookies already? I was only just thinking about baking some."

He smiled and went to give her a hug. "No, Mom. Though you know I'll take some when they're done. Is Dad around? I wanted to talk to you both."

She nodded. "He'll be back in a minute. Is everything all right?"

"Everything is great. I want to tell you both how great."

She raised her eyebrows and picked up her cell phone. "Dave? Come up to the kitchen a minute?"

A few seconds later, footsteps came up the stairs from the basement and his dad appeared. He looked from Shane to his mom and back again. "What's going on?"

"Shane wants to talk to us."

Shane grinned at his dad. "Nothing bad. There's nothing wrong. In fact something is going so right I wanted to tell you both about it."

His dad's grin surprised him. "Cassidy?"

His mom went and stood by him and he put an arm around her shoulders. "We have been wondering," she said.

"Wondering what?" asked Shane. "Can't a guy spring a surprise around here?"

His mom laughed. "You've got no surprises left, Shane. Not after Cassidy had you baring your all to half the townswomen."

Shane smiled through pursed lips. "Yeah, she got me with that one."

His dad nodded. "She's well and truly got you with everything hasn't she?" They were both smiling at him expectantly.

"She has. So much so, that I'm going to be moving in with her."

His mom's face fell. His dad raised an inquiring eyebrow. "And?"

"And what?" Shane was a little disappointed they weren't more enthusiastic.

"Nothing, dear." His mom shot his dad a warning look. "We're very happy for you." She didn't sound it.

Shane gave them a puzzled look. "Will someone tell me what's going on? At first I was nervous. Then I thought you were going to be pleased. Now I feel like you're disappointed in me, and I don't get it."

His mom came and put a hand on his shoulder. "Not disappointed in you, Shane. Not that at all. You'll have to forgive us."

That confused him. "For what?"

His dad smiled. "For getting carried away. We've both seen how you are with Cassidy and how she is with you. We're getting ahead of ourselves. And things were different in our day, you have to understand that."

He hadn't thought about that. "Oh. You don't think we should live together?"

"We do. We want to see you live together. We just thought that you'd be married when you did."

Married? He stared at them as if they'd both gone nuts. "Married?" he asked.

His dad nodded. "Forget we said anything. We were getting ahead of ourselves, that's all. We're very happy for you."

"We are," said his mom. "And we'll look forward to being invited over soon?"

Shane nodded. He looked forward to it. But married? That hadn't even occurred to him—*ever!* But everything about Cassidy was different—why shouldn't that be different too? He certainly didn't hate the idea. In fact, it made him smile!

He was still thinking about it when he pulled up at Cassidy's later that evening. He looked at his bags in the back of the truck—should he leave them there for now? He shook his head with a grin. Start as you mean to go on! He pulled them out and ran up the steps. He tried the front door, he didn't know if she kept it locked. She didn't. He let himself in and strode into the living room holding his bags up in the air. "Hi, honey. I'm home!"

She was sitting at her easel by the window. She looked so beautiful as she threw her head back and laughed. "And here I was wondering if you'd gone and chickened out on me."

He dumped his bags and pulled her to her feet so he could wrap his arms around her while he kissed her. He loved the way she kissed him, she certainly wasn't passive like most women he'd known. Oh no, not his Cassidy. She kissed him back, her tongue dueling with his, her fingers tangling in his hair, her soft breasts pushing at his chest. He loved it.

When he lifted his head, he smiled. "You thought I'd chickened out, did you? Well, nuh-oh. I'm a little later because I had to take time out at lunchtime to pack my bags." He held her gaze. "And to go tell my folks."

Her eyes widened in surprise. "You told your parents?"

He grinned. "I did. I want to tell the whole world. Don't you? You don't want to keep me as your dirty little secret, do you?"

She laughed and slapped his arm. "No, I don't and you know it. It's just, well, it's all a bit sudden us doing this—even *we* know it is. What did your parents think?"

"Actually, they were disappointed." He was pleased to see that she looked at little upset at that.

"Why?" she asked. Now he felt bad. He knew she liked his parents.

"Oh, don't worry. They love you. They think we're great together. They were disappointed that…" He hesitated. He'd been all gung ho to tease her and tell her about it a minute ago. Now he wasn't so sure he wanted to. What if she dismissed it as completely ridiculous?

"That what?"

He had to tell her; she looked so concerned. "They're disappointed that we're moving in together before we get married."

He'd never seen her speechless before. It made him smile. She sputtered for a moment before she could find any words. *"Married?"* was the only word she could muster. She was stunned, but she wasn't shooting the idea down as total lunacy.

He nodded. "So what to do you say? Do you think we should up the stakes even more and just go ahead and tie the knot?"

She searched his face, trying to figure out if he was serious.

He wanted to think that she might be giving it some consideration, but as the silence lengthened his confidence wavered. It really was ridiculous. He winked to let her off the hook. "I had you going for a minute there, huh?"

She blew out a big sigh. "You certainly did."

He brushed her hair away from her cheek and looked into her eyes. "It'd be way too soon right?"

She met his gaze, her honey-colored eyes soft and searching. "Yeah. Too soon."

Wow! There was hope then?

"Come on. I cleared out a closet for you. You can unpack your things while I fix dinner."

Up in the huge master bedroom, Shane looked around. For the first time he realized how real this was. Whenever he'd been in her bedroom before, all he'd noticed was Cassidy. She was so beautiful. And he usually had just one thing on his mind. Now he looked around. It was quite a room, with big picture windows and a fireplace in the corner. She said she'd cleared him out a closet. It was a huge walk-in deal that was as big as his bedroom back at the cabin. Even when he'd hung everything he'd brought, two rails remained empty.

He wandered through to the bathroom and unpacked his washbag. The double vanity ran the length of the room. Cassidy's makeup and girl stuff strewn around one sink clearly told him which one was his. He stood back and looked at his toothbrush standing solitary guard by the faucet. He smiled. That was just the difference between men and women.

When he was done in the bathroom he looked around. He'd get used to it. He noticed that he'd left the toilet seat up so he went back. When he turned, she was standing in the doorway watching him.

He gave her a sheepish grin, for some reason he felt embarrassed to be caught in the act of putting the seat back down for her. "You're not one of those kinky types who likes to watch bathroom stuff are you?"

"Eww! I am not," she said with a laugh. "She jerked her chin toward the toilet. "And I'm not a hypocrite either."

He didn't know what she meant by that.

"I've never understood why women make such a fuss about the seat. Why are you supposed to leave it down for us, but we're not supposed to leave it up for you?"

Shane laughed. "I've never questioned it before. It's just one of those things you learn. It's like saying please and thank you. It becomes engrained as a habit, you know you have to do it, even before you wonder as to the why."

"Well, just so you know. If you leave it up it's not a problem."

"Thanks. And in the spirit of equality, if you leave it down that's not a problem either."

She smiled. "Glad we've got that straight then. Are you ready to eat?"

He nodded. "Umm." He looked at the toilet and then at her. "I think I'll just wash my hands first."

After they'd eaten, they sat out on the deck above the river. Shane toasted marshmallows in the little tabletop fire pit and handed her one. "You've got the perfect spot here you know."

"I do know. I love it," she said as she squished the warm marshmallow between her fingers. He watched her with a smile on his face.

"What?" she asked as she popped it into her mouth.

"Nothing, you're just so cute."

She rolled her eyes. "I am many things, Shane, but cute is not one of them."

"You are to me." He held her gaze. "I want to make this work, Cassidy."

Her expression turned serious for a moment. "It scares the shit out of me, but so do I. Can we make a pact though, here and now, that if we don't, if we can't for whatever reason, we'll part as friends?"

He shook his head. "I don't want us to part at all." He realized what he meant as he said it.

Cassidy didn't seem to though. She just stuck to her point. "I know, but if we do. Please?"

He nodded. "I promise. If we do, we'll stay friends." The thought of going back to being her friend made his stomach churn. He didn't want that. But the enormity of what he did want from her was only just dawning on him.

Chapter Eighteen

Cassidy closed up the cash register with a grin. She hadn't had much foot traffic come through the gallery in the winter. She was pleasantly surprised by how many tourists were coming in almost every day now. She was glad that she'd taken the risk and had cards and smaller prints made up from her and Gina's Montana line. They were selling well. It wasn't as though they'd add to the bottom line in a big way, but they were samples of their work that were making their way out into the world. She had it in the back of her mind that at some point she and Gina might make a deal with Home Décor—the company who had bought up to the rights to much of the work she'd done in Florida. That deal had taken her from modestly successful, to…well… loaded was the word for it. She had boatloads of money, more than she knew what to do with, more than she even wanted. It had never been a primary motivator for her. However, feeling successful was a big motivator, and she wanted to know that she could repeat the success. Plus, she wanted to share it with Gina. Gina was far from loaded right now, and Cassidy was determined to help her change that situation.

She looked up at the sound of the door. Shane stood there. Damn he was gorgeous. He filled the doorway. His hat almost touching the frame above his head, his broad shoulders blocking the daylight behind him. His eyes shone, and that infuriating smile of his seemed a lot less infuriating today.
"Hey, beautiful. Do you want to come have lunch with me?"
She laughed. "We had breakfast together, we're going to have dinner together. You want to have lunch, too? Aren't you worried we'll get sick of each other?"
He shook his head and came inside. He made his way around the counter and planted a kiss on her lips. "You would think that'd be the case, wouldn't you? But it's not. You're like some addiction. The more time I spend with you, the more I want."
She wrapped her arms around his neck and kissed him back. "Aww, listen to you. I would never have guessed you could be such a sweet talker."
He gave her a hurt look. "It's not just talk. It's true. I would never have guessed I'd be like this either, but I can't help it. When I'm not around you, I miss you."
She smiled. She felt the same way. Instead of teasing him, she wanted to let him know. "I miss you, too. I don't know what you're doing to me, but, whatever it is, it's working." She nestled against his chest, loving the feel of him. She hated to admit it, but snuggled into him like that, she did feel all small and sweet. She smiled up at him. "So take me out to lunch, take me to bed, do whatever you want with me."
He grinned. "I like the sounds of that, but we don't have long enough to do what I want. We'll have to save it until tonight. We'll have to make do with lunch for now."
As they joined the line in the coffee shop, Shane grinned at her. "No chocolate mousse for me today?"

She laughed. "I thought I was the sweet something you crave?"

He cupped the back of her neck with his hand. "You are sweet, but also strong and smart. That's what has me addicted to you. I don't know why you ever thought I'd feel threatened by that."

She looked up at him. "You really mean that don't you?"

He nodded. "I do. And I think most men would feel the same way."

She had to laugh. "You couldn't be more wrong about that. You're just strange."

He pouted at her. "Here I am telling you that you're special and different and you tell me I'm just strange."

"And much as you put it on, it doesn't bother you at all, does it?"

"Not one bit. I know you love me really."

She stopped breathing as she looked up at him. "That's a strong word."

He grinned at her, but didn't reply as they reached the head of the line and he ordered their sandwiches."

Cassidy watched him as he ordered. *Did* she love him? Would she have asked him to move in with her if she didn't at least think it was a possibility?

They found a corner table and started to eat in silence. Cassidy thought it best to stay away from the L-word for now. She needed time to think about it.

Shane grinned at her as he picked at his chips. It seemed he wasn't ready to leave it alone. "What's up? Did I scare you?"

"Don't start down that road. That one's a bit too important to get into a war over."

"A war?"

"Yes, a bragging war. You're braver than me, so you'll tell me first."

He raised an eyebrow. "You don't want me to tell you?"

Her heart hammered in her chest. Was he about to say he loved her? "Do you want to tell me?"

He shrugged. "Not if you're not ready to hear it. Not if you think it's just some game." He held her gaze for a long moment, then winked. "It isn't." He took a big bite of his sandwich.

Cassidy just stared at him. She didn't know what to say. Love was such a big word. It was an even bigger commitment. Moving in with each other was one thing. Loving each other was a whole different proposition. But now she thought about it….She looked up as someone approached their table. Oh no, it was the girl who kept following Shane around. What was her name? Katie.

She stood next to the table and smiled at them. It was a tight, false smile. "How've you been, Shane? I've missed you."

He looked up at her. "I'm good. Thanks, Katie. I hope you are too, but right now I'm having lunch with my girlfriend." He shot Cassidy an apologetic look.

Katie looked at her; there wasn't even the pretense of a smile on her face anymore. "I thought you said you weren't interested in him?"

"I wasn't at the time." She smiled at Shane as he gave her a hurt look.

Katie scowled at her. "It won't last you know. You don't know him like I do. He fucks around, you're just the latest challenge. The novelty will wear off soon enough and he'll come back to me, he always does."

Cassidy took a deep breath. She did not want to lose it. Katie wasn't worth it, but her words grated. "Well, I guess I'll just enjoy it while it lasts then." She smiled sweetly. "If you'll excuse us, we're eating lunch. Don't worry, I'll send him on back to you when I'm done with him."

Katie glared at her, then at Shane. Then she turned on her heel and stalked out.

Shane looked at her. "You'll send me back when you're done with me, huh?"

"Well, it sounds as though you regularly find your way back into her bed."

He shrugged. "I used to for a while. As you've seen, she doesn't like to take no for an answer."

Cassidy let out a short laugh. "And poor little Shane is ever so obliging."

His smile faded. "Don't, Cassidy. I'm sorry, okay? She's persistent, but I just want her to leave us alone. I don't want you sending me away anywhere, and if you do, I sure as hell won't be going to her bed."

Cassidy felt bad, she'd snapped at him because she was jealous! That wasn't his fault. "I'm sorry. It just caught me off guard." She decided she may as well say it, since Katie's little appearance had made it very clear for her. "I was just building up to telling you that I love you, so I'm a bit pissed that she spoiled the moment, that's all."

~ ~ ~

Shane felt his jaw drop, but was powerless to stop it. He stared at her open mouthed for a moment before he could gather his wits. Part of him wanted to come back at her with something witty. All he could do though was reach across the table and take her hand. "I love you, Cassidy."

For a moment the world around them disappeared. All he knew was this beautiful woman was squeezing his hand, smiling at him, looking happier than he would have believed his words could make her.

"How about that? All our games, all our teasing, who would have thought they would have brought us to this?"

"Not me. At least not before. Now though, now I feel as though they were all just a testing ground."

"Testing for what?"

"To see if we were strong enough to handle each other. I didn't believe you were." She smiled. "I didn't believe I was."

That puzzled him. "Didn't believe you were strong enough for what? What's so hard to handle about me?"

She laughed. "You're full on, Shane. You're full of yourself, you're full of your own appeal. I didn't think I was strong enough to admit that I've fallen for you, hook, line, and sinker. But I have. Now all I can do is hope that we stay strong enough."

"We will." As he said it, he knew it. "We can handle each other's bullshit, but more than that we're learning to talk to each other, too. Do you know how many times these last few days, I've gone for straight up honest instead of going for the win?"

"I think I have some idea. I've done the same thing myself."

"I thought so. And the more you do it, the more I feel safe to do it."

She nodded, "And slowly we're making each other feel safe."

"I wouldn't say there's anything slow about it."

She laughed. "I suppose there isn't, is there? But I don't think that's a problem when you're as strong and smart as we are, you just get on with it. We don't need to be bound by what other people accept as normal—in time frames or anything else."

Shane liked the sound of that. "We don't, and don't you forget it."

She gave him a puzzled look, but he wasn't ready to explain yet. He just hoped she meant it because the beginnings of a plan were forming in his head, and if he was going to pull it off, he needed her to mean what she'd just said.

"Okay. But I am bound by a time frame right now. I need to get back to the gallery."

He smiled. "And I should be getting back down to the ranch. I've hardly been there lately."

"Is it causing problems for you? Spending so much time with me, not being right there?"

He shook his head. "No. I just need to get better organized. I'll figure out a new routine, now that I'm living in the lap of luxury up the road instead of in the shack on site."

They left the coffee shop and started making their way back to the gallery. He took her hand as they walked and she smiled up at him. He'd never got why people held hands before, it'd always seemed strange to him. Now he understood. He squeezed her hand.

"Can I ask you something?"

"Anything," he replied.

"What you said about living in the lap of luxury instead of your shack. Does it bother you?"

"Not at all. I love it. I love your place. I love that my woman is smart enough to be financially successful." A thought struck him. "Why, does it bother you that I'm just a ranch boy?"

"Not for me, no. My only problem would be if it was a threat to your ego."

He laughed. "I keep telling you, my ego is robust enough to handle whatever you throw at me."

She rolled her eyes at him. "You know what I mean though."

He did. "I know where you're coming from, but you're not taking into account that it's me you're dealing with. Not some big macho man. For starters, you being smart and strong feeds my ego, it doesn't threaten me at all. And as for your house and your money, it doesn't make me feel any *less* of a man. I like nice houses, the nice things money can buy, but they're not a priority for me. And just in case you're curious—if they were, I could have them. The guest ranch does very well. Success is important to me. Making a go of anything I set my mind to, that's important. But the money is just a side effect. I make plenty. I just haven't had anything I want to spend it on."

Her smile told him he'd definitely said the right thing, he just didn't know what it was. "Are you relieved I'm not after you for your money?" he asked, only half joking.

She slapped his arm. "No! And you know it. I'm just happy that money isn't a big motivator for you any more than it is for me. And if I'm honest, I suppose I'm a little relieved that you and the guest ranch are successful in your own right." She gave him a sassy smile. "Success is a turn on in a way that money never could be."

He laughed. "I won't argue with that." They arrived back at the gallery. "Well, this is where I leave you."

"Okay. Have a good afternoon. Any idea what time you'll be home?"

He shook his head at her. "There she goes nagging already, and we've not even been together a week. I'll be home when I'm ready woman and not a minute before."

She laughed and put her hands on hips. "Then your dinner will be in the dog and your woman will be out looking for a new man."

He pulled her to him. "There are so many things wrong with what you just said."

She laughed. "I know. I hope we don't ever get to that point."

"We won't; we don't have a dog." He winked at her, "But even more important than that, the man you've got is going to keep you so happy and so busy loving him, that you won't ever want to go looking for another one."

She looked up into his eyes. "Ever?"

He shook his head determinedly. "Never. Because I'll always come home just as soon as I can. Wherever you are is where I want to be." He smiled. "And you are what I want to do."

She laughed. "I want to do you, too. So I'll see you at home as soon as we can get there." She reached up to kiss his lips.

"See you later, Princess."

He was almost back to his truck when Guy Preston stepped out in front of him. Oh man…he did *not* have time for this guy.

"Shane."

Shane could tell by the look on his face that he was out to cause trouble. He looked way too pleased with himself.

"Guy," he replied with a nod and kept on walking.

"I see you're getting your share of the nice little piece of ass that owns the gallery."

He spun around fists balled at his sides. "I don't share." Shit! He knew as soon as the words were out that he'd played right into Guy's hands. The man was a master at honing in on whatever you held dearest and trying to use it against you.

"Oh, sorry."

Shane wanted to land a fist right in the middle of that sly smile.

"I thought she was up front about it. She doesn't strike me as the kind to be coy about getting it wherever she can. She doesn't try to hide it."

"What do you mean?" Shane knew he shouldn't rise to it. He knew that Guy was just trying to get him riled—but it was working. He needed to know what he was talking about.

"I probably shouldn't say any more. I just figured that since you both fuck around so much there'd be no secrets."

Shane's heart was hammering in his chest. Cassidy did not fuck around. Hell, he didn't anymore—not since he'd met her. So what the hell was Guy talking about? "There are no secrets, Guy."

The bastard smiled. "Good. I'd hate to think I landed her in it about the guy in Bozeman. I'm planning on taking a shot at her myself. I'd love to get that one in the sack, and you know I wouldn't want to go behind your back or anything."

Shane's blood was boiling. What guy in Bozeman was he talking about? And the very thought of Guy *taking a shot* at Cassidy had him ready to floor the idiot. He stepped toward him.

"Shane!" He turned at the sound of Gina's voice. She came hurrying down the street toward them.

Guy gave him that slimy bastard grin of his again. "I'll be seeing you." He left just as Gina reached them. Shane was tempted to grab him and teach him a lesson, but Gina put a hand on his arm.

"Don't, Shane. Whatever he's up to, don't let him get to you."

Shane scowled at her.

"What's he up to now? Is it about Cassidy?"

What did Gina know? What might Guy have on Cassidy that *he* didn't know? "Why what's she done?"

Gina glowered at him. "See. You've already let him get to you. You're already questioning what she might have done instead of recognizing what *he* is doing. He's playing you for a fool and you're letting him!"

He blew out a big sigh. She was right of course. He pursed his lips. "Thanks, G."

"Not a problem. I already learned the hard way what damage Guy can do if you let him. I would hate to see him do that to you. But the key is, you don't let him. You have to talk to Cassidy, and you have to keep talking to Cassidy. Whatever Guy says, you two need to talk—and most importantly listen—to each other. Not to him and his poison."

He knew she was right. He felt like a fool now. "You're right. It's hard though, not to get up in it when he starts."

Gina smiled. "Believe me I know. He told me Mason was Marcus's father, remember? And that was after Mason and I had sorted everything out. It still got to me, it made me doubt, but I went straight to Mase. I trusted him and I trusted in us. That's what you're going to have to do. I'm on my way back in to the gallery, do you want me to hold down the fort there while you talk to her?"

Shane shook his head. "I need to get back to the ranch."

Gina gave him a stern look. "If Guy has planted any doubts in your head you need to talk to Cassidy right now, not let them take root before you address them."

Shane grinned. "I know, bossy boots. It's all good. I appreciate the advice, but it's all okay. Okay?"

She held his gaze. "Honest?"

"Honest. Now please can I go get back to work?"

She laughed. "Yes you can. See you soon, I hope."

Chapter Nineteen

On Saturday morning Cassidy smiled at Shane over the top of the paper. "What do you want to do this weekend?"
He grinned. "Something fun. I think we've got the hang of domestic bliss at home. Now we should take it outside. Do you want to ride out with me again?"
"I'd love to. I've learned all about sharing my house with a predator. It's about time you taught me about the ones that roam around outside, too."
He laughed. "You don't need to worry; you've got me to keep you safe."
She was surprised by how much she'd relaxed into that. His first couple of weeks staying here with her had been great, easy, comfortable even. They seemed to just know what the other wanted and needed. She knew that he liked to go outside for a while after dinner. He needed downtime by himself just as much as she did. He understood that she enjoyed her little ritual of sitting outside looking at the stars with a glass of wine before she went to bed. She didn't necessarily need to be by herself, but she did like the quiet. Sometimes he joined her and they sat in companionable silence. And as he had just said, she

did feel like he kept her safe—and she loved it! She didn't resent it or want to prove herself his equal.

She wondered again whether it was because he was so admiring of her strengths. Every other guy she'd been with had had a problem with her art in some way. Al had been totally disrespectful, always making little throw away comments about how her job wasn't a real career, or how she didn't have to *work* like most people did. Adam had kept making excuses for her whenever he introduced her to anyone. She'd never understood how he found it perfectly acceptable that his friends' wives stayed home and raised kids, but he couldn't accept that she matched his income by doing something she loved. Shane couldn't be more different. He was genuinely interested in her work. He kept asking her questions about technique, about her motivation, about the business side. She'd been right that he had great marketing skills, too. He kept the guest ranch full and expanding by running constant promotional campaigns. Now he was offering suggestions about ways she could promote the gallery and the Montana line. She was revising her opinion about men with big egos. He certainly had one, but he wasn't trying to encroach on her. He was simply so full of himself in a good way, that he overflowed and wanted to share. His intentions were always to share, to move them both forward, not to step on her head to boost himself higher.

He raised an eyebrow at her now. "Did I say the wrong thing? Are you going to beat me up about how you can take care of yourself?"

She shook her head and went around the table to sit in his lap. She loved the way his arms automatically closed around her. She nestled against his chest. "No. In fact quite the opposite. I was just marveling at how much I love knowing that I do have you to keep me safe."

He hugged her to him. "It is weird, isn't it? You hate it when a guy wants to protect you, except when it's me. I hate it when a girl wants me to be there for her. Except when it's you."

"It's just that you're not overbearing. You're not trying to dominate me."

He winked at her. "I can do, if you're into that?"

She laughed. "Maybe we can play with that sometime, but you know the word submissive does not apply to me in any sense."

He grinned. "It doesn't have to be that way around. In fact I like the idea of you in black leather, whips…chains…"

She slapped his cheek gently. "Come back!"

"Oops, sorry." He gave her a sheepish grin. "What were we talking about?"

"We were saying how good we are together. And you were going to take me out riding again."

"Oh yeah. I remember. Let's go then."

Just as they were heading out the door, Cassidy's cell phone rang. It was Summer.

"Hey. How are you?"

"Umm. Not wonderful. Have you seen the paper?" Her voice was hoarse. Cassidy could hear how upset she was.

"Which one? Why?"

"The local one—for now. Would you mind coming over?"

"We'll be right there."

Shane gave her a puzzled look. "I'm sorry. I should've said *I'll* be right there. You go ride if you want, but I need to go see Summer."

Shane headed for his truck. "Jump in. Of course, I'm coming."

Cassidy scrambled into the passenger seat and he shot off up the driveway. "What's going on?" he asked.

"I don't know. She just asked if I've seen the local paper. She sounds upset."

"Oh shit. Those bastards at the Chronicle will print anything. It's just a gossip rag."

"But what could they have on Summer?" Cassidy was afraid she already knew though. Her fears were confirmed when they arrived at Summer's place to find her sitting out on the deck with Carter. They both looked pale.

"What does it say?" asked Shane.

Carter shook his head. "A load of lies."

Summer patted his hand. "It's okay."

Cassidy's heart hurt when she saw the look on Carter's face. "It's not though is it? Being seen with me has messed things up for you."

Cassidy didn't understand that. They were both single, it wasn't like either of them was cheating or hurting anyone. "What's messed up?"

Summer looked up at her. "Autumn," she croaked.

"Ah. Let me see."

She sat down next to Shane who was reading through the article. There were pictures of Summer and Carter together. One of them had been taken at Cassidy's house the night of her dinner party—which made it obvious who was responsible for the paper getting hold of the story—they were laughing together as they stood in the corner. Another photo showed them sitting on a bench down by the river out the back here. The way Carter's arm rested along the back of the bench behind her, and the way Summer was smiling up at him

portrayed a couple in love. She looked at them now. It seemed they were, she wondered if they didn't know it yet, or if they did and they were fighting it.
Shane looked up. "So that little bitch Angie took photos of you at Cassidy's place, took what you said about this place and turned it into some bullshit about you buying a secret love nest that you're going to run to because you can't hack it in Nashville anymore?"
Summer nodded. "That about sums it up."
Cassidy looked at her. "And Autumn heard about it already?"
Summer nodded. "You know what she's like, she'd been monitoring all the local media since before I came here. She likes to stay on top of things so she can exploit any opportunities and spot any potential troubles before they start."
"And what did she have to say about this?"
Summer hung her head. "She believes it all, and she's pissed at me."
"But why?" Cassidy was surprised that Autumn would be mad a Summer. She usually came straight to her defense.
"She's mad because she thinks it's true, and she knows what that would mean for her. She's mad I didn't talk to her about it."
"Why would she believe any of it?" asked Shane. "That doesn't make sense to me. She must know what local rags can be like."
Summer hung her head then shot a quick look at Carter. "She knows I haven't been telling her everything. And reading this makes her think that's why."
Carter looked about as uncomfortable as Cassidy had ever seen him. "I'm so sorry, Summer. It's all my fault."

"No!" Summer's voice cracked. "None of it's your fault, Carter," she whispered. "Please, I need you to understand that."

"She's right, bro," said Shane. "It's all down to that little bitch, Angie."

"From reading that it looks like she's trying to set herself up as someone Summer has taken into her confidence."

"Whatever she's doing," said Carter. "She wouldn't have had anything to use if it weren't for me. And now Summer's got problems with her sister. And it's all my fault." He pushed back his chair and stood. "I'm going."

Summer jumped to her feet and ran after him. "Please, Carter."

Cassidy's heart ached for them as she watched. Carter stopped and put his hands on Summer's shoulders. "I've been selfish and I'm sorry. I wouldn't do a thing to hurt you, especially not to cause you problems with your family. You'll be able to sort it out quicker if I'm out of the picture."

Summer's face crumpled as he turned and walked to his truck. The tears began to flow as he pulled away.

Cassidy exchanged a worried look with Shane. He sprang to his feet and went to Summer. Cassidy loved him all the more as he wrapped an arm around Summer's shoulders and let her cry into his chest. He stroked her hair gently and made soothing noises as he looked over her head at Cassidy. He really was one of life's good guys.

Cassidy joined them and put a hand on Summer's shoulder. "It'll be okay, sweetie."

"It will," said Shane. "Just you wait and see. I'm going to go after Carter and talk him down. He turned Summer over to Cassidy.

"Come on," she said. "Let's talk it through. We can call Autumn and set her straight."

Summer sniffed and looked at Shane. "Please bring him back. Let him know none of it's his fault."

"I'll do my best." The grim look on his face had Cassidy worried. She hoped he could talk Carter down. She knew he'd hate having his name plastered all over the paper, but more than that it would kill him to think that he had caused Summer pain—and trouble with her family. She knew how important family was to him.

Once Shane had gone, she made a fresh pot of coffee and sat Summer down out on the deck. "Tell me what Autumn said?" she began, then thought better of it. "On second thought, where's your pad?"

Summer pulled it out of her purse and began to scribble. It was long time before she held the pad up.

She called me as soon as she read the piece. Said now she knew why I was being so shady with her. I wasn't being shady Cass! I just didn't want to say too much about Carter because I knew she wouldn't like it. She believes everything in the story. That I've met a guy here and plan on buying a house and giving up my career. She thinks I'd dump her just like that—without a thought to what it would do to her. It's so not fair! That's all I've been thinking about. I wish the article was true! I wish I was that brave. But I'm not. It's not true because I'm prepared to pass up a chance at happiness for myself just so I don't let her down!

Cassidy read it and reread it before looking up at Summer. "Damn, chica! This is a fine old mess. You need to talk to her."

"I know," she croaked. "But now she won't even take my calls!"

Cassidy sighed. "I'll give her a try, shall I?"

Summer nodded.

She dialed Autumn's number, feeling a little guilty herself. Summer was only here because of her, after all. But no. She couldn't go down that road. Autumn's phone went straight to voicemail. Cassidy left her a message and hoped that she would call back soon.

When her phone did ring a little while later, it was Shane.

"Did you find him?" she asked.

"Yeah, but you're not going to like this."

She looked at Summer who was watching her hopefully. "He's packed up and gone."

"Gone?" She regretted saying it out loud, but it was too late.

"Gone where?" asked Summer.

"I'm putting you on speaker."

"Sorry, Summer," said Shane. "Carter's headed out. His way to resolve problems is to remove himself from the equation. He withdraws at the best of times. Family is the most important thing in the world to him and it's killing him to think he's caused problems for you with yours."

"But he *hasn't!* I just want to talk to him, I want to talk to Autumn. I want to sit down with the pair of them and talk all this through."

Cassidy felt so bad for her friend as she croaked the words out. Shane sounded as though he felt terrible, too, but there was nothing either of them could do.

"When's he coming back?" asked Summer.

Shane didn't reply for a long time.

"Shane?"

"I'm sorry, but he said he's not coming back until you've gone."

Wow! Cassidy was shocked. But she also knew enough about Carter to know that he meant it.

"He said to tell you not to worry, Cassidy. His guys can finish up on the work at your place."

"As if I care about that right now."

"I know, but you know what he's like."

"He means it, doesn't he?" asked Summer.

"I'm afraid he does. He can be pretty stubborn."

Cassidy knew that Summer could, too. "Okay then. I'm going," she said.

"What? When?" asked Cassidy.

"Just as soon as I can get hold of that pilot."

Cassidy wasn't at all surprised that Summer managed to get a flight lined up for herself for the next morning. She stayed the night with her—Shane was understanding about that. It seemed he was pretty good when a friend was in crisis. In the morning she followed her up to Livingston to return her rental car and then took her to the airport herself. Autumn still wasn't taking calls or replying to voice mail from either of them and Carter may as well have disappeared into thin air.

Shane had said that he'd gotten in touch with their folks, so they wouldn't worry. But other than that no one had heard from him. Shane seemed relieved that Summer was leaving so quickly. Cassidy had thought that it was just because he wanted his brother home but he'd surprised her. He still thought that things were somehow going to work out for Summer and Carter, but they wouldn't stand a chance of doing so until Carter came back and Summer had talked things through with her sister. He was smarter than Cassidy had given him credit for. She was hopeful now that Summer would find the strength to leave her career if she really wanted to. And if she did, that would open the door of possibility for her and Carter. But that was all a lot of ifs and buts. For now she was leaving.
She'd been quiet on the drive back to Bozeman. When Cassidy pulled into the parking lot at the airport, Summer looked over at her. "I'm coming back you know."
Cassidy smiled. "I believe it. I think Autumn will understand when you can sit down and talk it through with her."
"I hope so."
Cassidy carried the larger of Summer's bags. She was pleased that there were fewer of them than she'd had when she arrived. As they entered the building, two by now familiar faces came to greet them.
"It's a pleasure to be flying with you again today, Summer," said Carl.
Cassidy scowled at him. She wished the jet charter had managed to find a different crew to take her back. Summer didn't seem fazed at all though. She smiled and shook his hand. Of course he pulled her in for a hug.

The other guy, Justin, smiled at Cassidy. "Yet another near miss," he said.

"Yeah. I think we should take the hint. Don't you?"

"I don't. I think I'm just going to have to put in more effort."

Cassidy didn't have time for him. She turned to Summer. "Call me as soon as you get there, okay? And call me when you talk to Autumn. Tell her she needs to start returning my calls or I'm going to be flying out there, too."

"You should come," said Justin with a smile. "We've got an empty leg on the return. We could have you back by tomorrow night."

Cassidy shook her head. "I wish I could." She meant she wished she could go with Summer for moral support, but he seemed to think she meant go with him. Idiot.

"We need to go," said Carl.

Summer hugged Cassidy. "I'll call you, and I'll be back soon."

As Cassidy watched her walk away flanked by the two guys, she wanted to go and grab her and take her home again. Take her back to Carter and help her get started on a life she might enjoy. She walked back to her car. Who'd have thought that she'd turn into a dumb romantic? She smiled. It was all Shane's fault. He'd made her this way.

She was so glad to see him when she got home, she ran straight into his arms and wrapped herself around him. "I love you," she said before she planted a kiss on his lips. "I love you so much."

He laughed. "I love you, too. But you know acting like that when you've been out gallivanting in Bozeman could make a guy suspicious."

She stepped back, completely thrown by that. "What's that supposed to mean?"

He shrugged. "Like you might be trying to cover up for something?"

"What kind of something?" She couldn't believe this, it was so out of the blue and so unlike Shane.

He shrugged. "Nothing. I'm sorry. Ignore me. I just missed you."

Chapter Twenty

Shane left Cookie with the hands and headed up to the lodge. He'd enjoyed leading the picnic ride this afternoon. He was feeling as though he'd been neglecting the ranch and his guests for a while now. It was time to put some effort in. He wanted to get moving on the construction of the new cabins and he really needed to spend more time with the guests. He had a great team that could handle everything, but the business had thrived thus far because he was so hands on with it.

He headed back to his office. It was time to catch up on book work, too—his least favorite part of it all. He'd been working a couple of hours when his cell phone rang.

"This is Shane," he answered.

"Shane. It's Guy."

What the hell did he want? "What can I do for you?"

"Nothing. I was calling to apologize."

Bullshit! Shane knew this would be just one of the asshole's tricks to wind him up or to get to him somehow. He mustn't rise to it. "What for?"

"When I saw you the other day and talked about Cassidy, you know, about wanting to get between her legs…"

Shane bristled, but bit his tongue.

"I didn't realize that the two of you were an item. That was pretty crass of me. I mean it'd suck to even think about another man doing your girl, wouldn't it?"

Shane didn't trust himself to reply.

"So, yeah. I wanted to apologize."

Shane waited. No way was Guy Preston calling him simply to apologize. He was about to hit him with something else, Shane just knew it.

"And I'm sure the guy she was with over in Bozeman was just a friend."

"What guy?"

"The one who was all over her in the cafe. I can't stand public affection myself, that's the only reason I noticed them. They were pawing at each other. Her friend was the same with the other guy, too. I guess it's just me. Old-fashioned, I suppose. But then I was married for so long. I don't suppose you've heard anything about April, have you?"

Shane's mind was reeling. He was just making shit up, right? Trying to cause trouble. He sounded too smug though. He must know something. He wasn't about to let him know that it was getting to him though. "Well thanks for looking out for me. But you're right, Cassidy went to see friends over in Bozeman. She's an affectionate kind of girl, she's always hugging on people." What a lie! "Maybe April's gone to see friends, too? Gone looking for someone who'll show her some affection."

Guy laughed, but there was no humor in it. "Yeah right. We both know your brother had something to do with her leaving. I'm better off without the little bitch anyway. But when I find her…"

The unspoken threat made Shane shudder. He was glad April was safe and a long, long way from here. He doubted Guy would ever find her in California.

"They're all lying cheating bitches, Shane. You'd do well to remember that." He hung up.

Shane stared at his phone. He could not let the doubts creep in. Cassidy loved him. She wouldn't go cheating on him. He knew full well that it was just Guy trying to cause trouble the way he always did.

He called Cassidy's cell. He wanted to hear her voice. It went straight to voice mail. He called the gallery.

"Moonstone Gallery, this is Gina speaking."

"Hey G. Can I speak to Cassidy?"

"Oh, hi, Shane. She's not here. Try her cell."

"I already did; she's not answering."

"Oh. Shall I get her to call you back?"

"Do you know where she is?"

"Yeah, she's gone to the Mint."

"Why? Who with?"

Gina laughed. "You do realize you sound like the jealous boyfriend? Well, you might be right. Some guy came in and whisked her away for a drink."

"What? Who?"

"Oh, Shane stop it. I'm just teasing you. I don't know who he is, but I'm sure he'll be good for business."

Shane's heart was pounding. That was it, right? It was just some guy who wanted to buy paintings. Not anything else.

"What's gotten into you?" asked Gina.

Shane blew out a big sigh. "Sorry. I'm being an idiot. Guy-fucking-Preston has gotten to me—and the dumb thing is, I'm letting him. Ask her to call me when she gets back, would you?"

"I will. And in the meantime, you get your head straight. Do not let Guy screw things up for you. You know damn well what he's trying to do. And if you let him, you're a fool."

"I know, I know. Thanks, G."

He hung up. She was right. He'd be an idiot to let that asshole get inside his head. He tried to focus on his work again, but he couldn't help wondering who Cassidy was off having a drink with.

~ ~ ~

Cassidy locked up the gallery and headed for her car. It had been quite an afternoon. Justin showing up like that had surprised her, and she'd fallen for it, too. He'd come into the gallery saying he was concerned about Summer. There were people in the gallery when he came in, tourists who were looking to buy prints of some of Gina's photographs. Cassidy had wanted to get him out of there so Gina could make the sale. She'd taken him to the Mint for a drink so that he could tell her whatever it was he thought she should know. He'd said that Summer had been crying on the flight back to Nashville. That when they landed her sister had been waiting for her and they'd gotten into a fight. He seemed to be genuinely concerned. Though Cassidy doubted that if he would have come to tell her about her friend if he wasn't hoping for a date. She'd thanked him and made very clear that she wasn't interested. He'd been cool about it and that was the end of that. She was concerned that neither Summer nor Autumn had returned her calls though.

When she'd made it back to the gallery, she'd spent the rest of the afternoon talking on the phone with local retail distributors. She was on the verge of sealing a couple of deals that would get their new line into the local souvenir stores.

As she drove home she felt bad that she hadn't found time to call Shane back. But she'd see him soon enough. They had a quiet evening planned, dinner and a movie. After all the running around they'd both been doing over the last few days, they deserved it. They were trying to find a routine that suited them both—that would give them each the time and space to do what they needed and still leave time to spend together. She smiled as she pulled into the driveway. She was looking forward to spending some time in bed together tonight. She'd already grown used to sharing a bed with Shane. She loved to snuggle up with him.

She found him in the kitchen, sitting at the island with a glass of bourbon in his hand.

"Hey, you. How was your day?"

"It was a day. How about you?"

She made a face at him. "Better than yours by the sounds of it. Want to tell me about it? It's not like you to be sitting drinking with a grumpy face on you. What's wrong?"

He shrugged. "Nothing. What was it that made your day so good? Anything you want to tell me about?"

This wasn't like him. But everyone was entitled to an off day. She went to him and put her hands on his shoulders. She planted a kiss on his lips, hoping to make him smile. He didn't.

"Okay, well, I think I've got the distribution deal sorted out, which is great. Gina sold some of her photographs, so she's a happy bunny. I'm still worried about Summer. I haven't heard back from her yet."

Shane was scowling. "Anything else you want to tell me about?"

What was his problem? She put a hand on his shoulder, but he shrugged her off. "No, but if there's something you'd like to know, ask away."
"Why didn't you call me back?"
Oh, so that was it. "I'm sorry. I got really busy."
He scowled. "And where were you when I called anyway?"
That rattled her. Was she supposed to report her every move? "Living my life, Shane. I go places, I have things to do. Just like you. I have a business to run, remember? What is your problem? You don't really want to know what I'm doing every minute of the day do you?"
"No. Just the minutes that you're spending with some guy in a bar."
"What?"
"You heard me. Who was the guy you were with this afternoon?"
"His name is Justin."
"And how do you know *Justin?*"
"Seriously? That's what this is about? You're jealous?"
"I just don't like being played for a fool. Is he the guy you've been seeing over in Bozeman?"
Cassidy stared at him. This show of jealousy wasn't like him at all. It took her all she had, but she didn't lose her temper. She sat down on the stool next to him and looked into his eyes. "He's one of the pilots that brought Summer here. He came over today to tell me he was worried about her after they dropped her off."
Shane scowled.
"Why do you have a problem with that, Shane?"
"Because Guy Preston has gotten inside my head," he said with a sigh. "And he's good at it! He started planting seeds a

little while ago. Saying he'd seen you with some guy in Bozeman. Then he called me again today. I *know* he's just out to cause trouble, but it messes with my head. I'm all in here, I love you, I'm putting it all on the line for you, for us. So the thought that you might still be running around seeing other guys...Well, it hurts."

She nodded and put a hand on his arm. "I'm sorry. But I'm not running around. Or seeing anyone else."

He scowled again. "So how did this Justin know where to find you? And how come you're so pally that he would even want to tell you about Summer?"

Cassidy took a deep breath. "I met him before you and I got together...Slow down," she said as she saw the thunderclouds roll across his face. "He wanted to take me out. I wasn't interested. Summer and I bumped into him and his co-pilot in Bozeman. We were leaving as they were arriving at the café. That's all. That Guy Preston was there. Gina told me he was trouble."

Shane nodded. "He is. And I'm an asshole for letting it get to me."

"You are, but I'll let you off," she said with a smile.

"Yeah?" he smiled and the thunderclouds were gone. His eyes shone again and he wrapped his arms around her.

"Just this once," she replied. "But don't make a habit of going all jealous on me. I can't handle that."

"I won't." He grinned. "But don't you make a habit of taking little-dick guy out for a drink."

Cassidy threw back her head and laughed. "Little-dick guy?" she asked.

She loved Shane all the more as he held up his pinky finger and wiggled it at her. "*Just in*," he said with a wink.

She shook her head at him as she laughed. "It really is all about ego with men, isn't it?"
Shane nodded and took her hand, pulling her toward the stairs. "I admit it, it is. Come to bed and let me remind you."
She let him lead her. "What do you need to remind me?"
"That I'm so much better than *just in.*"

~ ~ ~

When he awoke the next morning, Shane watched Cassidy sleep on. He gently brushed her hair away from her face. He'd been stupid last night. Stupid to get caught up in jealousy, but that was exactly what it was. It was an emotion he'd never understood before. It was so ugly. He'd always thought it was about insecurity, and that was why he didn't do it. He knew differently now though. He wasn't insecure, not in any sense of the word. But Cassidy was just so damned important to him. He hated the thought of losing her. He never wanted to lose her; he wanted this life that they'd begun together to last.
He watched her as she slept. He wasn't going to say he couldn't live without her. That wasn't true. He could. He just didn't want to. He wanted to know that she felt the same way.
She stirred and opened her eyes with a smile.
"Good morning, handsome."
He dropped a kiss on her upturned nose. "Good morning, beautiful."
She held her arms up to him and he lay back down with her. "I don't want to get up, I want to stay here with you," she mumbled.
"I wish we could, but I have to get back to the ranch. How about Sunday morning we just stay in bed?"
She nodded. "Okay. I can wait till Sunday."

"We can make it our thing. That's what we do on Sundays—for the rest of our lives."

She opened her eyes. "The rest of our lives?"

He nodded. He knew it was what he wanted. He needed to know whether she did, too. "What do you think?" He sighed at the sound of his cell phone ringing.

"I think you'd better get that," she said.

He got up. The moment was gone even if he didn't take the call. It was Brandon asking if he could get down to the ranch in time to lead the morning ride. Shane said he'd be there as fast as he could. They were shorthanded with two guys out sick. He needed to take on more help, he needed to step everything up, if he was honest, and he needed to shift at least some of his focus away from Cassidy and back onto the ranch.

"I've got to go," he said when he hung up.

She smiled and slid her beautiful naked body out of bed. "Got time for a shower before you go?"

He shook his head sadly. He would love nothing more than to linger under the hot water with her for a while, but he needed to go. "I'll just jump in and out and get going."

He was ready to get out of the shower when she opened the door to join him. How was he supposed to resist? She pushed him back against the wall and he watched, mesmerized as the water ran over her, plastering her hair to her head, running on down in little rivulets between her breasts. His fingers itched to touch her nipples as they pebbled in response to the water running over them. He really, really wanted to stay, but he had to go. He couldn't keep neglecting the ranch just so he could indulge in his own pleasure. That wasn't who he was. He cupped her face between his hands. "Meet you back here tonight," he said, then stepped out of the shower while he still had the willpower to do so. She looked so disappointed, he almost stepped back in. But he couldn't. Part of him was glad to disappoint her. He wanted to know that she needed him, wanted him, as much as he did her. The look on her face claimed that she did.

~ ~ ~

Cassidy watched him step out of the shower. She didn't want him to go, but she wasn't going to beg him to stay. She was being unreasonable and she knew it. She'd told him last night that he shouldn't expect her to stop living her life just because she was with him. She couldn't be a hypocrite and expect him to stop living his—or even to delay starting his day because she wanted him to make love to her. She stood under the hot water, enjoying the feel of it running over her. *Make love?* Who would ever have thought that she and Shane made love? Screw each other's brains out? Fuck like bunnies? Yeah definitely. But no. They made love. Whether it was in bed, in the shower, on the island in the kitchen, or bent over the pool table in the basement—they made love. And she didn't ever want it to change. For two people who had been the way they were before they met each other—she hadn't wanted anyone, and Shane had wanted everyone—they'd come a long way in a short time. That thought bothered her. He had wanted everyone. Every time she'd rebuffed his advances he'd gone off with another girl. Was that why he'd been so upset about Justin? Did he really think that she might still go off with someone else? And if he did, then he didn't understand how much their relationship meant to her. And if he didn't—would *he* still go off with someone else? She blew out a sigh. She was being stupid. He loved her, she loved him. That was all that mattered.

As she soaped herself down, she smiled. She was happy, she was relaxed in her life, and she was in love. How about that? Her mind strayed to Summer. She wished she could help her friend find the same. Right now Summer didn't have any of it. She wasn't happy, she was far from relaxed in her life. How could she be, when she didn't know where it was heading? She might be in love though.

Cassidy stepped out and dried herself down. Today she was determined to get hold of Summer or Autumn—hopefully both. When she was dressed, she went to the window. It was a beautiful day already, she needed to get out there and get on with it. She looked down at the yard. The patio was almost complete, the flower beds were nearly done. The big trench was dug and ready for the line of Quaking Aspen Carter was bringing. She looked at the side yard where the mens' trucks sat. Carter's was there. Parked up with the others. He was back?

She ran downstairs and out into the yard to look for him.

"Carter!" she called. He was down in the side yard talking to two of his men. He looked up and made his way to her.

"Cassidy."

He was shut down. It was plain to see. "How are you?" she asked.

"I'm fine, thanks. Sorry about the delay, but the guys have been working to the plan. I think we'll still be finished up here on schedule.

She touched his arm. "I don't care about that. I care about you. How are you?"

He finally met her gaze. "I'm better, thank you. I just needed a little time to remind myself not to be an idiot."

"You're not an idiot!"

He shrugged and looked away. He scuffed the toe of his boot in the gravel. "How is she?"

"I don't know. I can't get hold of her."

"Give her my best when you do. Now if you don't mind I need to get back to work." He turned and walked away.

Cassidy wanted to go after him, but thought better of it. She needed to get to the gallery. Hopefully she'd manage to get hold of Summer today. She'd find Carter after she had and talk to him then.

Chapter Twenty-One

At lunchtime Cassidy and Gina decided to close up and head to the coffee shop for lunch. They'd just taken a seat at a table in the back when Katie and Angie came in.

"I could strangle her," said Gina as Angie gave them a dirty look.

Cassidy stood up. "I just might." She made her way over to the line where the two girls were waiting. "What the hell did you think you were doing?" she asked Angie.

"Leave her alone," said Katie. "What's it to you anyway? She didn't do anything wrong."

Cassidy was fuming. "She didn't do anything wrong? She came into my home, took photos of my friend, and abused my trust. She was very wrong, and I think she knows it."

Angie hung her head. "I didn't think she'd leave because of it."

"You didn't think at all, did you? I just don't understand what you were hoping to gain by it?"

Angie shrugged.

"Just leave her alone, would you. You think you and your friend can come in here and make a move on the Remingtons. It's not right. Everyone knows Carter will come around one day and be ready to take a wife. It should be someone local, not some stuck-up singer bitch. And you? Thinking you've got your claws into Shane. I've told you before and I'll tell you again. It won't last. He'll dump you and come back to me, just like he always does. You're just like the ones at Chico and the ones who come to the ranch. You're different, something new, but you won't last. You're just a novelty that's all."

Cassidy stared at her. Stupid little girl. She shook her head. "For starters don't you ever call Summer a stuck-up bitch again. You have no idea who she is. And I'm sorry to disappoint you, but Shane will not be coming back to you this time. We're together. Get used to it. And stay away from him." She turned on her heel and went back to Gina.

Gina gave her an odd look.

"What?" she couldn't believe she'd just made a scene like that, but she'd just seen red. She'd seen how sad Carter had been this morning, she still hadn't heard from Summer, and she was worried about them. And it was all down to that stupid little Angie and her attention seeking—or whatever it was she'd done it for. Then Katie butting in like that and telling her that she and Shane wouldn't last… She blew out a big sigh. "Sorry. I guess I over-reacted, huh?"

Gina nodded. "Maybe a touch. And I hate to say it, but you probably just set yourself up for more trouble. Telling Katie to stay away from Shane wasn't the wisest move."

Cassidy groaned. "I know. But she brings out the worst in me. And besides. He's hardly likely to go near her—is he?"

"No, but she's vindictive. Just remember that, if she sets him up somehow. Don't let her make trouble for the two of you."

Cassidy smiled. "Don't worry. I think we're past the stage where anyone can come between us." She met Gina's eye. "Love will do that to you, won't it?"

Gina's face lit up with a big smile. "Yes, it will! So you two are…"

Cassidy nodded. "We are. I love him, Gina. He's proved me wrong at every turn. Even last night, he was all jealous about me going for a drink with Justin, but we talked it through. He was open and honest and he listened. This feels like it's for real."

"I am so happy for you." She shot a wary look at Katie. "If it's for real, nothing will be able to mess it up for you."

Cassidy nodded. She was starting to believe that was true and wondering where it might lead. She hadn't forgotten his comment this morning about every Sunday morning for the rest of their lives. It seemed as though he was feeling the same way she was. They'd rushed into this so fast, but they were growing stronger with every challenge they faced. They were overcoming the hurdles together, helping each other over them. It was so different from anything she'd known before. Perhaps they really had found the real deal? And if they had, why not admit it and make a start on the rest of their lives together?

~ ~ ~

Shane ran up the steps to the main house. It had been a busy morning. He could have done with staying out at the lodge, working on the housekeeping orders, but his mom had summoned them all for lunch. She didn't do it often, but when she did, they dropped everything and came.

He kicked out of his boots in the mudroom and went through to the kitchen. He was surprised to see Carter sitting at the big table. He went over and slapped his back. "Good to see you home, Big C. How you doing?"

Carter nodded. "I'm back."

"What's his problem?" asked Beau. "I haven't been able to get a word out of him."

Shane shrugged. He didn't want to talk about it if Carter didn't. "You know what he's like. He just goes quiet on me sometimes, and I worry."

Beau gave him a puzzled look, but didn't get a chance to ask anything further as Mason came in through the back door. "What's with the family meeting?" he asked.

"I don't know," said Beau. "I could have done without it today though."

"Beau, Beau, Beau." His mom came up from the basement and smiled at him. "Always my impatient one." He smiled back. "Sorry, Mom."

Shane shook his head. Beau made out he was the hardheaded one, but he was as soft as the rest of them at heart. He may get prickly with his brothers sometimes, but he'd defend them to death against anyone else. He remembered what Carter had said about Beau just wanting love and approval. He could see it now.

Chance appeared at the basement door behind their mom. Beau's smile faded. Shane wished that tension wasn't there; he wished they could all just be brothers, but he did have a little more understanding now for the way Beau felt.

Their dad stuck his head out from the office. "Is everybody here?"

"Yep," said Mason. "All here and all ears."

"Well let's all sit down then, shall we?"

Once they were all settled around the big table, Shane thought he knew what was coming as his dad looked around.

"I'm sure it won't surprise any of you to hear that your mom and I are making plans to head south for winter."

They all murmured their agreement. "That's not news," said Beau with a smile. "So what is? What do you want to tell us?"
"Well, seeing as things are changing for some of you as well, we want to propose some major changes, but we want to ask what you all think first."
He looked at Mason. "You and Gina are going to be getting married soon. As the eldest, we wanted to know if you want to move in to the main house."
The silence around the table was deafening. They all knew the division of the ranch was coming, but Shane didn't think any of them had expected to take over the big house The look on Mason's face said that he'd had no clue this was coming either. He looked from his dad to his Mom and back again. "What's your reasoning?"
"It's quite simple really. We're going to be gone." He turned to Shane. "The littlest brother isn't living on the ranch anymore, and I have a feeling that's not going to change." Shane nodded. He saw his future as being with Cassidy, and he knew that would mean living at her house. She loved it, she wouldn't want to leave it, and he had no desire to ask her to.
"The ranch needs a family living in the big house," their dad continued. He looked at Carter. "You're settled where you are. You've built your home and your business." He hesitated, considering his words and then went on with an encouraging smile. "I have a feeling you might move back down the valley in the not too distant future, but even if you do, you won't make it all the way back down to the ranch."
Carter nodded, but said nothing.
"You," his dad looked at Beau. "You're off out in the world." Shane could tell that Beau was pissed, but he softened at his dad's next words. "You make me so proud, son. You've got all

the balls and the brains to go off and do what I never could. I don't want to tie you to this place. It's in your blood, but it's not in your heart is it?"

Beau's eyes glistened as he shook his head.

"And you, Chance. Don't think I'm forgetting you. You've got the cabin to yourself these days. I'm still hopeful that one day you'll bring home a girl and start a family of your own. And when you do, you'll have your share of the land to build on as you see fit."

Shane turned to Beau who made a huffing sound at that. All eyes turned toward him, but he just shrugged. Shane was glad he wasn't going to start the argument now. Chance was the only one who wasn't happy to let it go.

"I understand how you feel, Beau. I don't want to take what's rightfully yours."

"It's rightfully *yours,* Chance." Dave Remington's tone brooked no arguments. He looked at Beau. "You need to get over it, son."

Beau nodded but didn't meet his dad's eye.

"Mason. You need to talk to Gina and think about this. We decided to bring it up now, because we thought you might like to move in after the wedding. We're not going to leave until the end of September, but we can trade you for the cottage if you set a date before then."

Mason nodded. "I'll talk to her. But I don't see kicking you out of here so we can move in."

His mom laughed. "I'm hoping that you will. I want you to hurry up and set a date, and until we move out of this house and the routines of a lifetime, I'm not going to be able to get your father to go anywhere."

Their dad smiled. "Take your time, son. That's fine by me. Anyway, that's what we wanted to talk to you all about. Meeting over. Who's staying for lunch?"

"I have to go." Carter was out the door as fast as he could go.

Shane's mom put a hand on his arm. "Is there any word from Summer?"

How did she know everything? "No, Cassidy's still trying to get hold of her."

His mom nodded. "And you're okay with us assuming that you won't be moving back here?"

He knew what she meant. He smiled. "I am. In fact I don't think I should be disappointing you for much longer."

His mom looked thrilled.

"You don't think I'm nuts for moving so fast?"

"No, Shane I don't. In fact I've been wondering what's taking you so long."

~ ~ ~

Cassidy sat out on the deck with a glass of wine waiting for Shane to come home. She'd finally managed to talk to Summer this afternoon. It sounded as though she'd had a rough time of it with Autumn at first, but they had sorted things out. At least about the story that had run in the local paper. It seemed that Summer had backed down over the future and where her career was going. Cassidy understood that she didn't want to leave her sister in the lurch, but she had to put herself first in her own life. If she didn't want to sing anymore, she needed to be honest about it. And the sooner she was, the sooner Autumn could start figuring out what she was going to do next.

She took a sip of her wine. She needed to stop trying to solve other people's problems and focus on her own life. And life was good. She loved this place, she loved her work here, and most of all, she loved Shane. He was the partner she'd never thought she'd find. An equal, who not only didn't resent her strength, but admired it. She was realizing with him that true equality wasn't about two people who were both strong all of the time and who vied for supremacy. It was about two people who could each be strong when the other needed it. Two people who were confident enough in themselves and each other to allow themselves to be vulnerable. She smiled. That was them.

She stood up when she heard his truck coming up the driveway. It was funny, so many trucks came and went all the time with the guys working on the yard, but she knew and could distinguish the sound of Shane's big, red Tundra from the rest of them. She went to greet him at the front door.

"Hey, Princess. I missed you."

He closed his arms around her and she melted into him. Did she want to do this every day for the rest of their lives? Hell, yeah, she did. She looked up into his eyes. "I missed you, too. This place doesn't feel like home without you in it anymore."

There was something odd about the way he smiled back at her. "Do you want to keep me around then?"

She laughed. "Of course, I do." It was stupid but Katie's words came back to haunt her. "Why have you had enough already? Has the novelty worn off?"

He frowned. "No and it never will. You're stuck with me, if you want me."

"So what's the weird vibe you're giving off?"

He smiled. "You got me. I guess I'm just a little weirded out. We had a family meeting today. Mom and Dad are stepping back from running the ranch. They want Mason and Gina to move into the main house when they get married. They've given Chance the cabin since they assume that I have left the ranch and won't ever be moving back."

She studied his face. "And you're weirded out because you're thinking it's either me or homelessness?"

He held her closer. "I'm weirded out because I'm fine with it, but it kind of feels like I'm dumping myself on you whether you want me or not."

"Well, I do want you. So you've got no worries."

"I don't want to be just your boy toy though."

She laughed. "Aww. What else am I supposed to do with you?"

He hugged her to his chest. "Actually I'm not sure. Maybe we should practice that bit first?"

"How about we practice that bit later? I'm starving and I've been waiting for you to get home."

He followed her through to the kitchen, still looking thoughtful.

"What is it?"

He shrugged. "I don't know. I kind of feel as though I'm putting you in a tough position. That you might be getting more than you bargained for. I mean this, me living here with you, it started out as just a dare. Would you back out of it if you wanted to?"

This was new. A thoughtful Shane seeking reassurance—and looking out for her into the bargain. "I don't want to. You're right, it did start out as a dare, but only because we could see we had something worth gambling on. It looks to me as though we're onto a winner. And besides it's not as though you're throwing yourself at my feet and asking for charity. If we don't work out, it's not like you'd have nowhere else to go."

He nodded. "I know. On the practical side it's no big deal, but somehow it feels as though it is a big deal. I feel like I'm making myself vulnerable here, and I'm okay with it. I just need to know that you are, too."

She nodded. "I'm more than okay with it. I love it. I love you. But we seem to be doing an awful lot of talking about it. How about we just get on with living it and having fun?" It wasn't like either of them to get into deep and meaningful conversation for too long. But more than that, she kept having this crazy urge to just come right out and ask him. This conversation was giving her too many opportunities to do it. And she didn't want to ask him yet. She wasn't sure that she should at all. That really would be a challenge to a man's ego wouldn't it? "How about we go out for dinner tonight? Take me to Pine Creek? I haven't been there yet."

He nodded. "Whatever you say, Princess."

Chapter Twenty-Two

Over the next few days things finally settled down into an easy routine. Shane got up early and brought Cassidy a cup of coffee in bed before he left for the ranch. He spent most of his days working down there—not making nearly so many trips up to town as he had been doing since he met her. She went into the gallery most days and business really seemed to be picking up for her. He was glad to see it. She was happy and animated whenever she talked about her work and where she and Gina were going with it.

Carter settled back into his quiet ways. He was still working at Cassidy's and he'd even joined them for dinner one night. He'd come out of himself a little and had gone as far as to say that he wished things had been different for him and Summer. Shane had kicked Cassidy under the table when she'd started to reassure him that Summer would be back. He didn't know what Carter would do if she did return, but he didn't want his brother's hopes raised. Or worse, he didn't want him to take off again.

Last night, Chancc had come over. Shane loved the way he and Cassidy got along. He was just as relaxed around her as he was around the brothers. At least Shane thought it was that.

Or maybe that he was more relaxed altogether since his trip to Summer Lake. Shane hoped so.

It seemed that life was settling into a pattern he very much enjoyed. So much so that he was starting to get antsy about it. He knew he wanted to make this permanent, and he was pretty certain that Cassidy did, too. He had no qualms about their living situation. Yeah, he was living in her house, but that was fine by him. He was contributing. If she wanted, he'd buy half, make them equal partners. If she didn't, well that was okay, too. He was comfortable with it however she wanted to handle it.

Tonight they were heading out to meet Mason and Gina for dinner. He was really looking forward to it. It was hard to believe that he and his big brother had come so far in such a short amount of time. Not so long ago, Friday night would have seen the two of them heading out to Chico. They'd have been on the lookout for a couple of girls to spend the night with. Now they were going to the Valley Lodge, with a couple of girls—girls they wanted to spend the rest of the lives with!

He was about done at the ranch for the day and decided to take a quick walk through the barn before he left. As he walked down the aisle between the stalls, he smiled. He loved it out here, the familiar smells and sounds of the horses set him at ease. He stopped to have a quick chat with his old friend Cookie. Someday soon he wanted to get Cassidy out on him again. Every time he'd tried to get her out into the backcountry, get her used to being out there, and feeling confident about whatever they might run across, something had come up to cut it short. They'd had to come back that first time they'd gone out camping. The second time, Summer's call about the story in the newspaper had stopped them. Maybe he should try for third time lucky this weekend. If they did make it he knew that Cookie would play a big part, taking care of Cassidy while at the same time building her confidence just by being who he was.

He turned at the sound of footsteps approaching.

"Shane?"

Katie? What the hell was she doing out here? The sight of her told him what she had in mind. She was wearing a little white dress, under a jean jacket. The neckline was cut so low she was in danger of jiggling out of it. She was doing a lot of jiggling as she walked toward him in knee-high cowboy boots with ridiculous heels on them. There was an awful lot of thigh displayed between the top of those boot and the hem of her dress. He looked her up and down wondering what the hell she thought she was playing at. Well, he knew that. It was the same outfit she'd worn to Chico one night. He'd brought her back here afterward. Why would she think he wanted to recreate that? Why, when she knew he was with Cassidy and they'd both made it very clear that they intended to stay together?

She smiled at him, all pink lipstick and perfect white teeth.

"What do you want, Katie?"

"To remind you how much fun we have out here, Shane."

He shook his head. "We did have fun. I won't deny it. But not anymore. I'm with Cassidy."

She stepped closer, undeterred. "Yeah, but she doesn't have to know, does she? One woman has never been enough for you. You like variety."

He shook his head. "I used to. Not anymore."

She laughed and came to stand right in front of him, smiling up at him. "That's not true. You're just scared you might get caught. You're a fool though. She's still screwing around. Why can't you?"

He was not going to rise to that. He knew better. Guy had already tried playing that card. "Just go home, Katie. This is crazy. We had some good times together, but we're done. I've moved on, and I'm happy. I wish you all the best, and I hope you'll find the same."

Her smile faded. It was amazing how quickly the sweet little girl face turned into an angry bitter woman. She reached into her purse and pulled out a belt—his belt! He'd been wondering where that had gone for months now. "I was going to give this back to you after we got done here." She waved it in front of his face. "Now, I think I'll keep it."

He gave her a puzzled look. If keeping his belt was some kind of vengeance that made her feel better then so be it. She could have it. "Fair enough. You keep it." He checked his watch. "But I really have to get going. I meant what I said Katie, I wish you all the best."

The look she gave him made the little hairs on the back of his neck stand up. "You're going to regret this, Shane." She turned and tottered away.

Shane turned back to Cookie who head-butted his shoulder. "What did I ever see in her?" he asked. Yes he used to have fun in the sack with her, but damn. She wasn't a nice person. It made him wonder what kind of person he had been that he hadn't been able to see that.

He wasn't about to take her warning lightly. He knew she'd be out to make trouble for him. He headed for his truck. He needed to get home in a hurry now if he and Cassidy were going to make it to dinner on time. As he pulled out onto East River Road he decided he needed to tell Cassidy about Katie's little visit. She needed to know that Katie would be out to make trouble for them.

When he got back to the house, Cassidy was already showered and changed. She smiled and looped her arms up around his neck to kiss him. "We're cutting it fine, but you've still got time for a quick shower if you hurry."

He pecked her lips and ran upstairs, grateful that she wasn't the kind to ask why he was so late or to give him ear-ache for it.

Twenty minutes later they were in the truck and headed up the valley. He forgot all about Katie and her threats while Cassidy told him about Summer. She'd talked to her this afternoon, and she was planning on coming back on Monday. Apparently she'd been to see her doctor and he had recommended that she take at least three months to rest her voice. Cassidy was hoping that would be enough time for her to decide what she really wanted to do. And that it would give Autumn time to figure out what she would do if Summer wasn't going to sing anymore.

"So, is there a possibility that she won't be able to sing again, even if she decides she wants to?" he asked.

Cassidy nodded. "I didn't realize how serious it was, but I talked to Autumn today as well. Apparently she was so upset about the newspaper article, not because she was worried about her own career, but because she thought Summer was admitting defeat already. She thought Summer was buying a house and finding a man because she was afraid her singing days were over—whether she liked it or not."

Shane nodded. He could understand Autumn being concerned about her sister. After all he was concerned about his brother. He had to wonder what Carter would do when he knew

Summer was returning. He couldn't exactly run away and hide again. Not for three months. But at the same time, he couldn't see Carter getting involved with her while there was a huge question mark hanging over their heads—would she stay or would she go? He wouldn't want to take the risk of falling for her and being left behind. And perhaps even more so, he wouldn't want to be the reason that she didn't return to her career.

He shot a quick glance over at Cassidy. "I don't know what's going to happen with Summer and Carter, but I'm glad we're not them."

She smiled. "So am I." She reached over and took his hand. "Not because of the situation they're facing." She squeezed his hand. "I'm pretty sure that you and I can overcome anything. It's just that I'm really glad we're us." She laughed. "I like me. I like who I am." She stuck her tongue out at him. "And you're not bad either."

He laughed with her. "Yeah I know the feeling. Life would suck if I was anyone but me, and as far as sidekicks go, well you're pretty cool."

She made a face at him. "If anyone is the sidekick around here, it'd be you!"

He pulled off the road and into the parking lot at the Valley Lodge. Once he'd cut the ignition he pulled her to him and kissed her. "We don't have time to argue about it now…" He trailed his fingers down her cheek, over her throat, and on down, loving the color that touched her cheeks as he teased her nipple through her shirt. "But we'll revisit this later." He winked. "We'll see who comes out on top."

She laughed and then pulled his head down to her to kiss him. When she let him come up for air she said, "Well then we already know I win. You love it when I come out on top."

He nodded, he did. "Yeah, but I like making you work for it, too. I'm in charge the whole time; I just use your desires against you to get what I want."

She slapped his arm. "You keep on kidding yourself. Come on. Mason's truck's here already. We'd better get in there."

As they walked into the restaurant he patted her ass. "Come on sidekick, keep up."

She narrowed her eyes at him. "You're going to regret that, Shane."

Her words echoed Katie's earlier. Reminding him that he hadn't mentioned Katie's visit to the barn.

"Hey, you two!"

Gina waved at them from her perch at the bar. "Our table's not ready yet. They're busy tonight."

Shane led Cassidy over to the bar and pulled out a stool for her to sit while he stood behind her. Mason made his way through the bar and came to stand behind Gina.

"This is great, isn't it? The four of us out like this on a Friday night."

Mason smiled at Shane above the girls' heads. It seemed he was thinking the same as Shane had earlier. It was strange how much their Friday nights had changed.

"I love it," said Shane.

Cassidy smiled up at him, and he knew she did, too.

~ ~ ~

When their table was ready they took their seats. Cassidy loved it here. It was small and intimate. A fireplace blazed in the corner. She looked around, fascinated as always at the mix of patrons. Some faces she recognized. A writer was holding court at a large table in the center of the dining room. He seemed to be sitting there whenever she came in, though his audience changed, usually some mix of visitors and wannabes all dressed to the nines. He liked to wax loud and lyrical about the intricacies of his latest work in progress. She smiled to herself; she'd had no time for him since the first time they'd been introduced. He talked a good story, but she'd checked out his books—he didn't write one! It was the kind of dry literary navel inspection that bored her silly. She may be a heathen when it came to literature, but she was fairly convinced that it was more a case of the emperor's new clothes. A couple of critics had lauded his debut novel and since then he'd proclaimed to anyone who would listen that he was a literary genius. No one dared disagree with him for fear of being ridiculed as idiots who simply didn't understand.

In contrast to him a couple of old ranchers and their wives sat quietly by the back wall. They still wore work clothes, and their wives looked comfortable in jeans and sweatshirts. They were here to relax and enjoy themselves. Their conversation came easily, punctuated with much laughter. She wondered if someday that might not be her and Shane and Gina and Mason. The thought made her smile. Would they really all be married and still living out their lives here thirty years from now? For the first time in her life she wanted to stay here, wanted to put down roots and feel like she belonged here. She looked over at Shane as he studied his menu. She wanted to marry him!

When their food arrived she looked at Mason. The subject of weddings was dominating her thoughts. "So when are you going to make an honest woman of my partner?" she asked.

Mason grinned and looked at Gina. "Did you tell her?"

Gina laughed. "No, of course not. We're going to tell them tonight." She looked at Cassidy, "it's just that this one seems to have some eerie sixth sense."

"Tell us what?" asked Shane. Cassidy loved that he was so enthusiastic about Gina and Mason. Gina had been his best friend growing up and he loved that she and Mason had finally gotten back together and she was about to become family.

Gina looked at Mason. "You tell them."

"We've decided to get married at the end of August." He looked at Shane. "Given that Mom and Dad want to leave in September, we figured we can time it so that we move into the big house after the wedding."

Shane slapped his back. "Congratulations—and about time, too!"

Cassidy leaned over to hug Gina. "I love it!"

"Well I hope the timing works for you, because I want you to be my bridesmaid."

"You do?"

"Of course I do. If you will?"

"I'd love to. I'd be honored to."

"And it'll make life a lot easier that I won't have to worry about my Best Man getting in trouble with the bridesmaid." He looked at Shane. "Since he's already with the bridesmaid."

Cassidy loved seeing how thrilled Shane was. "Me?" he asked, his eyes shining happily.

Mason nodded. "Yes you."

"I mean I know I'm the obvious choice and everything. You want the best looking brother in your wedding photos," he said with a grin.

Cassidy slapped his arm.

He sobered slightly, giving Mason a serious look. "What about the others?"

Mason looked serious too for a moment. "You're right, you are the obvious choice. To me at least. If it weren't for you, there would be no me and Gina…first time around or second. Carter would hate to be asked, because he wouldn't want to upset anyone, plus he'd hate to do it. I can't ask Chance because I wouldn't want to piss Beau off, and to be honest, Beau and I just aren't that close." He grinned. "So I'm stuck with you."

Cassidy loved how close the two of them were as she watched them punch each other's arms. She turned to Gina who rolled her eyes. "What are we getting ourselves into?" she asked.

Shane grinned. "You're getting yourselves into the Remington clan, is what you're getting into." He held Cassidy's gaze for a moment. "Marrying into this family is going to be one hell of a ride. But I'm pretty sure you can handle it."

Oh, no! He wasn't going to ask her, was he? She'd already decided she was going to ask him. She smiled at him. "I can handle anything you throw at me. You already know this."

She was aware that Gina and Mason were watching them, no doubt wondering the same as she was—was Shane going to ask her?

"Oh shit!" The laughter faded from his face as he looked toward the door.

She followed his gaze and saw Katie Bell standing there. Ugh. Why did she have to keep turning up and trying to ruin things? She was surprised to see a guy come in through the door to join her. Good. Hopefully she'd moved on to him and would forget about Shane and leave them in peace.

After Katie arrived, Shane seemed edgy. He was quieter than usual and kept shooting a glance toward the table where Katie and her date were sitting. It bothered Cassidy. She didn't want that little cow to put a damper on their evening just by being there. The others noticed it, too, and once their plates were cleared, Mason called for the check.

He waved Shane off when he tried to take it. "This one's on me, for my Best Man and his girl." He grinned and added. "It'll be your turn soon enough."

Shane nodded, but he didn't look very happy about it. Cassidy had to wonder if she was wrong about him wanting to marry her. Surely if he did he'd be excited to think that he'd be buying dinner for his own Best Man soon?

She took hold of his hand on the way back to the truck. "Are you okay?"

He wrapped an arm around her shoulders and drew her close. She loved it when he did that! "I'm fine, Princess."

"You don't seem it. You haven't since Katie came in."

He nodded. "Sorry. There's something I need to tell you. Come on, let's get home."

Chapter Twenty-Three

Shane was quiet on the drive back. He was mad at himself and mad at Katie. He'd gotten caught up in the moment at dinner and had been on the verge of asking Cassidy to marry him right there. It would have been special. But Katie had to walk in. He didn't want her of all people to witness his proposal—to know about him and Cassidy getting engaged before even his parents or his other brothers. It just wouldn't have been right. So he hadn't done it. But it had spoiled the rest of the evening for him.

Now as they drove home, he realized that Cassidy might be thinking something else entirely. He looked across at her. "It's not what you think."

She raised her eyebrows. "I don't know what to think. All I know is that Katie still has enough power over you to spoil our evening."

"No! It's not like that!" He reached for her hand. "I need to explain."

"Yes, you do. But it can wait until we get home. You need to focus on the road for now." She gave him his hand back. She was right of course. You had to keep a sharp eye out for deer on the road at night. They drove on in silence.

Once they got home he poured them each a glass of wine and took them outside onto the deck over the river.

Cassidy took hers and went to lean on the railing. "So, tell me what the problem was?"

How could he tell her? That would mean telling her that he was about to ask her to marry him. He still wanted to ask her, but he didn't want to be forced into it by Katie Bell! He could tell her half the story at least though. "She came out to see me at the barn this afternoon. I was going to tell you as soon as I got home, but we were running late, and then we were at dinner, and I just didn't get a chance. When she showed up in there, part of me was afraid that she was going to come over and mention that she'd seen me today. I thought she was going to try to cause trouble, and I felt bad that I hadn't told you about her little visit."

Cassidy stared at him for a long moment, her expression inscrutable. He waited. He'd understand if she were pissed at him. He'd been pissed that she hadn't told him about that Justin guy. As the silence lengthened he could tell she was chewing the inside of her lip. What was she battling with herself about? Whatever it was she reached her conclusion and smiled at him. "I'll be glad when we're past the stage where other people can cause problems between us."

He grinned and went to lean against the rail beside her. "I think we already are, aren't we? We might both get wound up initially, but every time something like this comes up we manage to talk it through without it becoming a major issue." He turned and kissed the tip of her nose. "I'm proud of us. Some couples take years to get to where we are."

She smiled. "Yeah, I guess they do, but we seem to be on the fast track with everything we do."

"We do, don't we." Maybe it *was* time to ask her. "There's something else I've been thinking we might want to fast track."

She cocked her head to one side. Her smile was almost that scary one again. She had *something* up her sleeve. "Before you tell me what it is, do you mind if I ask you one more thing?"

He nodded. It was better that she get everything off her chest before he went for it. "Ask away."

He couldn't quite believe it when she dropped down on one knee in front of him and took hold of his hand. She'd never looked more beautiful than she did in that moment. Her honey colored hair shone in the moonlight; her honey colored eyes gleamed as she smiled up at him.

"Shane Remington, you cocky, arrogant, adorable man. I love you. Will you marry me?"

Damn! As his eyes filled with tears he understood how women must feel. He stared back down at her, momentarily stuck for words, but he knew the idiotic grin on his face was making his answer clear. He dropped to his own knees and took her face between his hands.

"Yes! Yes, I will marry you. And yes, I'm happy to give you the win on this one. I love you, Cassidy Lane, with all my heart and soul."

He wrapped her in his arms and kissed her as they both knelt there on the deck out under the big starry sky.

When they finally came up for air she grinned at him. "I beat you to it."

He had to laugh. "You did, and I love that you did, but don't get too carried away by your victory. It was a closer run thing than you think."

She laughed. "I thought you were supposed to be working on accepting defeat gracefully?"

"I am! And I don't consider this a defeat! But just so you know." He dug around in his jeans pocket and pulled out the little box he'd been keeping with him at all times for the last few days.

Her eyes widened as she watched him open it. "See?" He winked at her.

She nodded. "I'm happy to share this victory with you. But don't get used to it. This is a special exception."

He nodded. "I wouldn't expect otherwise. Now…" He took the ring out of the box and took hold of her hand. "Before you shut me down, this is what I wanted us to fast track. Cassidy Lane, beautiful, talented, challenging lady that you are, would you do me the honor of becoming my wife?"

Her eyes filled with tears as she nodded. "It'll be *my* honor, Shane."

He slid the ring onto her finger and wrapped her in his arms.

As they lay in bed later that night, Shane hugged her close as he spooned her. "Can you think of anything else we can fast track?" he asked.

"Umm, I think we just covered the biggie," she replied.

"What about babies?"

She rolled over to look into his eyes. "What about babies?"

He couldn't read her expression. "Do you want a family?"

She nodded. "But I'm not sure it's something I want to fast track." She laughed. "Unless you're going to stay home to take care of them?"

He grinned. "I was thinking that I could provide them with their good looks and you could provide them with the nurturing?"

She laughed and slapped his arm. "Don't be ridiculous. They'll get their good looks from their momma."

"Yeah, I can't argue with that one. Sure seems like you're winning them all tonight."

"Ha! You're the one winning, you got *me*. What more could you ask for?"

"Nothing, nothing at all. I hope we will have kids someday, but even if we never do, it doesn't matter as long as I have you."

She snuggled into his chest. "You'll always have me, and I'll always have you. I love you, Shane. And besides, no one else could handle you."

He laughed and kissed her neck. "No one else could handle *you*!"

She chuckled. "Very true. Now do you think we can stop arguing long enough to practice our baby making skills?"

He rolled her onto her back and pinned her wrists to the bed above her head. "I thought you'd never ask!"

~ ~ ~

Cassidy laughed at Shane as he tried to get comfortable in the passenger seat of her Beetle as they headed up to town. It wasn't made for someone his size.

"Remind me again why we couldn't bring my truck?" he asked.

"Because, much as you like to call me Princess, I have no desire to be chauffeured around everywhere the whole time. Whenever we go anywhere you always drive. Today is a big day, and I want to drive."

He closed his hand around the back of her neck. "It's a big day for me, too. Don't you think a guy would like to arrive in his own truck?"

She raised an eyebrow, but didn't take her eyes off the road. "Is that your ego talking, by any chance? Mr. Big Man doesn't want everyone to see him arrive in my girly little Beetle?"

He laughed. "No. More like Mr. Big Man, doesn't want to have to walk around crunched over all afternoon after being cramped into a vehicle that's way too small for him to fit in."

"Ah, sorry. Point taken"

"Thank you. Would you mind if, as a wedding gift, I buy you an SUV?"

She glanced over at him. "Mind? I'd love it. I've been thinking about needing one. Something with four-wheel drive?"

He shook his head at her. "Err, yeah! I can't believe you survived a winter here without it."

She huffed. "Well, I didn't know, did I?"

"Well now you do. But don't worry, you've got your big strong hubby to take care of you and all the practical details now."

She reached over and squeezed his hand. "If that was an attempt to wind me up, you failed."

"I did?"

"Yep." She grinned. "When it's you, I love the idea."

He squeezed her hand back. "You have no idea how happy that makes me. I don't want to smother you, and I do respect how strong you are, but I still want to be your man, you know?"

She nodded. She did know, and she loved it—loved him for it.

She found a parking spot close to the gallery and pulled over. "Well, are you ready to go do this?"

"I will be, just as soon as I can prize myself out of this tin can!"

She laughed. "Quit whining and get moving."

She did feel a bit bad as he got out and stretched his legs and rubbed his neck. Then he took her hand and they started walking toward the Railroad Café. Shane had called around the family this morning and asked them all to meet him there for lunch. He said his parents often had lunch there on a Saturday so it made sense to get everyone together while they were up there.

Cassidy had to wonder if they had any clue about the news they were about to hear. Once they entered and the hostess led them toward a long table, she got the idea that at least some of them did. Shane's parents were already there. She liked them. They greeted her warmly with hugs and what she had to think were expectant smiles. She'd been a little concerned that they might think she and Shane were moving too fast, but he had assured her that was far from the case. Mason and Gina were there, too. From the way Gina was grinning at her, Cassidy would bet that she'd guessed.

As they took their seats, Beau arrived. It was a nice change to see him all smiles. He even came and gave her a hug, though he seemed clueless as to why everyone had been summoned together again. Carter was the next to arrive. He was subdued and took a seat next to his mom. Chance came hurrying in a few moments later, apologizing for being late.

He grasped Shane's shoulder. "I hope this isn't going to take too long? I need to get back to it."

Shane grinned. "It won't take long, but I think you'll be glad you came."

"Do we want to order first?" asked his mom as the waitress hovered by the table.

"No," said Shane, holding up a hand to the girl to let her know to give them a few minutes. "Cassidy and I have something to tell you and we don't want to wait."

"We know that much," said Beau with a laugh. "So get on and tell us what it is!"

Cassidy loved Shane all the more as he looked at her, asking with his eyes whether she wanted to be the one to tell them. She gave him the slightest shake of her head and smiled encouragingly. She may love to take the lead, but this was for him to do. This was his family, and he was the man. The grateful smile he gave her confirmed once again just how right he was for her. If he'd wanted to, he could have just gone ahead and told them, but they were a team. He understood her and wanted to work with her.

He beamed around the table at his family and without preamble he simply stated. "We're getting married!"

Their reactions were everything she might have hoped for and more. There was much back slapping and hugging. Each and every one of them was genuinely pleased and happy to tell them both so. Even Beau came to give her a hug.

"I never thought he'd find the woman who could handle him, let alone tame him."

She laughed. "It's not that I've tamed him, Beau, it's just that we're the same kind of wild."

"Well whatever it is, it works for you. I couldn't be happier for you both."

She was pleased to watch him and Shane hug; it was the most genuine affection she'd seen between the two of them.

His mom, Monique, came and wrapped her in a hug. "I knew it the night you made him model for us."

Cassidy laughed. "You don't think it's too fast?" She'd hate to think that his parents had any reservations about this. Monique laughed. "Honestly, we've been wondering what was taking you so long!" She turned to her husband who was smiling at her side. "Isn't that right, Dave?"

He nodded. "Someday we'll tell you about how we got together." He put an arm around his wife, and Cassidy loved the smile that passed between them, hoping that someday wouldn't be too far away. She'd love to know their story.

Monique frowned as she looked toward the door. Cassidy blew out an exasperated sigh as she saw Katie standing there. Did she have a damned tracking device on them or something?

Shane had spotted her, too, and came to stand by Cassidy's side as she approached. Cassidy smiled up at him. "We *are* past the stage where other people can cause trouble for us, right?"

"Too damned right," he replied through gritted teeth. "But I'm getting pretty sick of her trying."

Cassidy took hold of his hand. "This'll be the last time she does."

Shane raised an eyebrow at her and chuckled. "Damn, that sounds scary. Remind me never to mess with you."

She had to laugh with him. "I don't need to. You know better. Now I just have to teach her the same thing." She turned to

Katie who had just reached the table. "Katie, what can I do for you?"

"Actually, it's what I can do for you."

"Oh, and what's that then?"

"I can save you from making a fool of yourself."

Cassidy deliberately brought her left hand up to tuck a strand of hair behind her ear. Katie's eyes widened when she noticed the ring. Her eyes flashed with anger.

"You really don't want to marry him."

"You couldn't be more wrong. I do want to marry him. I am going to marry him. You'd better get used to the idea."

"So you're happy to marry a man who is still…" she shot a look at Dave and Monique and chose her words carefully. "*Seeing* another woman?"

Cassidy laughed. "This is getting really old Katie. I suggest you grow up. It's not going to work. So leave us alone."

Katie looked at Shane. "You know she said she was just stringing you along to teach you a lesson, right?"

Shane gave Cassidy a puzzled look. Cassidy wasn't even worried. She knew by now that their bond was strong enough that he'd wait for her to explain. She turned to him. "It's true. I did. The night Katie came to the gallery after your modeling session." She smiled at him. "I'd told you I'd protect you and see her off. The easiest way to do it was to tell her she could have you back when I was done with you." She shot a quick grin at Chance who chuckled at that. Then she slid her arm around Shane's waist and smiled up at him. "Who would ever have guessed that we'd fall in love with each other?"

Shane hugged her to his side. "Sure as hell not me!"

She laughed and looked back at Katie. "So, you see, all you're doing is making a fool of yourself."

Katie rummaged in her purse. "I didn't want to do this here, but…." She pulled out a belt and waved it at Shane. "Remember in the barn yesterday? You left this with me."

Cassidy looked up at him. She recognized the belt as the same kind he always wore—she should do, she'd unbuckled it often enough. But she didn't feel any doubt, not in him, not in them. He looked down at her and she knew he could see the trust in her eyes. He smiled and spoke to her not Katie.

"Yep, it's mine." He shrugged and gave her an apologetic look. "And yeah, I did leave it with her. But months ago, not in the barn yesterday. I already told you what happened then."

Cassidy nodded at him then looked at Katie. "You should leave."

Katie burst into tears and thrust the belt toward her. "Here! You have it!"

Cassidy smiled. "No thanks, why don't you keep it as a reminder of the boy you knew." She smiled up at Shane. "I got the man."

And as Shane smiled down at her, she knew she'd never spoken a truer word;

A Note from SJ

I hope you enjoyed your visit to Montana and spending time with the Remingtons. Please let your friends know about the books if you feel they would enjoy them as well. It would be wonderful if you would leave me a review, I'd very much appreciate it.

You can check out the rest of the series on my website www.SJMcCoy.com to keep up with the brothers as they each find their happiness.

Chance has finally talked me into giving him his own three book spinoff – Look out for it in Spring 2017.

In the meantime, you'll see glimpses of him in my Summer Lake series, too. If you haven't read them, you can get started with Emma and Jack in Book One, Love Like You've Never Been Hurt which is currently FREE to download in ebook form from all the big online book retailers AND early in 2017 the whole series will be available in paperback as well!

There are a few options to keep up with me and my imaginary friends:

The best way is to Sign up on the website for my Newsletter. Don't worry I won't bombard you! I'll let you know about upcoming releases, share a sneak peek or two and keep you in the loop for a couple of fun giveaways I have coming up :0)

You can join my readers group to chat about the books on Facebook or just browse and like my Facebook Page

I occasionally attempt to say something in 140 characters or less(!) on Twitter

And I'm always in the process of updating my website at www.SJMcCoy.com with new book updates and even some videos. Plus, you'll find the latest news on new releases and giveaways in my blog.

I love to hear from readers, so feel free to email me at AuthorSJMcCoy@gmail.com.. I'm better at that! :0)

I hope our paths will cross again soon. Until then, take care, and thanks for your support—you are the reason I write!
Love
SJ

PS Project Semicolon

You may have noticed that the final sentence of the story closed with a semi-colon. It isn't a typo. Project Semi Colon is a non-profit movement dedicated to presenting hope and love to those who are struggling with depression, suicide, addiction and self-injury. Project Semicolon exists to encourage, love and inspire. It's a movement I support with all my heart.

"A semicolon represents a sentence the author could have ended, but chose not to. The sentence is your life and the author is you."

- Project Semicolon

This author started writing after her son was killed in a car crash. At the time I wanted my own story to be over, instead I chose to honour a promise to my son to write my 'silly stories' someday. I chose to escape into my fictional world. I know for many who struggle with depression, suicide can appear to be the only escape. The semicolon has become a symbol of support, and hopefully a reminder – Your story isn't over yet

Also by SJ McCoy

Remington Ranch Series

Mason (FREE in ebook form)

Shane

Carter

Beau

Coming next

Four Weddings and a Vendetta

Summer Lake Series

Love Like You've Never Been Hurt (FREE in ebook form)

Work Like You Don't Need the Money

Dance Like Nobody's Watching

Fly Like You've Never Been Grounded

Laugh Like You've Never Cried

Sing Like Nobody's Listening

Smile Like You Mean It

The Wedding Dance

Chasing Tomorrow

Dream Like Nothing's Impossible

Coming next

Ride Like You've Never Fallen

About the Author

I'm SJ, a coffee addict, lover of chocolate and drinker of good red wines. I'm a lost soul and a hopeless romantic. Reading and writing are necessary parts of who I am. Though perhaps not as necessary as coffee! I can drink coffee without writing, but I can't write without coffee.

I grew up loving romance novels, my first boyfriends were book boyfriends, but life intervened, as it tends to do, and I wandered down the paths of non-fiction for many years. My life changed completely a few years ago and I returned to Romance to find my escape.

I write 'Sweet n Steamy' stories because to me there is enough angst and darkness in real life. My favorite romances are happy escapes with a focus on fun, friendships and happily-ever-afters, just like the ones I write.

These days I live in beautiful Montana, the last best place. If I'm not reading or writing, you'll find me just down the road in the park - Yellowstone. I have deer, eagles and the occasional bear for company, and I like it that way :0)

Made in the USA
Lexington, KY
09 January 2017